Reunited

Reunited

HILARY WEISMAN GRAHAM

SIMON & SCHUSTER BFYR

New York   London   Toronto   Sydney   New Delhi

SIMON & SCHUSTER BFYR

An imprint of Simon & Schuster Children's Publishing Division
1230 Avenue of the Americas, New York, New York 10020

SIMON & SCHUSTER BFYR is a trademark of Simon & Schuster, Inc.
For information about special discounts for bulk purchases, please contact
Simon & Schuster Special Sales at 1-866-506-1949 or
business@simonandschuster.com.
The Simon & Schuster Speakers Bureau can bring authors to your live
event. For more information or to book an event, contact the Simon &
Schuster Speakers Bureau at 1-866-248-3049 or visit our website at
www.simonspeakers.com.
Book design by Lucy Ruth Cummins
The text for this book is set in Bembo Std.
Manufactured in the United States of America
10 9 8 7 6 5 4 3 2 1
Library of Congress Cataloging-in-Publication Data
Graham, Hilary Weisman.
Reunited / Hilary Weisman Graham. — 1st ed.
p. cm.
Summary: Alice, Summer, and Tiernan were best friends who broke up at
the same time as their favorite band, but four years later, just before they are
preparing to go off to college, the girls reluctantly come back together, each
with her own motives, for a road trip from Massachusetts to Austin, Texas,
for the band's one-time-only reunion concert.
ISBN 978-1-4424-3984-9 (hardcover)
[1. Friendship—Fiction. 2. Automobile travel—Fiction. 3. Rock groups—
Fiction.] I. Title.
PZ7.G7523Re 2012
[Fic]—dc23
2011024299
ISBN 978-1-4424-0689-6 (eBook)

FIRST
EDITION

To Sue and Sue

Acknowledgments

First and foremost I'd like to thank my manager, Seth Jaret. It is because of your wisdom and tireless support that I've been able to live out my dream of being a writer, and I feel incredibly blessed to have you shepherding my career.

To my editor, Alexandra Cooper—this book literally would not exist without you. Thanks for taking a chance on me, and for your creative vision and thoughtful guidance.

To my agent, Steve Malk—you are the man who Makes Things Happen. I feel lucky to have you on my team.

My deepest gratitude also goes to Lita Judge, Kim Dalley, and Lee Harrington for generously sharing your expertise in order to help me navigate the uncharted waters of the publishing world. Lee—you're the best mentor a newbie novelist could ever hope for.

To my mom, JoAnne Deitch—you have always been my first reader and biggest cheerleader.

Much appreciation goes to Tonya Dreher, Jennifer Duffy, Bethany Ericson, Andrea Summers, Bob Summers, Emily Coburn, Caitlyn Coburn, Janet Graham, Ron Smith, and Ceara Comeau for agreeing to read *Reunited* in its early drafts. Critiquing a novel is no small task, and your comments and insights were an invaluable part of my writing process.

To Cia and the Goddesses—thanks for your encouragement, for your friendship, and *especially* for your endurance in listening to me kvetch. I am deeply grateful to have you all in my life.

Brian Therriault, Emmanuel Ording, Bill Long, Kaori Hamura, Ethan May, Lisa Carey, Maggie Zavgren, Sadie Zavgren, Sofia Thornblad, Isabel Dreher, Anna Gombas, Rosemary Jo Crooker, Aidan Holding, David Stiefel, and Thomas Curran—I am hugely indebted to you all for volunteering your time and talents in order to help me turn my marketing pipe dreams into a reality. And I apologize for referring to you as my "army of slaves."

A big thanks to Ariel Coletti, Amy Rosenbaum, and the rest of the team at Simon & Schuster for all of the many wonderful things you do.

To the Society of Children's Book Writers and Illustrators— the benefits of winning the 2011 SCBWI Book Launch Award have been truly immeasurable. Thank you for bestowing this great honor on me and for helping *Reunited* achieve broader visibility.

And last but not least, my heartfelt thanks to Andy and Henry for your belief in me and for your constant love.

Reunited

Chapter One

"IS THE BLINDFOLD REALLY NECESSARY?" ALICE ASKED HER PARENTS.

"Yes!" they replied, in stereo.

Her mom tightened the bandanna around her head while her dad squeezed her shoulders. "March!" he commanded, steering her down the hall.

Alice tried not to get her hopes up about this mysterious graduation present—the Chia Pet they'd given her for her eighteenth birthday was still too fresh in her mind—but with all this hype, it was hard not to get a little excited. Especially if her parents remembered to consult the list of gift ideas she'd given them, typed up and organized by price. For a one-time event like high school graduation, Alice was hoping they'd spring for something from Category Two (iPad, camera, golden retriever) or maybe even Category One (laptop). After what happened yesterday, she could really use a good surprise.

"No peeking!" said her dad, guiding her through the living room and out the front door. Her mom made a drumroll sound with her lips, just in case the neighbors weren't already staring. The Miller family had a reputation as the neighborhood oddballs. Nothing too crazy, if you didn't count the garden gnome incident. But Alice was pretty sure that in all of white-bread Walford, Massachusetts, hers was the only house with a pea-green 1976 VW camper van up on blocks in the backyard.

"Okay," said her dad, "you may remove the blindfold."

It wasn't in the backyard anymore. The Pea Pod, as the van was affectionately known, was right there in her driveway. It looked shinier than she remembered, as if a clear coat of nail polish had been painted over a craggy old toenail.

"We fixed it up for you!" her mom announced, waving her arms like one of those ladies from *The Price Is Right*. "Completely restored, good as new."

"It's got new brakes, a new muffler, *and* a new paint job!" her dad said proudly. "We wouldn't let you and MJ drive cross-country if this baby wasn't safe."

Alice blinked a few times, adjusting to the bright summer sun and the shock of her disappointment. She still hadn't told her parents the bombshell that MJ had dropped on her yesterday. She was afraid if she said it out loud, she might have to accept it herself.

"My road trip with MJ," Alice began, tears welling in her eyes, "got canceled."

"Why?" asked her dad.

"Because Mrs. Ling is making her go to China all summer long," Alice stammered. She hated to cry in front of them. She hated anything that threatened her image as the Confident Girl Who Had It All Together.

"But you girls have been planning this trip for two years," said her mom.

"Exactly," Alice whined. She caught her reflection in the van's windshield, confirming that she looked as pathetic as she felt. Mascara—the only makeup she ever wore—was running down her cheeks, her long brown curls a frizzy fiasco, thanks to the blindfold.

Her dad wrapped her up in his arms. "Poor kid, you're not having much luck these days, are you?" *Understatement of the year*. Her best friend was on a plane over the Pacific instead of getting ready for their last big precollege hurrah. Not that Alice actually knew *which* college she'd be going to. She'd applied to Brown early decision and they'd put her on the wait list. *Hello, admissions people, it's the end of June . . .*

Her dad finally released her from the hug. "Well, like the great John Lennon once said, 'Life's what happens while you're making other plans.'"

"And that's supposed to be a good thing?" Alice asked. She wanted to believe that everything happened for a reason, that her canceled road trip and being wait listed by Brown were all part of the universe's grand scheme. But sometimes she wondered if destiny was just something people believed in to make themselves feel better when they didn't get their way.

"You know," said her mom, "there was a time when we couldn't get you out of the Pea Pod."

Yeah, thought Alice, *when I was twelve.* Back in middle school, when Summer Dalton and Tiernan O'Leary were still her best friends, the Pea Pod had been their clubhouse. "Three peas in a Pea Pod," her mom used to say. Alice always acted like the nickname embarrassed her, but secretly she'd liked it.

"Why don't we go give her a whirl?" asked her dad. "It might take your mind off things."

"That's a great idea!" said her mom. "It's a beautiful day for a drive."

Can't I just wallow in self-pity for one minute? Alice wondered. Then she looked at her parents. Her dad was buffing the van with his T-shirt. Her mom held the digital camera in her hand.

"Fine," she said, tugging on the van's sliding door. After avoiding the Pea Pod for the last four years, she had to admit, she *was* a little curious. Had they reupholstered the orange-and-green plaid seat cushions? Ripped down the limited edition Level3 poster signed by all three members of the band?

They hadn't. The inside of the Pea Pod looked exactly the same as she remembered it. Level3 memorabilia was still plastered on the walls—song lyrics written on heart-shaped pieces of paper, faded pinups of the boys ripped from the pages of *Rolling Stone,* glossy eight-by-tens covered with sloppy Magic Marker signatures. It was just like the sign taped to the dashboard said: LEVEL3 SUPER-FAN HEADQUARTERS.

HILARY WEISMAN GRAHAM

"We didn't want to mess with your stuff," said her dad.

Of course, he was living in the past, as usual. Level3 wasn't even a band anymore. They broke up the beginning of her freshman year, right before Alice, Summer, and Tiernan did. But back when they were together—when *everything* was still together—Alice and her friends had been diehard fans. Two all-ages shows at the Middle East, six at Boston Garden, three at the Orpheum, four at the Worcester DCU Center, and one at the Meadowlands in New Jersey, which resulted in their parents making a collective rule about not driving the girls to a concert more than fifty miles from home.

Alice couldn't help but smile as she took in the display of old collages. When they were young, Alice, Summer, and Tiernan were practically as obsessed with making Level3 collages as they had been with the band. These weren't ordinary collages, like the kind they used to make in their seventh-grade health class on the dangers of cigarettes. The Level3 collages were art (or at least they aspired toward it). Their final masterpiece consisted of hundreds of tiny cutouts of the boys in Level3, assembled into the shape of an eye. At the center—the pupil—was a photo of Alice, Summer, and Tiernan, age twelve, arms slung around each other, smiling.

"Why don't I start her up, and you can watch how I drive her for a while? The gear shift takes a little practice so—"

"I know how to drive, Dad."

"Not so fast. There's an art to driving the Pea Pod."

Alice rolled her eyes and flopped down on the bench seat in back, buckling herself in for the trip down memory lane. She'd been sitting right here the first time she'd listened to Level3. They were just eleven when Tiernan showed up with the CD her older brother burned for her—"Level3" scrawled in black marker across the front. It took Alice a few songs to get into it; the music was so different than the sugary Disney pop she was used to. Then something clicked and she started to really listen—not just with her ears, but with her whole body. It was an intense feeling, like she was hearing music for the first time. Like Level3's songs expressed all the things she felt but didn't have the words for. By the end of the album, she was hooked. They all were.

And that was *before* they found out that the boys in the band were cute. Alice liked Ryan because he played the bass with his back to the audience, and she had a thing for shy guys. Tiernan had a crush on Luke, poster child for crazy drummers everywhere. And Summer liked Travis, the lead singer-slash-guitarist-slash-total hottie.

Quickly, the Pea Pod morphed into a Level3 shrine. And like all worshippers, the girls had their rituals.

Step One: Crank up a Level3 tune and dance like crazed animals.

Step Two: Snack break in Alice's kitchen; check fan blogs, official band website.

Step Three: Back to the Pea Pod to discuss fantasies of meet-

HILARY WEISMAN GRAHAM

ing Level3 boys in real life, possible planning session about tri-ple wedding in Vegas.

Step Four: Put on a sad song, light some candles, lie down on the floor with eyes shut.

"Honey, are you coming?" her dad asked, snapping her out of her reverie.

"Sure, Dad, sure," Alice said, noticing that he'd actually pulled over and moved himself into the passenger's seat. It was funny: Alice thought she'd never step foot inside the Pea Pod again after the three little peas turned into split-pea soup, and now here she was, about to drive it.

"Now the clutch is finicky, so you have to push it all the way to the floor . . ."

Alice nodded patiently as her dad shouted commands all the way around the neighborhood loop. Twice. But by the third pass, even *he* had to admit she was Pea Pod proficient. So, she figured it was time for some tunes.

"What's the deal with this thing?" Alice asked, turning on the radio. "You and mom couldn't shell out for a new sound system?" She punched the preset buttons one by one. Nothing but static.

"Hands on the wheel, eyes on the road!" her dad yelled, noticing one of Alice's hands was missing from his mandatory nine-and-three o'clock arrangement.

"Dad, calm down." Alice kept her hand on the tuner. She scrolled past a Spanish talk radio show, then up through a long, staticky no-man's-land. She was about to lose all hope when she finally stumbled on a signal. The familiar song rang out loud and clear.

THE THINGS WE WISHED WE DIDN'T SAY
WE WENT AND SAID THEM ANYWAY
NO SAVING FOR A RAINY DAY
THAT'S THE WAY IT WAS

Of course, it was Level3. Who else could it be? Being in the Pea Pod had somehow channeled their music into existence.

"Hang a right," her dad said, pointing to the street up ahead.

Alice might have laughed out loud at the coincidence if it wasn't the one Level3 song that always made her cringe. Back before that disastrous night at the freshman winter dance, "Heyday" used to be one of her favorites. Now it just brought back ugly memories.

IT'S A ROAD I CAN'T GO DOWN AGAIN
A STREET CALLED I REMEMBER WHEN
IF WE COULD DO IT ALL AGAIN, WE WOULD
WE WOULD . . .

Alice took the turn a little too fast. At the same exact moment, the song changed into its thumping chorus.

HILARY WEISMAN GRAHAM

IT WAS OUR HEYDAY, HEY DAY, HEY! OUR HEYDAY, HEY DAY, HEY!

"Slow down!" her dad yelled as Alice jerked the wheel seconds before hitting a mailbox. She stomped on the brakes as the Pea Pod lurched forward with a loud grinding noise, then immediately stalled out.

WHY DID WE REFUSE TO STAY, ANYWAY?

Her dad drove the rest of the way home. By the time he pulled into the driveway, Alice practically leaped out of the van while it was still in motion. Clearly the universe was trying to send her a message. First, there was the canceled road trip, then her "gift" of the Pea Pod, and now "Heyday."

She hurried inside to the den, desperate to soothe herself with some junk food and mindless TV. That's when she saw it: the photo of Level3, right there on the TV screen. And unless the van had somehow transported her back in time—which she was pretty sure it hadn't—she had no choice but to believe that the image was real. It had to be real; the old guy from *MTV News* was talking about it. She hit the TiVo rewind button three times just to make sure she'd heard Kurt Loder (*that* was his name!) correctly.

"Level3, the pop-rock trio that broke up at the height of their success nearly four years ago, has announced they will be getting back together for

a one-night-only benefit concert next Friday in their hometown of Austin, Texas. Tickets go on sale at noon and are expected to sell out within minutes. According to lead singer Travis Wyland, 'A reunion show is the fastest and most effective way to raise money for a cause we all firmly believe in and which has affected my family personally: finding a cure for Duchenne muscular dystrophy.' The band has denied rumors they will be permanently getting back together."

Alice shoved a handful of Doritos in her mouth and crunched them up without even tasting them. How could one day be this crazy? And yet, it was how everything had always been with her old favorite band—meant to be. Tiernan used to have a Yiddish word for all the coincidences between Level3 and the girls. *Beshert*. And when something was *beshert*, you didn't tune it out. When something was *beshert*, you went with it. It was all you *could* do.

It was 11:56 a.m. Four minutes from now, the ticket website would be a feeding frenzy. Alice ran to her bedroom and turned on her computer, the thrill of a new plan formulating as the screen tingled to life. So what if Austin, Texas, was two thousand miles away from Walford, Massachusetts? Or that tickets started at two hundred dollars apiece? Alice was going. *They* were going. How could they not? Especially now that they had the Pea Pod to get them there. But how could she justify spending six hundred dollars on tickets without even knowing if her old friends would agree to go along with her?

She and Tiernan were at least civil to each other. But Summer would pass by in the halls and barely make eye contact. Still, this was Level3, and however Summer and Tiernan felt about her now could never take away the fact that they'd once considered themselves the band's biggest fans. And what was the worst-case scenario? If Summer and Tiernan said no, she'd just sell the tickets on eBay.

Alice rifled through her desk drawer for the credit card she'd borrowed from her mom two months ago and "accidentally" forgotten to give back. *Whoops.* After a few clicks of the mouse, she was on the ticket site. A photo of the band appeared above the words, "Reunited—for one night only!"

She carefully typed in the numbers on her mom's Visa. At the bottom of the screen, an ominous line of text read: "By clicking continue, you agree that your credit card will be charged and your nonrefundable ticket(s) will be processed." If she didn't buy the tickets now, there'd be no other chance.

Well, Alice thought to herself as she clicked the button, *if you guys can get back together for a one-time reunion, why can't we?*

Now she just needed to convince her ex–best friends to join her.

Chapter Two

SUMMER SQUISHED A MOSQUITO ON HER ARM AS SHE WATCHED Alice Miller cross the stage to take her diploma. *Ugh, they were only on the M's.* She lifted her thick strawberry blond hair from her neck, wiping away the sweat with the back of her hand. At this rate, it would be at least another hour before she could ditch this yawn-fest and dive into Jace's pool. Up in the grandstands, her parents were laughing and talking with their old high school friends like a bunch of rowdy teenagers. If she and Jace were back here with their kids in twenty years, somebody might as well just shoot her now.

"Heads up!" a voice shouted at the exact same moment a beach ball slammed into the head of a nerdy boy sitting in front of her. Summer picked the ball up off the grass. From a few rows back, she could hear Maz's obnoxious laugh. *Typical.*

Summer looked at the boy who'd been hit, the pink flush of embarrassment rising up his neck. She wished she had the nerve to say something to him. To tell him that high school would probably be the pinnacle of Maz's pathetic life. But before she had the chance, the boy turned around and shot her a dirty look, as if the ball in her lap made her guilty by association.

Summer glared back at Maz, then opened the valve and squeezed. The ball collapsed in her hands, air whistling as it escaped.

"Chill out," said Jace, giving her a finger flick to the neck. By some fluke, he was seated right behind her. Jace Fitzgerald and Summer Dalton, high school power couple extraordinaire. The way the girls in school treated her, you'd think being popular and having a cute boyfriend were the keys to eternal happiness.

Summer never understood what made her and her friends so "popular" anyway, considering half the school hated them. Not that there was any point in bringing this up. Every time she tried to talk about something other than:

1. Who was getting fat

2. Who hooked up with who

3. How wasted they were last weekend

her friends would accuse her of being a nerd. *As if.* Summer was pretty sure that she'd be the laughingstock of her Poetry 101 class in college. It hadn't stopped her from signing up, but still, the fear was real. So far, the only person to read her poetry was Jace, and he'd said it was amazing. But how much could she trust a boy who considered *Maxim* magazine heavy reading?

And it wasn't like her parents understood it any better. They could barely wrap their heads around the fact that she wasn't going to school with all her friends at UMass Walford. But Summer couldn't wait to go to Boston College in the fall. She wanted to hang out with people who had their own opinions; people who argued with her; people who weren't so afraid to just be who they were and live or die by the consequences.

"Tiernan O'Leary!" Principal Roberts's voice boomed through the loudspeakers. *God, they were only on the O's.*

"Freak!" Maz shouted as Tiernan crossed the stage. Like a girl with blue hair, combat boots, and red day-glow lipstick would consider that an insult.

"Can you tell your monkey to shut up?" she whispered to Jace.

"You know I can't control him," Jace said, shrugging his shoulders.

On the stage, Tiernan curtseyed to the crowd, while raising her middle finger in Maz's general direction.

Thankfully, Summer only had to deal with Maz for one more week. For the month of July, it was good-bye Walford, hello Martha's Vineyard.

"Tell me again what your beach house is like," Summer said, fanning Jace with her diploma. She needed to work up a good daydream if she was going to make it through the rest of commencement.

"Uh, it's gray," Jace replied. Vivid descriptions were never the boy's strong point.

Not that it mattered. Summer had already painted the picture in her mind. Picnic dinners of boiled lobster and corn on the cob; sandy games of touch football on the beach; sunsets spent writing poetry in her journal.

Hopefully, Jace wouldn't mind if she slipped away now and then to write. Knowing Jace, he'd probably be fine with it as long as she didn't miss out on any important beach activities—especially the kind that happened *after* dark. Summer closed her eyes, imagining the sunsets off of West Chop.

She must have drifted off because the next thing she knew, loud clapping and a chorus of "Woo hoos!" and "Hell, yeah, babies!" jolted her awake. She turned around to ask Jace why he hadn't woken her—well, to yell at him, really—but he wasn't there. Lately, he was always disappearing like that. Summer scanned the crowd. Her parents and their friends were still chatting away up in the bleachers, enjoying their own party too much to notice that graduation was actually over. But Jace was nowhere to be seen.

She headed toward the edge of the field, weaving her way through the throngs of people, dodging tossed caps and that infernal beach ball (reinflated courtesy of Maz). *Where on earth had Jace gone?* Summer was almost at the bleachers when a familiar hand tapped her on the shoulder. Only, it didn't belong to the person she was looking for. It belonged to Alice Miller.

"Hey, there," said Alice casually, as if it wasn't the first time they'd spoken in nearly four years. "Happy graduation."

"Happy graduation," Summer answered by reflex. As far as Summer was concerned, she and Alice had drawn a line in the sand freshman year, one they'd both agreed never to cross. Now, for some unimaginable reason, Alice was acting like the line had never been there to begin with.

"Well, I know this might sound crazy . . . ," Alice began. Then, without even taking a breath, Alice launched into a rambling account of her last twenty-four hours—her parents giving her the newly refurbished Pea Pod, then learning the news of the Level3 reunion show. Since it was impossible to get a word in edgewise, Summer just stood there, trying her best to absorb Alice's onslaught of information. It was hard to decide what bothered her more—that Alice had totally glossed over everything that had happened that night at the Winter Wonderland Dance or that she was dredging up the past in the first place. *Note to Alice: High school's over.*

"Sorry," Summer said, "Jace and I are going to the Vineyard for all of July. But have fun, okay?"

For a second, Alice just stood there looking as if someone had let the air out of her, like the beach ball from before. "Well, if you change your mind . . . ," she finally stammered, walking away before she even finished the sentence.

Summer was surprised Alice had the audacity to speak to her after all this time, let alone invite her to a concert halfway across the country. But even more shocking was how willingly she took no for an answer. Suddenly Alice stopped.

"He's still got those dimples!" she shouted through the crowd.

Summer didn't have to ask who "he" was. She had already googled Travis's picture when she'd heard about the Level3 reunion on the radio. Not that she would admit it to anyone—especially not Alice Miller. What was more embarrassing than being eighteen and having a crush on some rock star she didn't even know?

And why was she thinking about Travis's dimples when she already had a boyfriend? A *real* one. Maybe Jace didn't have the soul of a poet, but at least he wasn't some adolescent fantasy. In fact, he was right in front of her.

"Where have *you* been?" Summer asked, flustered.

"I've been looking for *you*," he said.

"Uh-huh," said Maz, nodding his head in confirmation while his eyes stayed firmly planted on the cleavage of a girl walking by.

"I was talking to Alice Miller. She just came up out of the blue and asked me to go to the Level3 reunion show with her in Austin. It was totally messed up."

"Austin, Texas?" Jace asked, confused. "Why is she asking you?"

"We used to be friends. Back in middle school."

"That sounds psychotic," Maz butted in. "Like what if she goes all Leighton Meester in *The Roommate* on you and she tries to kill you and take over your life?"

"Funny," Summer said, wishing she could have had this conversation without Maz's interference.

"I think you should go," Jace suddenly declared. "You listen to that stupid band all the time."

Jace had a point. Summer still loved Level3. But not enough to get her to spend ten days in a van with Alice Miller.

"Even if I wanted to, how could I? We're going to the Vineyard, remember?"

"Right," said Jace, fanning himself with his customized "Hawks Rule!" cap, "about the Vineyard . . ."

Maz punched Jace in the bicep, then ran off into the crowd.

"I was thinking, actually"—Jace stopped to rub his freshly shaved chin—"that it might be better if you . . . didn't come."

Summer could feel her stomach in her throat. She knew this tone. She had *invented* this tone. Jace was breaking up with her.

"And I was thinking about the long-distance thing in the fall," Jace continued, "and how hard it's gonna be to only see each other on the weekends . . ."

Summer couldn't believe that in all her years of dating, up until this moment, she'd never been the one at the receiving end of these words. She'd dumped David Long in an e-mail. She'd had a friend tell Brian Rourke that she didn't want to see him anymore. And poor Scotty Weishaupt, she'd simply shown up to his state finals basketball game holding hands with Chris Hedison.

Jace was still babbling away, doing everything he could to say *I don't love you anymore* without actually coming out and using those words. But Summer had plenty of words: mostly the four-letter kind.

"Enough!" she finally said. "I get it, okay?" It always annoyed her when the boys she broke up with wanted to "talk it out," when clearly the best thing to do was make a clean break, then disappear as quickly as possible. So that's just what Summer did. She ran through the crowd, hiding under her graduation cap so as not to be spotted by her friends or, even worse, her parents.

"Congratulations" was the last thing she needed to hear right now.

Out in the parking lot, traffic was already at a standstill. Part of her wanted to go back to the stadium and punch Jace right in his rock-hard abs. But instead she kept running—past the gym, up the hill by the science labs—as if it were possible to outrun that feeling in her gut.

For months she'd waited for this day to come, for the chance to start over, to have a clean slate. *Clean slate, indeed. Jace sure took care of that.*

At the top of the hill Summer stopped to catch her breath. Her parents were probably looking for her by now. No doubt, they'd heard the news of the breakup and were ready to console her, right there in front of everyone. Like she needed more humiliation. Just the thought of it made her want to run again. The only problem was, she wasn't sure which way to go.

What if her parents and Maz were right? What if high school was as good as it got? Or worse: What if there was a better life out there, but Summer didn't know what it was or where to find it?

That's when she saw the bright-green van pulling out of the parking lot. It was strange to see the Pea Pod out on the open road after all those years of sitting in the same spot. But there it was, cruising down East Walford Street, just like all the other cars leaving high school forever. It wasn't until the van drove out of sight that Summer realized she was smiling. If the Pea Pod could get it in gear, maybe there was hope for her yet.

Chapter Three

TIERNAN UNZIPPED HER GREEN POLYESTER GOWN AND CHUCKED it onto the heap of clothes in the corner. She couldn't believe she'd just spent the last four hours in that hideous muumuu, let alone the ridiculous cap. And what the hell was a mortarboard, anyway? Wasn't that some kind of torture our military used to make terrorists spill their secrets? Or maybe that was waterboarding. Whatever. Wearing it *felt* like torture.

Tiernan looked in the mirror, curling her short blue bob behind her ears so that it ended in two perfectly defined points midcheek. Being back in her normal clothes made her happy. Of course, the term "normal" was relative. But Tiernan liked the way her look perfectly captured her personality and at the same time made her look taller than her 103-pound, five-foot-one self. It was one part wacky (vintage Kermit the Frog T-shirt), one part sexy (short skirt, fishnet tights), and one part dangerous (knee-high Doc Martens boots).

Her mother had begged her not to wear the boots to graduation, and after a long knockdown drag-out battle (was there really any other kind with Judy Horowitz?) Tiernan had promised not to wear them. *Oops.*

"Tiernan?" her mother called from upstairs. "Are you down there?"

Where'd her mother think she'd be? Ever since she'd found that 1.5 liter bottle of vodka in Tiernan's closet, sneaking out of the house had become harder than busting out of Shawshank.

"Tiernan Horowitz O'Leary!" Her mother's red Dior pumps were already clomping down the stairs into Tiernan's basement room. So much for the little things, like privacy.

"If you're here for happy hour," Tiernan said, "I don't start mixing martinis till five. But help yourself to a cocktail wiener."

Judy didn't even crack a smile. "That's not why I'm here," she said, her eyes scanning the room for more contraband. Like Tiernan managed to duck into the liquor store in between getting her diploma and the ride home.

"Then why *are* you here?"

"I'm here because you have a visitor." Her mother's gaze landed at Tiernan's feet. No comment from the shoe police.

"I thought I didn't get to have visitors when I'm grounded."

"Well, I'm making an exception."

Her mother didn't make exceptions. She certainly didn't make them for any of Tiernan's "weirdo, delinquent" friends.

"It's Alice Miller," Judy said, smiling.

Tiernan had always feared that this day of reckoning would come, but she didn't expect it to be right after graduation. Now that high school was over, what was the point? But if Alice had finally uncovered Tiernan's big lie freshman year, Tiernan was toast. She should have just 'fessed up ages ago. Not that the debacle at that stupid dance was all her fault anyway. Alice wasn't exactly innocent. Plus, it was only a matter of time before Summer finally exposed herself for the superficial Abercrombie that she was. All Tiernan had done was speed up the process. In a way, she'd probably done Alice a favor. Right?

"Tell her I'm busy," Tiernan said, grabbing her iPod.

Her mother came closer and yanked the little white earbuds from her head. "I am *not* going to lie to your friend," she whispered angrily.

"Since when is Alice Miller still my friend? The girl hates me."

"Don't be ridiculous. Why would she be here if she hated you?"

"Good question," Tiernan shot back. "Did you pat her down for weapons?"

Tiernan's mother just looked at her and waited. It was one of her favorite tools in her arsenal—the Stare of Shame. Then she turned on her heel and hurried back upstairs. Obviously, the woman was pumped to have a normal-looking teenager in the house.

Sometimes Tiernan wondered if she might still be friends with Alice if her mother hadn't shipped her off to New Jew freshman year. New Jew (known to the rest of the world as Jacobs Academy of New Jewish Studies) was the pricey Jewish boarding school Tiernan's Jewish mother insisted she go to for the sole purpose of making Tiernan's Irish father (Judy's philandering ex-husband) foot the bill. But Tiernan just wanted to go to Walford High with her friends. Not that her mother ever cared about what *she* wanted.

So, Tiernan fought back with the only real power she had—the power to piss her mother off. It was funny how much damage a six-dollar bottle of "Raven" Manic Panic and some scissors could do. Add in a nose ring and an eighteen-year-old boyfriend with dreadlocks (standard issue at all the finest Jewish prep schools) and her transformation into a punk-rock badass was complete.

To Tiernan, the change wasn't all that radical. She'd just turned up the volume on her already quirky personality. To eleven. But the whole thing had seriously wigged Judy out.

Summer didn't have time to notice Tiernan's makeover, what with her newfound hobby of letting every jock at Walford High ram his tongue down her throat. And Alice (in typical Alice fashion) tried to act like nothing had changed. She pretended it didn't matter that Tiernan went to a different school. She ignored the fact that Tiernan's wardrobe was growing freakier by the day while she and Summer still dressed like Banana Republicans. By the time New Jew booted Tiernan's butt back to public school sophomore year (a story for another day), Summer and Alice seemed like strangers.

Upstairs, Tiernan heard her mother laughing. Of all Tiernan's friends, Alice had always been Judy's favorite. Even back when Tiernan was still a "good girl" (well, if not "good," at least "better") her mother often wondered (aloud) why Tiernan couldn't be more like her well-mannered, overachieving friend. "Did you know that *Alice* started an after-school environmental club?" Judy would ask, all mock-innocence. "I bet her mother must be proud." Insert knife, twist.

Not that Tiernan held a grudge against Alice for it. Their friendship was fun while it lasted. Then they grew up and drifted apart. The real question was, Why had Alice drifted back into her life now?

And yet, Alice Miller was in her house—the only visitor Judy had *ever* let into chez Horowitz while Tiernan was grounded. (And she spent plenty of time being grounded.)

In every prison break movie, the inmates waited for a chance like this—a guard with a drinking problem, a crack in the fence. Maybe (for once) instead of fighting with her mom, Tiernan would just nod her head and smile. If her mother wanted Tiernan to be Alice's best friend again, then she would play the role the best she knew how. (And Tiernan *did* know how.) After all, if her performance was convincing enough, Alice just might be her ticket out of here.

Tiernan kicked off her combat boots and slid on some boring ballet flats. She dug through the mound of clothes piled in the corner until she found the Level3 T-shirt Alice had given her as a birthday present back when she'd turned thirteen. It smelled a bit moldy, but Tiernan was willing to tolerate a little mold. Hell, she was ready to endure Alice's wrath, just as long as it came with a Get Out of Jail Free card. Maybe with Alice at her side, she'd be able to hit a few graduation parties after all.

"Mom!" Tiernan yelled, her voice straining under its own forced sweetness. "Tell Alice I'm ready for her." She took a quick look in the mirror, admiring herself in the costume of the girl she used to be.

"Knock, knock," Alice said in a timid voice. *Some wrath.* All it took was one look at Alice's face for Tiernan to see that her secret about that night at the freshman dance was still safe. Then why *was* Alice here?

"Howdy, stranger," Tiernan said.

"Nice T-shirt," said Alice.

Oh, this old thing? Tiernan thought, but instead said, "Yeah. It's funny, seeing you when I'm wearing this."

"Well, considering why I'm here," Alice replied, "it's totally *beshert.*"

Tiernan was surprised Alice had hung on to that Yiddish word she'd taught her all those years ago. She also wondered what she meant by it. But before she had a chance to ask, Alice was off and running.

"So, I was watching MTV yesterday—well, I wasn't really watching it, but I had it on and—I don't know if you heard about this—I mean, it's been on the radio but I'm not sure what station you listen to, but anyway . . ."

Alice had always been a fast talker, but whenever she felt uncomfortable or nervous, she bordered on unintelligible. Unfortunately, Tiernan's Alice decoder had grown rusty over time.

"So I was looking on Mapquest and I figure it's about a five-day drive to get to Austin. And I thought we could share the driving once I show you how to handle the stick shift. Plus, I was thinking we'd alternate between staying at motels and sleeping in the van."

Tiernan thought cozying up to Alice might get her out of the house for a night or two—but a full-fledged ten-day vacation? *Jackpot!* Sure, it would be awkward to go on a road trip with her ex–best friend to see a band she hadn't listened to in years, but it still beat living with the dragon lady under house arrest. Just as long as she wasn't stuck in a van with Summer Dalton for ten days (and Alice said she wasn't coming) the whole thing would be totally bearable. Who knew? Maybe they'd even end up having some fun.

Tiernan climbed onto her desk so she could see out the high basement window. Sure enough, there was the Pea Pod parked in front of her house. Her getaway car.

"You're sure Summer's not coming?"

"She can't," Alice said, shaking her head. "She's going away with her boyfriend."

There was only one possible catch in this impossibly perfect plan. What if her mother said no? Tiernan *was* still grounded, and, as a rule, Judy's punishments were nonnegotiable. Unless Tiernan didn't try to negotiate. If she just slipped away under the radar, by the time her mother figured out she was missing, she'd be halfway across the country.

Technically, it wasn't running away. She'd give Judy a courtesy call from the road. Let her know there was no need to slap her picture on a milk carton or anything drastic like that. And how angry could her mother get if she was hanging out with Alice Miller? That was like the woman's wet dream.

Tiernan stared at the Pea Pod. All she needed now was her retainer and her natural hair color and it'd be eighth grade all over again.

"So," Tiernan whispered so her mother wouldn't hear, "anything special I should bring along? Some back issues of *Tiger Beat*? Maybe my old training bra?"

"Well," Alice said, deadpan, "if it still fits."

Tiernan smiled. Unlike her friendship with Alice, her love of Level3, or any of the other stuff she'd be putting on for this trip, the training bra was probably the one thing she hadn't grown out of.

"UNADULTERATED"

THE SCULPTORS WHO CARVED YOU OUT OF STONE

HAVE GONE AND LEFT YOU ALL ALONE

THEIR WELL-ETCHED DETAILS ARE YOUR LEGACY

BUT THEY'RE NOT WHAT YOU WERE MEANT TO BE

DADDY SPLIT,

YOUR MOMMA'S GONE,

YOU'RE UNADULTERATED,

BETTER GET REACQUAINTED

WITH YOU.

—*from Level3's self-titled first CD*

Chapter Four

ON MONDAY AT 8:32 A.M.—PRECISELY FOUR MINUTES AFTER HER mother left for work—Tiernan threw on her army-store back-pack, slapped a Post-it note on the kitchen table, then zipped down the driveway on her skateboard. She needed to haul butt over to Alice's pronto, before some friend of her mom's spotted her and called Judy up to report an Unidentified Tiernan Sighting.

She cruised out of her neighborhood in no time at all. But the closer she got to Alice's house, the slower her skate-board seemed to go. Sure, her mother could nab her at any minute—and if she did, she'd probably be grounded right up until she got dropped off at the dorms in September. But at least Tiernan knew what she was running from. What was she running to?

A gawker in a beige Lexus wagged his head disapprovingly as Tiernan rolled across Main Street, making a sharp left into Dunkin' Donuts. Like ugly overpriced sedans were the only vehicles with drive-thru privileges.

And why shouldn't she stop to grab a bite? Now that half the town had seen her, there wasn't a reason to rush. Judging from the number of stares she'd gotten, you'd think blue-haired girls on skateboards sporting thirty-pound backpacks weren't a standard part of the Walford morning commute.

"Welcome to Dunkin' Donuts," a female voice crackled over the loudspeaker. "What can I get for you this morning?"

Tiernan scanned the menu board for something she felt like eating. Part of her wanted to bail right now—to just go back home, lock herself in her room, and pretend like this morning's little field trip never happened.

"Ma'am, what can I get for you?" Clearly Tiernan's indecision was twisting this woman's panties into a major bunch. The skateboard probably wasn't helping.

"Ummmm . . . how 'bout a large chai?" Tiernan asked, like it was a question.

She paid for her drink, then scooted back to Main Street, struggling to stay on her board between the weight of her pack and the steaming, twenty-two-ounce beverage in her hand.

Normally, Tiernan was all about sugar. But the chai was so disgustingly sweet it actually made her teeth hurt. Who knew what it would do to her stomach lining if she somehow managed to finish the thing? Her belly had been feeling funky all morning, anyway. Ever since she left the note for her mom.

Don't worry. I'm safe. Be back soon. —T.

She could just see the look on her mother's face when she came home and discovered the note on the kitchen table. Judy probably wouldn't waste any time before she put out an APB to all of Tiernan's friends, who of course knew nothing, which meant she'd have to suck it up and call Tiernan's dad, which would only piss her off more. But the only person who knew where she was going was Alice.

Or so Tiernan assumed until she rounded the corner onto Alice's street and saw Bill and Sarah Miller smiling and waving at her from the front lawn. *Crap.* She hadn't thought of the parents factor.

"Hey, it's the T-Bird!" Bill called out as she skidded into the driveway. "Long time no see."

T-Bird was Tiernan's old nickname. Summer had made it up back in fifth grade, a blatant rip-off of skateboarding legend Tony "Birdman" Hawk. Of course, Hawk was way past his prime even back then, but he was probably the only boarder Summer could actually name.

"Hey, Bill, Sarah." Alice's parents were the first names kind. Every evening they ate dinner together as a family. On Friday nights, they played board games.

"Happy graduation!" Sarah said.

"Thanks." Tiernan smiled, praying for Alice to come and save her from this dreaded small talk.

"So, Tiernan, how's your mom doing?" Sarah asked.

Fine, until she realizes I'm gone, Tiernan thought. "Uh, the same."

Just then Alice flew out of the house, arms loaded high with blankets, making a beeline for the back of the Pea Pod. No high-fructose caffeinated beverages necessary for this girl.

"Tiernan! You're here," Alice said, raising her eyebrows, which Tiernan interpreted to mean *Tiernan! You're late!*

"Helluva commute this morning," Tiernan said, holding up her Styrofoam Dunkin' Donuts cup as evidence. Disturbingly, it was almost empty.

"So, Tiernan, where are you going to school in the fall?" Bill asked.

"In Boston. Emerson College."

Sarah nodded her approval. "I have a friend at Emerson. She teaches in the drama depart—"

"*Mom*," Alice snapped. "We don't have time for chitchat if we're going to make it to West Virginia by tonight."

"Aye-aye, Captain!" Sarah said, shooting her a look of exaggerated deference.

"You forgot to salute, hon," Bill added, elbowing his wife.

Alice gave Tiernan an eye roll. "Just toss your stuff in the back."

For the first time in her life, Tiernan was grateful for Alice's anal-retentive need to be on time. She wedged her skateboard behind Alice's suitcase, remembering to grab her iPod from her backpack before tossing it on top. With ten straight days of unadulterated Alice ahead of her, odds were that she'd give it some serious use. Might as well grab her camera, too. You could never have too many distractions to fill up those long stretches of uncomfortable silence.

"Water, sunglasses, cell phone, map," Alice was reading off a typed-up checklist. "Okay, looks like we're good to go," she said, smiling at Tiernan.

Sarah rushed over to hug her daughter. "Just promise me you'll drive carefully, okay? Never when you're too tired."

"And call us. At least every five hundred miles," Bill said, moving in to give Tiernan a squeeze, which, shockingly, turned out to be *less* awkward than Sarah's squishy mom-boob embrace.

Tiernan climbed into the Pea Pod, face-to-face with a sign written in her own handwriting, circa sixth grade: LEVEL3 SUPER-FAN HEADQUARTERS. *More like Super* Dork *Headquarters*. It was strange to be back in the van with all their old stuff just as they'd left it—their posters, their precious Level3 collages.

"Okay, let's do this thing," Alice said, starting the Pea Pod.

The thrum of the engine sent shivers up Tiernan's spine.

"Bon voyage!" Bill shouted from the front steps as the Pea Pod slowly backed down the driveway. Tiernan waved politely out the window and Alice gave the horn a quick double-beep, then Bill and Sarah disappeared inside their house and she and Alice were alone.

Tiernan was tempted to take a picture of this moment just to prove it was actually happening. She was really running away.

Not to mention driving cross-country with Alice Miller. It was hard to say which made her more nervous.

"Stop!" shouted a voice from behind the van.

Alice's eyes flew to the rearview mirror and the van screeched to a halt. *Shoot.* Tiernan couldn't believe her luck. *Busted while she was still in the driveway.* Her heart hammered in her chest as she turned to face the one person in Walford she'd been trying to avoid.

Okay, make that two people.

"Oh my God!" Alice squealed. She flung open her door and leaped out onto the pavement. "Don't tell me you're coming?"

Yeah, don't tell me.

Summer Dalton strutted over to Alice in a form-fitting yellow tank top and khaki short-shorts, an oversize green Walford Hawks duffel bag in hand.

"I thought I might miss you guys, so I ran the whole way here," she said breathlessly.

Alice snatched the duffel bag from Summer's hand, like she was the girl's personal bellhop. "I can't believe it." Alice giggled. "All three of us, together again!" Then she quickly turned away, fiddling with Summer's luggage in an effort to cover up the embarrassment of her own enthusiasm. Not that Summer noticed. She had already let herself into the back, filling the van with a cloying flowery smell, like a women's magazine after somebody ripped open all the perfume samples.

"Wow, this looks exactly the same! Are you guys having

flashbacks, or what?" Summer asked, smiling at Tiernan.

"Yeah, but it might be from all those mushrooms I ate back in ninth grade," Tiernan replied.

Summer freaking Dalton. There was something behind that superfake smile of hers (a whiff of desperation?) that made Tiernan pretty sure Summer wasn't here to reconnect with her old middle school pals. A runaway can always spot another runaway.

"Okay, ladies, take two," Alice said, getting back behind the wheel.

This time they made it out of the driveway.

"Just so you guys know," Alice began, "there's plenty of fruit in the built-in coolers in back, and the water tank's full, so you can just fill your water bottles at the sink. First-aid kit's in the storage space above your head, Summer. Scrabble and Pictionary are in the one at your feet."

"Did you remember to pack the Belgian waffle maker?" Tiernan asked.

Of course Alice hadn't overlooked a single detail. Back when they were all friends (as opposed to whatever they were now—van-mates?), Tiernan and Summer used to have a running joke that they lived life like they were vacationing on a luxury liner and Alice—hyperorganized child that she was— was their cruise director.

"I brought my GPS along!" Summer announced, pulling it from her trendy oversize purse. It was still in the box, unopened.

"It was a graduation gift from my parents," she explained. "They're worried about me driving in Boston. All those one-way streets."

Tiernan rolled her eyes. Boston College wasn't technically even *in* Boston. It was in Newton, which was a suburb almost exactly like Walford, full of wide *two*-way streets, sprawling green lawns, and rich people in khakis who cared about sports.

"Tiernan, you want to set it up?" Alice asked.

"Maybe Summer should do it. It's her thing."

Summer shook her head. "You know I'm terrible with directions. Plus, you *are* in the co-pilot's seat."

Summer handed the box up to Tiernan, but she refused to take it. "Just so you both know, I'm not planning on being van bitch for the next two thousand miles."

"Why not?" Summer asked cheerily. "You seem to be doing a pretty good job so far."

Tiernan gave a small chuckle. She had to admit, Summer could really dish it out when she wanted to.

"You guys," Alice chided, "once I teach you how to drive the Pea Pod we'll *all* have a turn at copilot, o—?"

But a loud thump interrupted Alice's peacemaking.

"Stop the van!" Summer screeched from the back. "Alice, pull over!"

"Shoot!" Alice hit the steering wheel with her hand. "Shoot! Shoot! Shoot!"

Tiernan hadn't seen what they'd hit, but judging from

Alice's and Summer's reactions, it was either the most ador-
able puppy in the world or a wagon full of preschoolers. But
just as she was about to ask, Tiernan spotted the lifeless clump
of gray fur through the rear windshield, lying by the side of
the road about twenty yards back. A squirrel. It was only a
squirrel.

Not the best omen for the start of their trip. That is, if
Tiernan still believed in any of that *beshert* crap anymore.

"PARADE"

DON'T TELL ME YOU'RE GONNA BE LATE,
YOUR P-P-PARADE WILL JUST HAVE TO WAIT.
'CAUSE YOU KNOW, I'M GONNA BE THERE
RIGHT ON TIME

I WAS RIGHT HERE WHEN WE MET
AND N-N-N-NO, NO I'M NOT HERE YET
BUT YOU KNOW, I'M GONNA BE THERE
RIGHT ON TIME

—*from Level3's third CD,* Natural Causes

Chapter Five

the squirrel. "Just perfect." Three minutes on the road and already they were leaving dead bodies in their wake.

"The poor little thing," Summer gushed, leaning over the corpse as if it were a beloved family pet.

Of course, Alice felt terrible about killing an innocent creature. But it wasn't as if it were premeditated. The truth was, if Summer hadn't freaked out over it, she might not have even bothered to stop.

"Chief, we've got a 419 at the middle school soccer fields," Tiernan said in her best policewoman imitation, focusing her lens on the victim like she was a detective on *CSI: Pea Pod*.

Alice approached the body cautiously. Despite the gut-wrenching sound it had made on impact, she was relieved to find the squirrel unbloodied and intact.

"I think we should call the police," Summer said.

Do the cops even deal with road kill? Alice wondered. And supposing they actually did, they'd probably make her give a statement and fill out a police report. Like she didn't have enough stress in her life without having to worry about a vehicular squirrelcide on her record. At least not until she'd heard back from Brown.

"We are not calling the po-pos for some smelly, disease-infested rodent," Tiernan said, snapping another photo. "It probably had rabies anyway."

"Stop taking pictures!" Summer barked. "Give the poor creature some dignity."

"It's only a squirrel." Tiernan shrugged. "What do you want us to do? Go casket shopping?"

"*Ladies*," Alice said sharply. This situation was already bad enough without having Tiernan and Summer at each other's throats.

"We don't need a casket to bury it," Summer shot back.

"You actually want to bury it?" Tiernan asked, incredulous.

"I think this is public property." Alice pointed to the fields beyond the patch of road where they stood—the same place they used to play soccer as kids. "I'm not sure it's even legal to bury a squirrel here."

"All I know is that it's the right thing to do," Summer said. Normally, Summer was a strict rule-follower, but she'd always had a soft spot for nature's innocent creatures. Unless, of course, that creature happened to be Alice.

"Ooh, I have an idea!" Tiernan squealed. "Maybe we can hire Elton John to perform a personalized version of 'Candle in the Wind' at the funeral!"

Alice let out a long, heavy sigh. Five minutes ago she'd been thrilled to learn that Summer was coming along for the trip, that all three Peas would be back together for the Level3 show, just like she'd planned. Of course, back then, she'd naively assumed Summer and Tiernan had let go of the past and were capable of acting like mature, reasonable people.

"Listen," Alice began. "I think we should all take a minute to say our good-byes to the squirrel, then get back on the road. We've got a lot of ground to cover today."

"I wasn't kidding." Summer planted her hands on her hips. "It's bad mojo not to honor the dead."

And what about starting off our trip with a funeral? Alice wanted to ask. *What kind of mojo is that?* Instead, she just glanced at her watch. At this rate they'd be lucky to make it out of Walford.

Tiernan bent down and snapped a close-up of the squirrel "Just gathering some forensic evidence," she mocked. "In case the CIA gets involved."

"Hilarious," Summer spat, turning her attention to Alice. "So, what does our fearless leader think?"

Fearless leader? Ha! Alice didn't know what terrified her more—saying no to the funeral and have to deal with Summer's sulking, or saying yes and being the butt of Tiernan's jokes for the next two hundred miles.

She coiled a lock of hair around her finger, trying to buy herself some time while the squirrel's black, glazed-over eyes appeared to stare at her expectantly, as if waiting for her to issue a verdict. Being the leader had always come naturally to Alice. It was being in the middle she'd always hated.

But what choice did she have? She could stand around all day waiting for Summer and Tiernan to come up with a compromise on their own (not likely), or she could save them all some time and step in and do it for them. "I say we have a *short* memorial service," Alice finally declared. "But let's be quick about it. I want to make it to West Virginia by sundown."

The Pea Pod's emergency road kit contained a new roll of duct tape, a flashlight with fresh batteries, two kinds of screwdrivers, but no shovel—a rodent funeral being the one crisis Alice *hadn't* anticipated.

"Well, I'm not digging by hand," Summer cried, showing off her perfectly manicured French nails.

"Uh-oh," Tiernan chuckled. "Summer's got her claws out."

"We just need to keep looking," Alice said, before Summer had the chance to fire back. Alice opened the supply cabinet below the sink, unpacking its contents just as carefully as she'd packed them only hours ago. "There has to be *something* in here we can use."

Out came the Tupperware and plastic spoons, the boxes of of trash bags and rolls of toilet paper.

"What about this?" Summer asked. She held up Alice's stainless steel travel mug, the words #1 DAUGHTER emblazoned on the side. "We can use it like a scoop to dig the squirrel's grave!"

A grave-digging scoop, Alice thought to herself. Not exactly what she'd envisioned with the gift her parents had given her for making National Honor Society. And sentimental value aside, how was she supposed to drink her green tea every morning if her favorite mug was defiled by dirt?

Alice looked at the collection of kitchen accessories and cleaning supplies on the floor of the van—all of them useless as digging implements. She wasn't exactly thrilled about sacrificing her "#1 Daughter" mug, but if it would get them back on the road faster, she'd take one for the team.

Summer used the mug (which proved to be a surprisingly effective shovel) while Alice, who wasn't afraid of a little dirt, did her share of the digging by hand. For ten minutes they toiled on their knees in the grass, as Tiernan (who was boycotting the funeral) kicked back in the comfort of Pea Pod, munching on a Hostess Snowball. Normally, Alice would have complained about such slackerly behavior. But with Tiernan and Summer separated, there had been a ceasefire in their bickering, and she didn't dare risk starting it up again.

Except for a few rare occasions, Alice avoided conflict at all cost. She and MJ never fought—unless you counted their heated debate over which font to use for the school's literary magazine. In fact, ever since the debacle at the Winter Wonderland Dance (the most infamous of Alice's infrequent outbursts), her teenage years had been almost abnormally peaceful and calm. She didn't have backstabbing friends or screaming fights with her parents. She didn't get grounded for staying out past curfew, or wind up crying over some boy in the bathroom at the big school dance. Though she'd have happily shed a few tears in the handicapped stall if it meant actually *having* a boyfriend.

"It's done!" Summer stood up, wiping her hands on her shorts.

Alice peered into the hole. Personally, she would have dug another foot, but if Summer was happy, *she* was happy. And the sooner they were back on the road, the better.

"Okay," Alice agreed. "So how do we get him in there?"

"Hmm." Summer wrinkled her nose and looked around. The squirrel lay at least five feet from the open grave.

"We could just kick him in," Tiernan called out from the passenger's seat. "I've still got a pretty good chip shot."

"Since when was your chip shot good?" Summer asked.

Can you two just let it go already? Alice wanted to scream. *The past is over. What's done is done.* Alice wished she were the type of person who could just let it slide. After all, Tiernan and Summer were the ones with the issue, not her. But here she was, trying her best to make things pleasant and happy again and getting sucked into the drama in the process.

"Help me find something to pick him up with," Alice said, searching the grass for the perfect corpse-moving tool. If she didn't find something fast, that squirrel might not be the only thing dead around here.

"How about chopsticks?" Tiernan offered, wiping a flake of pink coconut from her lip.

Tiernan's sharp sense of humor was one of the things Alice had always loved best about her. But sometimes a person's best qualities have a funny way of being their worst qualities too.

"Can you just try to help us out here?" Alice asked, losing her patience.

"I *am* trying to help," Tiernan continued. "What I meant was"—Tiernan pulled herself from the van and picked two sticks off the ground—"you could use a couple of sticks like chopsticks to pick it up."

After the gruesome task was done (by none other than Tiernan herself, *thankfully*) they gathered around the grave and filled it with dirt.

Alice didn't want to oversentimentalize it, but it *did* seem like a rather strange coincidence that the three of them had wound up at the edge of the very same soccer field where they'd first met and become friends back in fourth grade. Even stranger was the fact that they'd now spent more time giving closure to a dead squirrel than they had to the death of their five-year friendship.

When they were done, Summer patted the earth flat with her hands. "Would anyone like to say a few words?"

Tiernan stifled a laugh. "He was a good squirrel," she said in her best spiritual-sounding voice. "He really loved his nuts."

"Can you just be serious for one second of your life?" Summer asked.

"I'd like to say something," Alice jumped in. She wasn't sure where she was going with this, but it had to be easier to eulogize a dead squirrel than to play referee to these two. "I'd just like to, ah, tell the squirrel that . . . I'm sorry. For killing it. It was all my fault, really. And if I'd been looking where I was going, he—or *she*—would probably still be alive today." Alice hung her head, making it look like she was extra reverent, though, in truth, she'd been so swept up by the sentiment of her own words she was afraid that if she made eye contact with Summer or Tiernan, she might actually start to cry. Her rational side told her it didn't matter, that it was only a stupid squirrel. Yet, the fact remained that she'd killed an innocent creature, just like that, without meaning to.

Summer cleared her throat. "Let's all pause for a moment of—" But the driving techno beat of her cell phone smothered the word "silence."

"Sheesh," Tiernan said under her breath. "If that ringtone was any louder, it'd wake the dead."

"Sorry 'bout that." Summer quickly slid the phone from her pocket, glanced at the caller ID, and silenced it. She may have been trying to hide it, but Alice still knew Summer well enough to tell when she was pissed.

"Let's continue," Summer said evenly, letting the call go to voice mail.

Alice took a long deep breath, then exhaled it slowly (just like her yoga teacher instructed) while reciting a calming mantra in her mind. *The past is past. What's done is done. It was an accident. It was only an accident.*

But no matter how many mantras she said, nothing could erase the fact that some mistakes have consequences for which there are no second chances.

When she looked up at Tiernan and Summer, she could swear they felt it too. A shared grief. A silent moment of understanding. But as soon as they noticed her staring, Summer quickly hid her face while Tiernan reverted to her usual smirk.

Back in eighth grade, Alice had been both confused and in awe as she'd watched Summer and Tiernan develop this new air of cool detachment, like they'd suddenly become above it all, no matter what "it" happened to be. At first Alice assumed the same thing would happen to her eventually, that she'd grow into it, the way some girls developed later than others. But that moment never came. She may have been the first to wear a bra, but Alice was the last to grow into this studied indifference. Try as she might to be guarded and apathetic, she was (and probably always would be) the type of girl who walked around with her heart on her sleeve.

It was especially bad during those first few months after the Winter Wonderland Dance. Alice did her best to hide the hurt expression on her face whenever she bumped into Summer in the halls or drove past Tiernan's street, but whomever she was with only needed to take one look at her face before they would inevitably ask what was wrong. Just another example of the many differences between the person Alice wanted to be and the one she actually was.

"Any final words?" Summer asked, opening her eyes.

But there would be no words for what happened next, as a paw, then two, then the squirrel's entire gray furry head thrust its way through the earth. For what felt like a good ten seconds, nobody moved or spoke—the only sound came from the squirrel, whose twitchy black nose sniffed the air as its eyes darted from Alice to Summer to Tiernan, then back again, as if they were all stuck in some strange interspecies staring contest.

Even Tiernan was too stunned to utter a snarky remark.

For a creature that had just been buried alive, the squirrel looked surprisingly chipper, as if things like this happened to him every day. And before Alice's brain could even begin to process what her eyes were seeing, the little rodent gave one final wriggle and freed himself from the hole—sending Alice, Summer, and Tiernan straight from their stupefied states into pee-in-their-pants hysteria.

By the time the squirrel had scampered off into the woods, all three of them were howling and crying and rolling around on the grass in a good old-fashioned laughing fit, just like they used to do, back in the day.

But as happy as Alice was to be sharing this hilarious moment with Summer and Tiernan, the shock of it all left her feeling strangely off-balance. When the squirrel was dead, the world was a place Alice was familiar with—a place of unwavering certainties, where what was buried *stayed* buried, and what was done (like she'd said in her mantra) was most definitely done. But if a squirrel could rise from the dead, maybe the past had more power than Alice had previously given it credit for. Maybe the past was only the past until it decided to claw its way back to the present.

"THE COUNTDOWN"
THE ROCKET I BUILT
OUT OF PAPER AND GLUE
JUST BROKE APART IN THE ATMOSPHERE
OVER YOU.

AND NOW ALL THE PIECES
ARE FALLING TO EARTH
AT THE SPEED OF LIGHT,
WHAT AN AMAZING SIGHT.

—*from Level3's third CD,* Natural Causes

Chapter Six

THEY WERE BARELY THROUGH THE TOLLS ON THE MASS TURNPIKE and already Jace had called and texted twice. It was hard to say which annoyed Summer more—being stalked by the guy who just dumped her, or being forced to endure Alice and Tiernan's not-so-subtle digs at her expense.

"Summer, I actually think you were right." The sarcasm oozed from Tiernan's voice. "I think it *was* dead, and the thing that crawled out of the grave was a zombie squirrel."

"Either that, or maybe the rodent Jesus?" Alice joked, ever the faithful sidekick.

Somewhere between the "gravesite" and now, the ice that had been broken by their laugh had quickly refrozen again. Summer assumed things would be different after four years' time. But apparently old habits (like Alice and Tiernan ganging up on her) died just about as easily as squirrels hit by vans.

So, she'd made a mistake. *Whatever.* It wasn't as if either of those two rocket scientists could tell the different between an unconscious rodent and a dead one.

"Hey, Summer," Tiernan called. "Maybe we should swing

by the cemetery and check on your grandma. Just in case."

Summer didn't even dignify that remark with a response. It was classic Tiernan. The girl never knew when to quit.

"Summer, what does your GPS say?" Alice asked, thankfully changing the subject. "I already mapped out our route on paper, but I'm a little confused about what we do when we get to Connecticut."

After a little trial and error, Summer finally had the GPS up and running and she handed it up to Alice. "According to what this thing says, we don't make a single turn for the next forty-five miles."

"You never know," Tiernan said gleefully. "A bird could fly into the windshield."

Summer was about to respond when her cell phone vibrated in her pocket. Jace again. She didn't much feel like talking to him, but given the conversation in the van, it seemed like the lesser of two evils.

"H-hey, it's you." Jace sounded surprised that she answered.

"What's up?" Summer kept her voice all business.

"I've been trying to call you for the last half hour."

Summer didn't reply. Why was it any concern of his whether or not she answered her phone?

"S-S-Summer?" Jace stammered. "Are you still there?"

"Yes." Summer kept her voice low. "I'm here."

"Well, the reason I've been trying to call you"—Jace paused dramatically—"was to say that I made a mistake."

Summer felt her blood rush down her neck and arms.

"I acted like a fool," Jace continued. "And I'm calling to say I was wrong. I want us to be together again, Summer."

Summer waited a good five seconds before she spoke. *Let him suffer.* "So, what happened between today and yesterday?" she whispered angrily. Up in the driver's seat, she could see Alice trying her best to pretend she was concentrating on driving as opposed to, say, blatantly eavesdropping.

"Maz was talking trash about how I needed to be free my last summer before college," Jace explained. "And I'm not *blaming* Maz. I know it's not his fault. I'm the one who listened to him. But I just thought, well . . . your parents started dating in high school, and then they got married. And I started thinking that if the same thing happens to us, then we will have only been with each other, and, well, you know what I mean. . . ." Jace let his voice trail off.

Even right now, mad as she was, whenever Jace mentioned marriage, for some strange reason, Summer couldn't help but smile. It was completely lame. Not to mention delusional. She hated the idea of people marrying their high school sweethearts. And it wasn't like Summer ever took Jace's talk of getting married seriously—*they were only eighteen, for God's sake.* But something about it made her happy—knowing that he *wanted* to marry her, someday, even if she didn't want to marry him.

"I know it was stupid, Summer. *I* was stupid. But I want you to go to the Vineyard with me on Friday. I just want everything to be back to normal again."

The thought of going to the Vineyard made Summer snap back to reality. On the one hand, at least Jace was admitting he'd made a mistake. But dumping her on graduation day just so he could spend his last high school summer hooking up with randoms? It was gross. Not to mention demeaning.

"Well, it can't be normal again," Summer hissed. "You humiliated me. Not to mention ruining my summer plans. You can't just change your mind on a whim and expect me to come running back to you."

"I love you," Jace pleaded. "I said I was sorry."

"I'm on a road trip right now," Summer said coolly. "I'll be home in ten days. We'll talk then." Jace had just started to speak when she snapped the phone shut.

Up in the driver's seat, Alice whistled a Level3 tune, trying to act nonchalant. Proof that she and Tiernan had heard absolutely everything.

"Hey, you guys." Alice kept her voice extra casual. "Remember how the van has electrical outlets? Well, if you want, we can plug in my iPod dock . . ."

Summer knew Alice was just trying to lighten the mood, but the last thing she wanted was Alice's help. *Although* . . . if they cranked up the music loud enough, at least she'd be spared from Alice's inevitable onslaught of probing questions about Jace. *Stupid Jace.* Summer had barely wrapped her head around the idea of being without him, and now here he was, trying to pull her back in.

"Summer? Summer!" Alice was commanding her to do something, but she didn't know what. "I said the iPod dock's in the cabinet above your head if you want to go ahead and grab it."

Summer nodded and did as she was told. It was strange to see such sleek audio gear in the Pea Pod when they used to listen to CDs from Alice's crappy old boom box. Their technology may have been upgraded, but in that same amount of time, the people inside the van seemed to have hardly changed at all.

"Backseat gets to deejay," Tiernan said, handing back her iPod. Of course, Summer was "allowed" to deejay, as long as the songs were from Tiernan's music library. *Typical.*

Most of the bands Tiernan listened to, Summer had never even heard of. But it didn't take her long to find what she was looking for. The only Level3 album on Tiernan's iPod was their first, but it was just the hard-driving, angst-ridden music Summer wanted to hear. She pressed play and the baseline of "Jackie Needs New Glasses" filled the van.

NOW YOU'RE PROMOTING—YEAH, YEAH
PROTECTIVE-COATING—YEAH, YEAH
AND I'M JUST NOTING,
THAT IT MIGHT CHANGE THE VIEW.

Reunited

Yesterday when Jace dumped her, Summer felt nothing but anger. But now that he wanted her back, it was all she could do to not break down and cry. Not that she'd ever let that happen in front of Tiernan and Alice.

Maybe Jace was right. Pretending like the whole thing never happened *would* be the easiest thing to do. Then again, Summer wasn't exactly the type to forgive and forget. But what was there to forgive Jace for, really? *All* guys thought about being with other women. And there was a difference between thinking about something and actually doing it.

"Up ahead, take the motorway," a British voice blasted out of nowhere, making Summer jump.

Alice put a hand on her heart. "That was a wake-up call."

"In eight hundred yards, take the motorway." The voice was coming from Summer's GPS.

"Sheesh!" Tiernan snatched it off the dash, randomly prodding the touch screen with her finger. "How do you turn this thing down?"

"Give it to me," Summer said.

"Turn right!" the GPS commanded from her hand. Just what Summer needed, one more voice in her life trying to tell her what to do.

"You know who that thing sounds like?" Tiernan asked.

Summer thought for a second. The voice *was* oddly familiar. "Coach Quigley!" she and Alice shouted simultaneously while Tiernan chuckled to herself.

The *real* Coach Quigley, their first soccer coach, was a former professional "football" player from Manchester, England, who had the rather unseemly habit of barking at the Walford Girls Age Eleven and Under as if they were playing Brazil in the final game of the World Cup.

"So, should I change the voice?" Summer asked. "It has other options."

"No way!" Alice whined. "Coach Q was the best!"

From the backseat, Summer could only see Alice in profile, but it was enough to make out the self-satisfied expression on her face. Ever since she'd known her, Alice had been a sucker for nostalgia. None of them would be here right now if she weren't.

"Look." Tiernan pointed to a sign for 84 WEST—HARTFORD/ NEW YORK CITY. "You guys want to stop in the city for lunch? I know this place in the Village that makes a killer broccoli-garlic pizza."

"Sounds good to me," Summer said. She'd been to New York one other time, on their seventh-grade class field trip. But she'd only made it as far as the Statue of Liberty, never to Greenwich Village, once home to such greats as Allen Ginsberg, Maya Angelou, Dylan Thomas . . .

"We can't," Alice said matter-of-factly. "Manhattan has way too much traffic. By the time we get in and out, there's no way we'd still be able to make it to West Virginia by tonight."

"So?" Tiernan asked. "What's the big hurry to get to West Virginia?"

"Well, for one thing, we already lost time this morning, and I don't want to end up rushing to Austin at the last minute because we've wasted time in a city that's not even four hours away from where we live . . ."

Summer closed her eyes and let out a sigh. Even Coach Quigley seemed irritated by Alice's blathering, shouting directions over her as she talked. It took some trial and error, but Summer finally figured out how to adjust Coach Quigley's audio level. Sadly, Alice didn't come with volume control.

". . . which I've calculated specifically so that we'd spend an average seven hours on the road each day . . ."

Tiernan turned around, pretending to adjust her seat belt, and shot Summer a knowing smile. Summer smiled back. Maybe they still had something in common after all. Alice was still a control freak. And it still bugged the crap out of them.

"Anyway, I'm not taking Route 84," Alice continued. "I'm taking Route 91."

"So, should I just turn it off?" Summer asked, gesturing to her GPS.

"I guess for now, if you want to," Alice said.

Summer shoved Coach Quigley into her purse and pulled out her phone. She had four new text messages. The first was a mushy apology from Jace. The second three were from Melanie, Claire, and Jocelyn asking, "Where r u?" and "Jace still luuuvs you," and "Austin, TX! WTF?" Summer hadn't told anyone other than her parents she was going on this trip. Then again, she hadn't decided whether to come on this trip until this morning. What did her friends expect her to do—post her entire life on Facebook?

When she'd left her house a few hours ago, getting some distance from the grapevine of gossip back in Walford seemed like a great idea. Of course, that was before she knew Jace wanted her back.

Summer's cell phone buzzed in her hand with yet another text from her oh-so-remorseful ex-boyfriend. And as good as it felt to know she was wanted, part of her couldn't help but wonder—as she read Jace's fifth sappy apology—if the only reason he wanted her back was because she'd actually gone away.

"HEY, STRANGER"
I OVERHEARD PEOPLE
TALKING 'BOUT YOU.
I DIDN'T KNOW THEM,
BUT YOU SOUND LIKE A STRANGER.

THEY SAID THINGS ABOUT YOU
I KNEW WEREN'T TRUE
EVEN THOUGH THEY SOUNDED JUST EXACTLY LIKE YOU.

—*from Level3's second CD*, Rough & Tumble

Chapter Seven

TIERNAN OPENED HER EYES AND CHUGGED A LARGE GULP OF HER lukewarm blue Gatorade. Shortly after scarfing down lunch at a New Jersey Turnpike rest stop (ugh!) she'd slipped into a long, fast-food-induced coma. Either that, or being forced to listen to the Queen Bee blabbing to her drones back in Walford had rendered her unconscious.

One hundred fifty miles later, Summer was still going strong. Apparently, her breakup with Jace (if it even *was* a breakup) was happening by committee.

"Are we there yet?" Tiernan asked groggily.

"Nope," Alice answered. "Still in Pennsylvania."

In the backseat, Summer flipped her phone shut, then immediately opened it back up and dialed another number. "Hi, Melanie? It's me. Listen to what Sierra just told me."

Tiernan raised her eyebrows and shot Alice a look. This *90210*-style drama was definitely not how Tiernan's posse rolled. Then again, Tiernan could actually make decisions all by herself.

"Hang on a sec, Mel. Claire's beeping in."

As long as Tiernan could remember, Summer was all about

the boy drama. Even back in fourth grade, when the only boys in their lives existed in Level3 fantasy world, Summer could get bent out of shape if she and Travis failed a compatibility quiz in *Seventeen* magazine. Once, Summer saw a video of Travis kissing a Victoria's Secret model on tmz.com and had actually cried real tears.

It wasn't as if Tiernan had never crushed on a rock star before. As a kid, she'd had a major infatuation with Luke from Level3. Hell, she'd *still* jump his bones in a heartbeat, given the chance. But, unlike Summer, Tiernan always knew the difference between a celebrity crush and reality.

"That's weird," Summer whispered. "Jace didn't tell me he went to your party."

Tiernan gave Alice another sidelong glance. If even *Alice* knew, then everyone at school had to know about Jace and that perky sophomore chick. Everyone, that is, except for Summer. The girl had an army's worth of blond frenemies back in Walford, and not one of them had the cojones to tell her Jace was stepping out on her. Not that Tiernan was about to drop that bomb.

"I thought you said you didn't go to Melanie's party. . . ." From the sound of things, Summer was back on with the cheater himself.

Tiernan leaned in toward Alice and cupped a hand over her ear. "Well, Bob," she whispered in the nasally voice of some old-timey sportscaster, "Dalton started out with a weak first quarter, but now it looks like she's turning her game around."

"Bob?" Alice asked with a chuckle.

"That doesn't make sense, Jace. How do you forget to tell me something like that?" Summer was growing impatient, louder.

Tiernan held up a fake microphone this time. "The defense is giving it everything they've got, but wait—it looks as if Dalton has rallied and—hang on—she is heading into the end zone and—oh!—out of bounds!"

"Shhhh." Alice gave her a reprimanding look Tiernan interpreted as *lower your voice*, not *stop altogether*.

"I have to say, Bob," Tiernan went on. "Dalton looks determined to take that ball to the goal line even if it means going into overtime."

Somewhere in northern Maryland, Summer (halle-frickin'-luyah!) lost cell service. If Tiernan had still been sportscasting, she would have declared it a tie.

Part of her felt a little guilty for mocking Summer's breakup. She'd had her own share of guy trouble over the years. She knew how much it sucked. Then again, it wasn't as though Tiernan had been the one yammering on the phone for the past two hours with no regard to the bleeding ears of the two *other* people in this traveling sardine can.

Plus, someone needed to cheer Alice up. Maybe Summer was too self-absorbed to notice, but it was pretty obvious to Tiernan that being left out of the loop was still Alice's number-one pet peeve. And the fact that Summer had now shared her trauma with five zillion or so of her closest friends back in Walford, and specifically *not* with the two people who were actually in the car, had to be driving her crazy.

"Hey, Summer." Alice's voice was tentative. "I just wanted to make sure you're . . . that everything's . . . okay."

Summer stopped to think, like she was pondering this for the first time. "I don't know," she finally said. Then she put Level3 back on—*loud*.

Good old Level3—more emo than 30 Seconds to Mars, less poppy (and decades younger) than U2, and just enough edge to get play on both the Top 40 *and* the alternative radio stations. Tiernan hadn't listened to Level3 in years, but in honor of the road trip, she'd loaded their first album (and their best, as far as she was concerned) onto her iPod last night. Surprisingly, their music still held up.

But even Luke Dixon's hard-core drum solo couldn't break through the walls of tension between them. And as much as Tiernan tried to kick back and enjoy the music, she couldn't help feeling twitchy and restless, like she wanted to find the nearest mosh pit and dive in headfirst. The shrink Judy forced her to see after the divorce always used to tell Tiernan that being angry was just a way people protected themselves from feeling hurt. But as far as she was concerned, the only thing that hurt was her butt from sitting on it for the past eight hours straight.

They listened to the album twice and not one of them spoke a word.

Back when they were young, Tiernan always had a knack for snapping Summer out of one of her sulky moods. It wasn't like Alice didn't try. The girl was constantly going out of her way to do something nice if Tiernan or Summer was sad, like when Tiernan told them her parents were getting divorced and an hour later Alice showed up on her doorstep with a plate of her famous chocolate-chip oatmeal cookies, still warm. But as much as Alice tried to break through to Summer, Tiernan was always the one with the magic touch. She wasn't sure how it managed to work out that way, but she figured it probably had something to do with the way Alice took things way too seriously and Tiernan never took anything seriously at all.

Not that Tiernan thought for a second that she *still* had that power over Summer. And even if she did, there were certain unwritten rules for the three of them being together again: invisible DO NOT ENTER signs; topics they dared not mention.

They finally crossed into West Virginia and Alice broke the long silence. "Check it out! We're here!" She pointed to a large WELCOME sign at the border. "What do you say we find a cheap place to stay and call it a night?"

"Works for me!" Tiernan said enthusiastically.

Summer just nodded.

At the bottom of the off ramp, they followed the blue signs toward a strip of fast-food restaurants and chain hotels.

"Just so you know," Alice began. "I'd rather stay in places

that are small and locally owned, as opposed to, say, corporate and franchised."

Tiernan had to hand it to Alice—the girl not only talked the talk, she actually walked the walk. It wasn't as if Tiernan didn't have strong beliefs about things; it was just that she showed them more in a bumper-sticker kind of way.

"Well, I don't think any of these chain hotels can take us anyway." Tiernan pointed out the window. "The Red Roof Inn says 'no vacancy.' Same with the Travelodge across the street."

They drove past four more hotels, each with a NO VACANCY sign.

"Since when did West Virginia become such a vacation hot spot?" Summer asked, suddenly perking up.

"They're probably just here for the free HBO," Tiernan offered.

Alice shook her head. "There has to be something going on. I mean, it's a Monday night."

Soon they were past the big-box stores and strip malls into a less-developed area. But even the locally owned fleabag had a NO VACANCY sign.

"Maybe we should get back on the highway and try the next exit," Alice suggested.

"Hang on." Tiernan turned to Summer. "I think we should see what Coach Quigley has to say about this."

Summer pulled out the GPS and handed it up to Tiernan.

After a bit of poking around, Tiernan found what she was looking for. "Check it out." She held the GPS up for Summer to see. "According to Coach Quigley, the Happy Beaver Campground is just eight point six miles up the road."

"*The Happy Beaver?*" Alice sounded dubious.

"*Please*, Alice," Tiernan begged. "*Please* can we stay at the Happy Beaver?"

Alice shrugged. "As long as they have vacancies, it's fine by me."

"Whatever," Summer said.

Ten minutes down the road, an enormous wooden beaver came into sight. It was only when they got closer that Tiernan noticed the little white sign the beaver held in his teeth: FULLY OCCUPIED.

"Looks like the Happy Beaver's already getting plenty of action tonight." Tiernan shrugged.

"Bummer!" Alice whined. "Now what?"

"I'm starving," Summer said. "I think we should find someplace to eat first and then figure out the hotel situation later."

From Tiernan's unscientific observation, the only thing Summer had consumed all day was a small bag of fries and a Diet Coke.

"I brought along plenty of snacks, you know," Alice offered. "Apples, clementines, granola bars, sesame rice cakes, soy crisps . . ."

"*This*, my friend, is what we call a road trip," Tiernan said, a note of authority in her voice. "Which means we should be adhering to the road-trip food pyramid, not that mini version of Whole Foods you stashed in the back."

Summer stifled a giggle.

"I guess I must have missed that day in health class," Alice said.

Tiernan went on. "On the bottom of the pyramid, you've got your snack cakes—your Ho Hos, your Twinkies, your Little Debbies. Next up, you have gummy animals, which includes your Gummi Bears, gummy worms, as well as Swedish Fish and Sour Patch Kids, all of which are considered subspecies within the gummy kingdom."

"What's at the top of the pyramid?" Alice asked, playing along.

Tiernan rolled her eyes. "Funyuns. *Duh.*"

"I think we all need to get out of this van and get some fresh air," Summer declared.

A red neon sign for Lucky's Diner flashed in the distance, so Alice headed toward it, without even bringing it up for a vote. Lucky's looked like an old-school greasy spoon, the kind of place where if it wasn't cooked in a fry-o-lator, they probably weren't serving it. When they pulled into the parking lot, Tiernan could see that the neon *L* on the Lucky's sign flickered on and off so that LUCKY's temporarily turned into UCKY's.

Alice parked in the only empty spot she could find next to a long-haired dude by a motorcycle.

"Nice wheels," he called out as they exited the Pea Pod.

"Thanks," Alice said.

The motorcycle dude was older than them, but not by much—twenty-one or twenty-two—and cute in a scraggly sort of way. Tats on both arms, three days worth of stubble on his chin, the kind of wiry, skinny guy muscles that come from working outdoors. Tiernan usually went for guys with more of an indie rock vibe to them, but there was something captivating about this one—the hint of a bad-boy gleam in his eye.

"Is it a 'seventy-seven?" he called out.

"'Seventy-six," Alice said, quickly wiping the sweat off her forehead before turning to face him. Without the breeze of the moving van, the heat was stifling.

"It's in good shape," he said, moving his gaze from Alice to Tiernan. "*Damn* good shape."

Tiernan smiled back at him, but only with the corner of her mouth. Maybe she liked him; maybe she didn't. Of course, Summer hadn't even bothered to acknowledge his presence and was already halfway across the parking lot.

"Thanks." Alice giggled. "My parents just had it redone for me as a graduation present."

Tiernan cringed. Nothing like mentioning the 'rental units to kill a good flirtationship. But, in a way, Tiernan always thought it was kind of sweet the way Alice had absolutely no moves whatsoever. She was just 100 percent pure Alice, take it or leave it.

"Anyway," Alice kept blathering, "we're pretty hungry, so we should probably go." Then she turned around and actually started to jog toward the Ucky's entrance.

"See ya around," said the dude, his gaze lingering on Tiernan.

"Maybe," Tiernan replied, giving just a hint of the other half of her smile as she slowly walked away. Mona Lisa had nothing on her.

When she entered Ucky's, Tiernan was hit with a much-needed blast of air-conditioning, and she stood under it until the breeze made the hair on her arms stand on end. She'd just started to shiver when the hostess came over, pointing them toward the last available booth.

Summer sat down first and Tiernan plopped herself onto the bench across from her, which left poor Alice with the unfortunate task of choosing sides. Tiernan could practically hear the silent eenie-meenie-minie-moe going on in Alice's head before she finally slid in next to Tiernan, her bare legs making a farting noise against the green vinyl seat.

"You gals here for the festival?" A chunky waitress with streaky blond hair and eighties bangs plunked three ice waters on the table. She was about Tiernan's mom's age and she wore a polyester uniform two sizes too small. Her name tag said WANDA.

Tiernan looked up from their menu. "What festival?"

Wanda flashed her a big gummy smile, shaking her head like Tiernan was being sarcastic, which, *for once*, she actually wasn't.

HILARY WEISMAN GRAHAM

"Y'all are pulling my leg, right?" she asked in a sticky Southern drawl.

According to Wanda, the Eyes of the World Music Festival—named after a song by the Grateful Dead (barf)—was starting tomorrow, in the next town over. Hotels, motels, and campgrounds for miles around were filled to capacity with (Wanda's words) "Birkenstock-wearin' patchouli-oil smellin' hippies." Hence all the NO VACANCY signs.

"Shoot," Alice said, when Wanda had walked off. "I really don't feel like driving another thirty miles tonight."

"Can't we just stash the Pea Pod in a parking lot and camp there?" Tiernan asked.

Alice shook her head. "Aside from the fact that it's illegal, I promised my parents we'd only stay at campgrounds."

Again with the parents. Tiernan wouldn't be surprised to find out Alice was rooming with them in her college dorm.

"Well, camping in a parking lot does not sound safe to me at all," Summer added. "Who knows what kind of random people might be roaming around at night?"

"Bunch of folks are camping out in this farmer's field off of East Mountain Road."

Two boys in tie-dye T-shirts had slumped into the booth across from theirs while Wanda was still busy clearing the dishes from the last people. From the newness of their Tevas, Tiernan guessed they were frat boy hippies as opposed to the genuine article (the key differences being showering on a daily basis and listening to Dave Matthews). The one who spoke to them was tall and skinny, with a puka-shell necklace and a patchy goatee. His friend had a stumpy ponytail and Guatemalan print shorts.

"Guy who owns the place charges five bucks a head," the one with the ponytail added.

"I don't think so," Summer jumped in. "But thanks."

"You are most definitely welcome," said the tall one, who, judging from his bloodshot eyes, was either highly allergic to something in the West Virginia air or, more likely, just plain high.

Wanda gave the boys' table a perfunctory wipe with her gray dishcloth, then hurried off. The short one adjusted his ponytail and leaned across the aisle. "So, where you guys from?"

"Massachusetts," Alice offered, after no one else did.

"No way." The stoned one laughed. "We're from Vermont!" Tiernan wasn't sure why, but New Englanders away from home were always jazzed to meet other New Englanders.

"We came down with a bunch of people from school. This band we know from UVM is opening up for RatDog."

Summer rolled her eyes.

"We're not going to the festival," Tiernan explained. "We just happened to be passing through."

"Crazy," Ponytail added.

"Totally," said Tiernan, openly mocking him. Not that he noticed.

"My name's Toad." The long-haired one pointed to a silk-screen picture on his T-shirt of a toad driving a car. Underneath it read, "Mr. Toad's Wild Ride."

"And I'm Phred. Phred with a *P-H*." The ponytailed one extended his hand.

Tiernan smirked. These guys were priceless.

Alice was the only one to return Phred's handshake.

"I'm Alice. And this is Tiernan and Summer."

"You've got extremely soft skin, Alice." Phred grinned, still holding her hand captive.

Alice blushed, slipping her fingers from his grasp. "Thanks. So do you. I mean, your skin's not *too soft*. For a man. It's, like, totally normal."

As opposed to the way Alice was acting. Someone needed to jump in and save her fast, or the girl might end up drowning in her own words.

"So, what's it like out in this field?" Tiernan asked. "Is it total hippie bacchanalia, or what?"

"Kinda," said Toad. Phred just laughed.

Wanda distributed their dinners—a basket of Lucky's country fried chicken for Alice, Cobb salad (no cheese) for Summer, and a plate of buffalo wings and an orange soda for Tiernan (from the "orange" food group, naturally).

"Maybe we should go stay in the field," Alice said, chomping into a chicken leg. "I mean, it's only one night."

"More like a night*mare*," Summer said, under her breath. "Surrounded by a bunch of dirty hippies with greasy, unwashed hair and smelly bare feet? No thanks."

"Oh, come on. They seem like nice enough guys to me," Alice said, her voice extra casual.

"Only because P-H Phred wants to get in your pants," Tiernan whispered.

"Shhh!" Alice put a finger to her lips, glancing over to Toad and Phred's table to see if they'd heard. Fortunately, the boys were both deeply entranced in a game that involved a fork, a balled-up straw wrapper, and Toad's open mouth.

"I just figure it's the simplest option," Alice continued. "Plus, I might end up going to school with them at UVM if Brown doesn't let me in."

"I don't know if that's such a great opener," Summer cautioned. "Hey, guys, guess what? *Your* school is my *safety*."

Tiernan sneaked another look at Toad and Phred just as the projectile straw wrapper pegged Toad in the eye. So, they were a little on the dorky side. But if Alice was into Phred, who were they to put the kibosh on her hookup? Clearly the girl needed all the help she could get in the romance department. And going to a hippie party was bound to be more fun than being holed up in some boring motel room with Alice and Summer.

"My vote is that we stay in the field," Tiernan announced.

"Great!" Alice smiled, turning her attention to Summer. "I mean, if that's okay with you?"

"Does it matter?" Summer asked flatly.

Tiernan licked some buffalo sauce off her thumb. "Well, it *is* two against one."

"So, my opinion doesn't even count?" Summer sounded snippy.

"Last time I checked, we still lived in a democracy," Tiernan shot back.

"Guys," Alice tried to interject, but Summer wouldn't let her.

"First off, we don't even *know* them," Summer said. "And second, spending the night at some loud, sketchy hippie-fest isn't exactly my scene."

"Maybe instead of just thinking about yourself you should think about *Alice*," Tiernan spat. "Not to mention the fact that she's been driving all day long. I don't think it's fair to make her get back on the highway for another thirty miles. Do you?"

Summer sighed, then leaned across the table, whispering, "And neither of you are concerned about heading off into the middle of nowhere with Ben and Jerry over there?"

Alice shrugged. "They said there's a whole field full of people. It's not like you have to be their best friends."

Tiernan stole a french fry off Alice's plate. "Sometimes the devil that you don't know," she said, winking at Summer, "is actually better than the one you do."

"FINDERS, KEEPERS"
I'M CALLING THE COPS 'CAUSE
YOU STOLE MY HEART
AND NOW.
NOW, NOW.
NOW YOU WON'T GIVE IT BACK TO ME

AND YOU SAID IT'S NOT A CRIME
BUT I'M BETTING YOU'LL DO TIME
FOR TAKING SOMETHING
THAT NEVER BELONGED TO YOU

—*from Level3's second CD,* Rough & Tumble

Chapter Eight

SUMMER LOOKED OUT THE WINDOW AS THE PEA POD RUMBLED past a slant-roofed barn, then out onto the farmer's field. She couldn't believe Alice and Tiernan had just forced her to come to this freakapalooza, especially after the day she'd had. It wasn't as if she needed their sympathy, but a shred of ordinary human compassion would have been nice. Then again, this wasn't the place for ordinary anything.

High school and college kids milled around the field decked out with rainbow clown wigs and glow-stick necklaces. Older people in Grateful Dead T-shirts and Indian-print skirts sat in lawn chairs swilling microbrews. In the middle of the field was a bonfire surrounded by the largest drum circle Summer had ever seen, with dancers flailing and twirling all around it, hypnotized by the steady rhythm.

Not exactly like the last time she'd gone camping with Alice and Tiernan back in sixth grade at the Girl Scout jamboree. Unless you counted the two-hundred-pound bearded guy in the Girl Scout uniform.

Alice followed Toad and Phred's beat-up Honda Civic to a quiet area at the far edge of the meadow. In the campsite next to them, two bikini-clad girls stood in an inflatable baby pool, painting their bodies blue.

"Welcome to the neighborhood," Toad said, hopping out of the van and nodding at the blue girls. Apparently he and Phred had appointed themselves their personal tour guides for this circus sideshow.

"You guys wanna check out the bonfire?" Phred asked.

"Hells yeah," Tiernan said, pulling her camera from her bag. She was never one to miss a party, even if it meant hanging out next to a raging inferno in hundred-degree weather.

"I need to make a quick phone call first," Alice said.

"No worries," said Phred. "We can wait."

Alice shook her head. "That's okay. I'll catch up with you."

"I think I'm just going to stay in and read," Summer said, getting back in the van. She would have given anything to be back home in Walford right now, curled up in her bed, alone with her thoughts. But since she was stuck here, she figured she might as well nab the top bunk before Alice or Tiernan got the chance. It *was* her old spot, after all.

"You don't mind if I pop the top, do you, Alice?"

"Go for it." Alice said, using her hands to sweep the crumbs from Tiernan's seat onto the grass.

"Well, I guess it's just us then, eh, boys?" Tiernan stood between Toad and Phred, linking her arms through theirs. Then the three of them skipped off into the night, with Tiernan leading them in an obnoxiously bad rendition of "We're off to See the Wizard."

Summer tugged on the metal bar to release the pop-top, just like she remembered, but the roof wouldn't budge.

"Alice, I think it's stuck."

Alice let out a sigh, tossed a Hostess Snowball wrapper into her trash bag, then came around to the back of the van. With one forceful tug, she pulled down on the bar, instantly transforming the Pea Pod from regular old van into a two-story living space.

"Thanks," Summer said as Alice snapped the pop-top into place. "And if I'm asleep by the time you get back, then I guess I'll see you tomorrow."

But Alice just stood there looking at her. "You know . . . if you want to talk about it—"

"That's sweet of you," Summer said, smiling, "but I think I just want to sleep." It wasn't a lie. Everything about this day had completely exhausted her. Not that spilling her guts to Alice was ever an option.

"Okay, then," Alice said. "I'm heading out after I check in with my parents."

Summer smiled just thinking of the Millers and the way they'd always doted on Alice. A total contrast to her own parents, who, when Summer had asked them if they wanted her to call them from the road, had basically just laughed in her face.

Alice hopped outside to make her call and finally, blissfully, Summer had the van all to herself. She placed her right foot on the well-worn groove next to the sink, then hauled herself up to the top bunk. When they were kids, she'd clocked hundreds of hours nestled away up here, listening to Level3, or talking with Tiernan and Alice, even though all they could see of her was a pair of dangling legs. The top bunk had always been her special place, her cocoon.

Summer unzipped the screen window in the unlikely event that there was a breeze somewhere in this stagnant West Virginia night. It also gave her a perfect view of the bonfire with its frolicking tribal dancers. There was one girl—long flowing dress, unruly tangle of hair—whose entire body was silhouetted by the fire as if she were the flickering blue heart at the center of the flame.

Summer had never danced like that, not even in the privacy of her bedroom. And here was this girl, dancing so freely in front of hundreds of strangers. Summer stared at the fire, surprised by the sudden onset of hot tears spilling down her cheeks, tingeing her lips with salt. She buried her face in her arms in case Alice was still close enough to the Pea Pod to hear.

Yesterday, when Jace had dumped her, she'd felt nothing but anger. But now that he wanted her back, it was as if those other feelings she'd held inside burst open. So why was she crying now? If Jace truly wanted her back, that was a good thing. *Wasn't it?*

Summer wiped her eyes and lay back on the scratchy plaid padding. Life had been so much simpler the last time she'd gone camping with Alice and Tiernan, when the closest any of them got to boys was in their fantasy world. She could picture it all so clearly in her mind, the three of them staying up past lights out, whispering their Level3 dream dates to each other in the darkness. In Tiernan's fantasy, she and Luke usually spent the night club-hopping in New York while Ryan whisked Alice away to a romantic dinner in Paris on his private jet. Or was it London?

But unlike Tiernan and Alice, who were constantly coming up with new scenarios and exotic locations for their fantasies, Summer's dream date with Travis was always the same. She could still remember every detail; she'd lived it so many times in her head. The date started with the two of them meandering down Main Street in Walford, arm in arm, laughing, talking, window-shopping. And at the end of the night they'd wind up back at Summer's house on her porch swing while Travis serenaded her on guitar. Then after he was done, a kiss. Never a full-on make-out session—just a sweet solitary kiss and a whisper, nose to nose. *I love you.*

I love you. She and Jace had said it to each other a million times. But never once had it felt like it did in that silly daydream.

Stupid Jace. Summer wanted to believe him. She really did. But she couldn't get over the feeling that there was something he wasn't telling her. Some detail he was leaving out. According to Jace, the reason he hadn't mentioned going to Melanie's party on graduation night was because he hadn't wanted to make Summer feel bad about the fact that he was out celebrating their breakup while she was home, crying in her pillow. But for some reason Summer couldn't shake the aftertaste of her initial doubts. It was like the way a bad dream could ruin her whole day, no matter how many times she told herself it wasn't true.

Summer pulled her journal from her purse. It was the only chance she had to sort out all the turmoil in her head. She flipped past her diary entries, poems, fragments of poems, and random doodles looking for a blank page. To a stranger, her journal probably looked like the ramblings of a lunatic. But Summer liked the way her mind spilled out onto the page in all its unedited messiness. It didn't have to be prettied up for anyone but herself.

She wrote feverishly, until her hand hurt, filling ten pages by the time she was done. Most of what she'd written was about Jace. But the lines she liked best were the ones about the girl by the fire.

Her eyes are closed,

But she is open.

Spinning, Smiling, Alive,

Burning as bright as the fire at

her back.

Dancing, just for the joy of dancing.

Dancing for no one but herself.

HILARY WEISMAN GRAHAM

"Knock, knock," said a voice from below. Summer peered over the edge of the bunk just as the back door slid open. Outside the van, Tiernan stood next to the motorcycle dude they'd seen back in the parking lot of Lucky's. A shark-tooth necklace hung off his collarbones. They both had beers in their hands.

"Good. You're awake," Tiernan said.

Summer closed her journal and tossed it back in her bag. If Tiernan was hoping to get busy in the Pea Pod, she was sorely mistaken.

"This is Michael. Michael, this is Summer."

"Hey," Summer said, sizing him up. She had to hand it to Tiernan, Michael was pretty hot for a biker—skinny but muscular, with broad shoulders and a devilish smile.

"Hey," Michael said.

"Guess where we're going?" Tiernan didn't wait for an answer. "Michael knows about a secret swimming hole a couple miles from here. He says it's the most pristine water you've ever swum in."

Summer wrinkled her nose.

"Aw, don't say no, darlin'," Michael begged. "It's a night destined to be spent swimming under the stars." He pointed to the sky—*as if Summer didn't know where the stars were*—his eyes lit up in the moonlight.

"What about Alice?" Summer asked. "Is she going?"

"She sure is," said Phred, ambling up to the Pea Pod, his

arm slung around Alice's shoulder. "We gotta find some way to cool off from this heat."

Toad trailed behind Alice and Phred, shooting Summer a hopeful smile. *In your dreams, kid*, Summer thought, quickly extinguishing his grin with an icy stare.

"I think it would be fun for all of us to go for a swim," Alice said perkily. She and Phred were wearing matching green glow-stick headbands, like halos. "But I don't think we should leave anyone here by themselves."

"I don't mind," Summer said. "I was just about to go to sleep anyway."

They probably all thought she was a big old stick-in-the-mud, when in reality it was more like, *Been there, done that.* Summer and her friends back home partied at the Walford quarry zillions of times. She didn't need to tag along for amateur hour.

"But you *have to* come." Michael frowned at Summer, then Tiernan. "I thought you said this could be our party bus."

"Wait a minute." Alice looked concerned. "You didn't say anything about taking the Pea Pod."

This was the Alice Summer remembered. The girl didn't let just anyone inside her precious Pea Pod.

"Well, how else are we gonna get six people to the swim-min' hole, darlin'?" Michael asked. "On the back of my bike?"

Summer's throat loosened. If Alice shut down Michael's plan, Summer didn't have to be the bad guy. And Alice would never agree to pile everyone back into the Pea Pod after she'd spent all night complaining about how sick of driving she was.

"It's only a couple miles away, right, Michael?" Tiernan asked in that sugary high-pitched voice she used whenever she was trying to get her way. The sad thing was, the girl spent so much time being ornery that people fell all over themselves whenever she showed the tiniest ounce of sweetness.

"Come on, Alice." Phred gave her a pitiful-looking pout. "You know we'll have fun."

"Well . . ." Alice was wavering. "If it's okay with Summer."

Now everyone was staring at her, making it impossible to say no without seeming like a total bitch. And even if she did, Tiernan and Alice would probably just overrule her anyway. The dynamic duo had already shut her down once today in the oh-so-democratic vote that had brought them to this hippieville.

"Dude, you're either on the bus or off the bus," Toad chimed in. Of course the two stoners of the group were on their side.

"Fine," Summer said, against her better judgment.

"Alrighty then," said Tiernan. "Let's load her up."

Summer stood on the grass as they piled into the van—Alice behind the wheel, Michael in the passenger's seat to navigate, Tiernan on a milk crate in the back, which left Summer stuck sitting between Toad and Phred on the bench seat. Joy.

By the time pavement turned to dirt, Summer knew she should have stayed in Walford, where there were streetlights on the roads and cars drove in straight lines instead of twisting and turning in all directions. Her friends had lectured her all afternoon that coming on this trip was a bad idea. But, of course, she'd refused to admit it.

"Are you sure I shouldn't have taken a left back there?" Alice asked.

"Nope, you're doing fine." Michael pointed to some pine trees at the top of a hill. "It should be just down past there." He sounded so confident, despite the fact that they'd been driving around the woods for the last fifteen minutes and he'd said that exact same thing three times so far.

"Hey, I've got an idea," Tiernan said. "Let's give ol' Coach Quigley a try."

"Who's Coach Quigley?" Phred asked.

"He's our GPS," Tiernan explained. A few miles back, she'd been defending Michael. Now she was trying to overthrow him.

"We don't need any technology, darlin'. I grew up in these woods."

Summer couldn't help but grin watching Tiernan bristle at the word "darlin'."

"Spent three weeks campin' out by that swimmin' hole back when I was your age," Michael added.

"That must have been fun," Alice said.

"Not really." Michael shrugged. "Only reason I did it was 'cause the cops were lookin' for me."

"You were a fugitive from the law?" Tiernan gasped with

delight, as if someone had told her she'd just won the lottery. "What did you do?"

"I didn't do nuthin'." Michael's voice was suddenly angry, defensive. "But I'll tell you one thing. Don't matter what the truth is. After that, people 'round here ain't never treated me the same."

Summer's breath quickened as she reeled through a list of potential crimes in her head. *Was it a drug deal gone wrong? Rape? Kidnapping? Murder!* A half hour ago she had been nestled away on the top bunk, perfectly content. Now there was a high probability she was going to die at the hands of this psychopath, with no one to help her but her ex–best friends and two ridiculously named strangers.

"Crap," said Tiernan. "No signal." Coach Quigley's display was TV screen blue, the words "Searching for Satellites" blinking in the center like an error message.

This entire fiasco was Tiernan's fault. *She* was the one who'd brought this lunatic into their lives. The one who'd encouraged Alice's flirtation with that loser Phred. But did anyone ever listen to what Summer wanted? If they did, by now they'd be in an air-conditioned hotel room twenty miles up the road instead of trapped in this hillbilly hell.

Or maybe she was overreacting. After all, this wouldn't be the first time Summer let her imagination get the best of her. She glanced over at Toad and Phred, hoping their mellow, glazed-over expressions might offer a bit of reassurance.

But the looks of sheer terror on their faces only fanned the flames of Summer's fears. Either all that pot they'd smoked was making Toad and Phred paranoid, or coming out here with Michael Crazy-Eyes was starting to seem like a really bad idea.

"I think we ought to just turn around," Alice said, her usual self-assured tone betrayed by only the slightest quaver.

Summer looked out the window into the blackness. Next to her, Toad was shaking his head back and forth, as if to say, *Not good, not good at all.*

"Hey, Michael," Tiernan said, trying desperately to keep her voice light and airy. "You're not, like, taking us out to the woods to, like, kill us or anything, are you?" Then she gave a short chuckle just to show everyone that she wasn't genuinely scared or anything, that she was just being her usual brash, irreverent self.

Michael spun around to the back, his mouth stretched in a wide skeletal smile. "I ain't gonna kill ya." He laughed, his sharp collarbones heaving up and down under his tank top. "In fact, I'm probably the safest guy you could be out here with."

He twisted his torso some more, pointing to the tattoo on his right bicep. "You see that?" Summer leaned in to see an image of a winged man with a sword in his hand hovering over the devil. "I got it when I was in jail. That's me—Michael the Archangel. Prince of Light."

Well, Summer thought to herself, *that makes me feel so much better.* As if the nasty prison tattoo wasn't bad enough, it was now obvious to everyone that the man was certifiably insane.

Summer was in the midst of trying to figure out if it were possible to lean over, open the passenger's side door, and push Michael out of the van while it was still moving when the swimming hole came into view.

"Look!" Summer shouted, even though they were all within three feet of each other. "There it is!"

A wave of relief flooded through her body as she noticed the silhouettes of at least a dozen other cars parked along the road, and further on down the hill the glimmer of their headlights in the water. Summer had no clue where they were, but in all of her life, she couldn't recall a moment she'd been happier to arrive at a place that she'd never wanted to be.

"TIME, TRAVEL"

WE WENT TO ANCIENT ROME AND 3018
IN MY BROKEN TIME MACHINE.

THE LANDSCAPE CHANGES
BUT THE PAST STAYS THE PAST
THE FUTURE'S MECHANICS
SAY MY PROBLEMS WON'T LAST.

BUT I KNOW MY TIME MACHINE IS BROKEN
'CAUSE I SEEM TO BE STUCK IN RIGHT NOW.

—*from Level3's second CD*, Rough & Tumble

Chapter Nine

ALICE JAMMED ON THE BRAKES, FLUNG OPEN HER DOOR, AND leaped out of the Pea Pod, landing smack in the middle of a pricker bush. Compared to the heart attack she'd been having for the past ten minutes, a few minor scrapes were nothing. Her brain screamed directions at her body like it was shouting through a megaphone: *Keep moving forward. Get away from the archangel. There's nothing to see here, people. Just go! Go! Go!*

How had she let this happen? How had she ended up in Lord Knows Where, West Virginia, with a man who at best was a known criminal, and at worst—well, she didn't want to go there.

She took off down the hill after Summer, Tiernan, Toad, and Phred—all of whom had bolted from the van before it was even in park. *Gee, guys, thanks for waiting up.* But Alice was too scared to bother staying mad. She just wanted to get to the swimming hole. *Alive.*

"It's only me," Alice whispered, the sound of her footsteps joining Summer's and Tiernan's in the darkness. She could just make out Toad's and Phred's bodies running away in the shadows ahead.

"Hurry up," Summer hissed.

"No need to rush!" Michael's voice made Alice jump. "That swimming hole ain't goin' nowhere." From the sound of it, Michael wasn't right behind them, but he was getting close.

"We'll meet you there!" Summer called back. She sounded polite, even cheerful. It was a strange gift she had—making everything seem fine no matter how un-fine things actually were.

Without a word, all three of them quickened their stride, entering a dark, thickly wooded area where the treetops blocked all the moonlight.

"Shoot!" Alice cried out, stumbling over something on the trail—a rock or a root. *Prince of Light.* What they needed was a Prince of Flashlight. That, and an exit strategy.

"Here's my plan," she whispered. "I say we go down to the swimming hole, grab Toad and Phred, then, when Michael's not looking, the five of us hop in the Pea Pod and cruise on out of here."

"I'm down with that," Tiernan agreed.

Summer was about to answer when Michael's voice leaped out of the darkness. "Last one in's a rotten egg!"

Alice didn't turn to look, but she could *feel* Michael gaining on them—his towering frame looming behind her, those stringy, muscular arms of his swinging apelike at his side. The guy gave off so much crazy energy, Alice wouldn't be surprised to hear a sizzle when he touched the water.

"Darn it." Tiernan slowed her pace as she spoke. "We forgot

our bathing suits. We're just gonna run back and get—"

But there was no point in finishing her sentence. The swimming hole emerged out of the darkness like a silvery oasis. And from the looks of things, the only suit you needed to wear here was the one you'd been born in.

"Water's nice and warm tonight," a completely nude man called out from a rock in the middle of the pond. He was in his sixties, white hair, full white beard, and a twinkle in his eye. It was Naked Santa Claus, and his stocking was most definitely hung. *Well, that just ruined Christmas forever,* Alice thought to herself as Naked Santa did a swan dive into the water.

Alice looked at Tiernan and Summer. *Must flee now,* she said telepathically. She was pretty sure they'd understood her message but she kept her eyes on theirs, the one view in the entire place guaranteed to be free of saggy man butt.

Michael didn't seem to notice or care that it appeared to be Senior's Day at the swimming hole, happily undressing not two feet from them, without even the slightest bit of self-consciousness.

Alice pretended to pick at a hangnail as she listened to the clink of his belt buckle, then his jeans crumpling to the grass. She didn't dare look up again until she heard the sloshing noise of Michael's legs hitting the water.

"Water's nice and warm, ladies," Michael called out when he was up to his knees (it was just a quick peek, but the guy was definitely no Santa). Then he was gone.

"Let's get out of here," Summer whispered, turning back toward the van.

"Wait." Alice pulled Summer's arm. "What about Phred and Toad?"

"They're way over there." Tiernan pointed to the opposite side of the pond. "By the time we go get them, Michael could come back."

Summer nodded. "I say we bolt without them. They're big boys."

"And personally"—Tiernan leveled Alice with a look—"I think you can do better."

"What are you talking about?" Alice asked. "Phred and I are only friends, and we—"

Alice was about to list the many reasons why saving Toad and Phred was the right thing to do (none of which had anything to do with the fact that Phred had been hanging all over her) when Michael emerged from underwater, howling like a coyote and pounding his chest. That was all the convincing it took for her to turn tail and run—across the wet spongy grass, through the low brush, then back inside the dark cover of the woods. Man, was she out of shape. But she kept on running, even as Summer and Tiernan overtook her, trying her best to ignore the burning feeling in her hamstrings and focus on the noise of her shoes against the slippery gravel, the rhythm of her own labored breath, the blood whooshing through her veins. And then the one sound she was hoping never to hear again.

"Wait up!" Michael called out. Or was she imagining it? There was no way Alice could have heard him from all the way back at the water. But that would mean—could it even be possible?—that Michael the Archangel was chasing them through the woods. *Naked?*

Alice's heart pounded in her chest, in her throat. *Don't turn around. You're just imagining it.* Why were Summer and Tiernan so much faster than she was? *She* did power yoga three times a week. Okay, maybe two. *Don't think about that. Just concentrate on running.* Alice reached into her pocket, digging her keys into the palm of her hand.

The Pea Pod was finally in sight. Alice's lungs were on fire, her eyes blurry with sweat. They were so close she could almost touch it.

Summer got there first, opening the back door and flinging herself inside in one seamless motion. Tiernan was right behind her. Alice ran around the front of the Pea Pod—straight through the pricker bush, again, *duh*—scrambling in through the driver's side door. She was breathing too hard to speak.

"Headlights!" Summer shouted as Alice threw the Pea Pod in reverse.

When she turned on the lights, Alice half expected to see Michael in front of them, wild-eyed and naked and holding a bloody butcher knife. But the woods were empty and still. She could kill MJ for dragging her to all those stupid horror flicks. Not that she ever watched the really scary parts. Now that she was actually *living* a horror movie, she still wanted to hide behind her hands.

It was hard to steer in the darkness with only the dim rear lights, but backing out was definitely faster than making a twelve-point turn. She could only imagine what her father would say if he saw the Pea Pod doing thirty, backward, up the bumpy dirt road, but the wider the distance grew between the van and Michael, the safer Alice felt. Finally, at a bend in the road, she stopped to shift it into drive.

Up until this moment, Alice's sole mission had been getting them away from the swimming hole. Now they were finally away. The only question was—*where?*

"We came in on that road, didn't we?" Alice pointed left.

"I don't remember taking a turn there," Summer sounded uncertain.

"Don't ask me." Tiernan shrugged. "I couldn't see crap."

Nothing looked familiar, yet everything looked the same.

"Turn on Coach Quigley!" Alice commanded, taking the left.

Tiernan, the de facto copilot, sprang into action. "Still no signal," she said, holding the GPS up to the windshield.

"Damn it." Alice thought she knew where she was going. But the road she'd chosen quickly dwindled away into nothing more than a hiking trail. She backed out, continuing in the opposite direction.

"Aren't you supposed to just stop?" Summer asked. "If

you're . . . you know, lost?" There it was. She'd gone and said the *L* word.

They'd been driving for at least ten minutes. They had to be close to the main road by now, didn't they? Up ahead, Alice saw another crossroad and she took it. She was just starting to get a good feeling that this way their way out, when she saw the enormous pine tree lying across the road and jammed on the brakes.

"Why me?" Alice yelled, lifting her hands to the sky. Just then, the sky answered back as a curtain of rain pelted the Pea Pod's roof like an audience bursting into sudden applause. It was a summertime downpour. *Point one for Mother Nature.*

Alice put the van into park. The rain was coming down so heavily, the droplets on the windshield had merged into a single, thick sheet of water.

"Why aren't we moving?" Summer asked.

Um, maybe because I can't see anything, Alice wanted to say. Instead, she took a long deep breath, determined not to let stress get the better of her. "I think it's probably safer to wait out the storm here."

Summer and Tiernan were quiet as they took this in, the rain drumming against the rooftop. All Alice wanted was one trouble-free minute in this godforsaken day. Just one tiny moment where they could all get along.

"We could play Scrabble!" Tiernan said, her eyes all lit up. She sounded more enthusiastic than anyone should ever sound about a board game. And Alice *liked* board games. But considering that they'd just cheated death at the hands of a delusional maniac, her next thought hadn't necessarily been Q words that didn't require the letter U.

"Come on," Tiernan whined. "It'll be a good distraction."

"Yeah, the last distraction you had for us turned out great." Summer glared.

Alice bit her lip. She needed to find something they could all agree on, something with the potential to be a bonding experience (and that didn't involve burying live animals or fleeing through the woods from a deranged maniac).

"How was I supposed to know he was crazy?" Tiernan asked as a flash of lightning illuminated them all in white.

Summer just shook her head, the din of rolling thunder filling their silence.

In the two short days between buying the Level3 tickets and now, Alice had done nothing but prepare for this trip. She'd planned their route, precalculated the cost of gas, and cross-referenced weather reports from three different websites. Aside from occasional late-night thunderstorms north of the Alleghenies (cue thunder now), their trip was supposed to be sunny and clear. But the meteorologists gave no forecast for the storm brewing *inside* the Pea Pod.

And then it came to her. "I have something we can do," Alice said, trying to make it sound like a casual suggestion as opposed to a desperate plea. "A distraction," she added, giving

Tiernan a nod. "What would you guys think about making a collage?"

"Hmm." Summer smiled. "The old standby."

Tiernan stood up to review their old masterpieces. "Sure. Let's do it."

Alice hadn't realized how tense her shoulders were until she felt them relax away from her ears back to their usual position. A collage. They'd always worked so well together when they were making collages, each of them so essential to the process that Alice wasn't sure if she'd even know how to make one if she had to do it alone.

Tiernan usually came up with the concept. Alice was the detail person—selecting all the right pictures, then meticulously cutting them out. Summer handled the assembly, arranging and rearranging the pieces to make sure they all came together in the most artistic way possible.

"What about a map?" Tiernan asked, looking directly at Alice. "I know you've got some kind of plan about where we can and can't stop on our way to Austin. But maybe, between the three of us, we could come up with something more . . . more . . ."

"Democratic?" Summer offered.

Tiernan just smiled.

It was interesting, Alice noted, how Tiernan and Summer always got along best when they were trying to overthrow one of her own well-laid plans. Oh, well. At least when those two were in cahoots against her, it meant they were getting along. And Alice was more than happy to volunteer herself as the sacrificial lamb in exchange for a little peace and quiet.

"What I was thinking was"—Tiernan looked inspired—"that maybe *the three of us* could decide where to stop between here and Texas based on places that have to do with Level3. Like the stopping points on our map could come from things mentioned in Level3 songs, you know?"

"I have one!" Summer said enthusiastically. "You know the song 'Rock Me To and Fro'?"

Alice nodded.

"Well, we could make a collage for that and put it in Little Rock, Arkansas. Get it? 'Rock Me,' Little Rock?"

"Exactly." Tiernan had a satisfied look on her face. "That's just what I'm talking about."

Alice sighed. She was resistant to change by nature, not to mention the fact that she'd spent hours planning their route. But she could already see that Summer's and Tiernan's wheels were turning, and once those two got brainstorming, it was safer to just move aside and let their creative genius flow. Whether or not she actually *adhered* to the route on this new collage map was a different story. That is, if they ever made it out of the woods.

"Well, did anyone bring glue or scissors?" Summer asked.

Had the girl not been her best friend for five years?

"Don't let the shovel incident besmirch my good reputation," Alice joked, pulling a small plastic bin marked "Craft Supplies" out from under the sink. Just one of the many boxes she'd started to organize for Brown. *Knock on wood.*

"The only thing is . . ." Tiernan carefully peeled an old collage off the wall. "We're gonna need to cut up these old collages to make the new one."

"But we put so much work into those," Alice cried. She knew she was probably being overly sentimental, but could she help it if she hated to throw things away? Whenever MJ looked inside Alice's closet, she'd pretend she was making an emergency phone call to the producers of the TV show *Hoarders.*

"Think of it as a tribute to the past," Tiernan said. "It's not like we're getting rid of the old collages. We're just repurposing them. Like an extended remix."

Alice shot her a skeptical look. It was a well-known fact that Tiernan got off on destroying things.

"I say out with the old, in with the new," Summer said. She held a heart-shaped collage of Travis in her hands, circa fifth grade.

"Okay, I guess." Alice shrugged. She had to admit a collage map *was* a pretty cool idea. And why hang on to faded memories when making a new collage would give them new ones?

By the time they'd finished, the storm had passed. On the surface, their new collage looked like a map, only without the benefit of being geographically correct or even remotely to scale. But what it lacked in accuracy, it made up for in heart.

Most of the stopping points were selected at random, like the snow-cone collage (inspired by the song "Snow Cone") Tiernan had stuck in the center of Kentucky, implying they'd stop to get snow cones sometime on their way through the state. But where the lyrics or a song title allowed, their stopping points were location specific, like the T-Rex-shaped collage Alice had placed in Nashville, Tennessee, (based on the song "Dinosaur"). *"Jeff Goldblum may have died in Jurassic Park, but I swear that I saw him in Nashville."*

"You guys just want to sleep here for the night?" Alice asked.

"You don't think he might be out there lurking, do you?" Summer nodded toward the window.

No one had mentioned Michael's name for hours, but Alice had locked all the doors and closed the curtains just in case.

"I don't think we should even start *thinking* about that," Alice said. As time passed, the less anxious she felt about Michael attacking them and the more guilty she felt for abandoning Toad and Phred.

"What do you think happened to Toad and Phred?" Alice asked.

"Maybe they hitched a ride back on Santa's sleigh," Tiernan said. "Did you guys *see* that dude?"

"In way too much detail." Summer yawned.

"Who knew Santa was packing that kind of heat?" Tiernan said with a laugh.

Clearly, Summer and Tiernan weren't wasting their time

worrying about Toad and Phred, so why should she? Sure, Alice liked Phred's attention, but she'd only known him a couple of hours. Sometimes she felt like she spent so much time concerned with everyone else's happiness, she ended up sabotaging her own.

"I vote we stay here," Tiernan offered. "Not that you guys want to listen to any more of *my* suggestions."

"You can say that again." Alice smiled. She could tell Tiernan felt bad about the Michael incident. But poking fun at herself was about the closest Tiernan ever got to an apology.

"Fine by me." Summer nodded. "But first, we make a rule." She stuck out her hand like she was getting ready to do a soccer cheer. "No more strangers in the van."

"No strangers in the van." Alice placed a hand on Summer's. Tiernan slapped her hand on top. "Ditto."

It took Alice a long time to fall asleep that night, but it wasn't from fear of Michael the Archangel. This was a different kind of nervousness keeping her awake, making her all too aware of the high-pitched whistling sound coming from her left nostril, the creak of the bed every time she shifted positions.

It should have felt familiar, sleeping in the Pea Pod next to Tiernan, with Summer up on the top bunk in her usual spot. But for some reason the Pea Pod never felt so small as it did right now.

Had Alice made a mistake coming on this trip with them? After all, knowing who someone *was* was different than knowing who they *are*. And what had she expected? That things would be the same as they were four years ago?

When Alice finally drifted off, she was thinking about the rule they'd all agreed to, wondering if "no strangers in the van" was meant only for outsiders, or if it also applied to the people inside.

"BURIED TREASURE"

IT WAS YOUR IDEA
TO GO INTO THE DIAMOND MINE
SO I FOLLOWED YOU
DEEP INSIDE THE EARTH.

WE WERE LOOKING FOR TREASURE
BUT ALL WE FOUND WAS COAL
SO I PUT SOME IN YOUR POCKET
AND YOU CRIED.

AND I SAID, DON'T CRY, DON'T CRY
JUST GIVE IT TIME
AND THEY WILL BE DIAMONDS
IN TIME, THEY WILL SHINE.

—from Level3's self-titled first CD

Chapter Ten

TIERNAN WAS NOT A MORNING PERSON. BUT APPARENTLY THE bird that had been screeching since the butt crack of dawn hadn't gotten the memo. Not that it was easy to sleep in the Pea Pod anyway, between being crammed in next to Alice (mouth breather), Summer tossing and turning in the bunk above their heads, and the knot tightening in Tiernan's stomach every time she thought about her mom finding the note.

She'd been MIA for almost twenty-four hours now. Chances were, whatever worries her mom had yesterday had turned into full-scale panic. Tiernan felt bad she hadn't called home last night. Not that she was looking forward to Judy's tirade. But she'd intended to call. Really. At least that was the plan until the party at the field distracted her. A few Magic Hats later she'd forgotten about her mother altogether. Then she'd stumbled into Michael the Archangel playing bongos by the fire. *Drummers.* She should have known he was trouble right then and there.

The problem was, Tiernan had a bad habit of judging books by their covers. Just about every guy she'd ever dated turned out to belong in the category of either Beautiful Poser or Beautiful Loser. But she could never seem to get past the looks part. Like with Michael. At first glance, Michael had *appeared to be* cool, so, like a total idiot, Tiernan had assumed his coolness went all the way inside. Of course, if she'd just listened to her gut instead of ogling Michael's rear end, they wouldn't even be here right now. But when had she ever done that? Even at this very moment, when her gut was screaming.

She'd been fighting the urgency to pee for the last half hour, deluding herself that she'd be able to just ignore it and go back to sleep. As if *that* ever worked. And yet, Tiernan just lay there, squirming uncomfortably, trying to sleep, as the crisis in her bladder elevated to Threat Level: Yellow.

Now she'd waited so long it was hard to sit up. Somehow she managed, scooting out of the bed past Alice, opening the sliding door as quietly as possible so as not to wake them up and start the day off on their bad side. She was actually kind of shocked Summer and Alice weren't more pissed off at her for dragging Michael the Psycho into their lives. No nasty digs from Summer, no lectures from Alice about using "good judgment." Either those two had seriously mellowed over time, or, like so many of the people who knew Tiernan well, they'd decided it was easier to just lower their expectations.

Tiernan tiptoed far enough away from the Pea Pod to have some privacy, but close enough to still feel safe—then squatted behind a large pine tree.

Oh, sweet relief.

Now that her bladder wasn't bursting, she could actually

focus on her surroundings, maybe even explore a little. It was an exhilarating feeling to be the only person awake in the woods, so Tiernan ventured in farther while, all around her, rays of watery sunshine flickered through the trees, wet green leaves yawning to meet their light.

Back home, Tiernan wasn't exactly the outdoors type. Between the mosquitoes and her mother making her rake leaves every fall, she'd be fine if they paved over the whole unpleasant business. But for some reason these woods seemed to quiet her. Like the only thing more chaotic than her own mind was the anarchy of nature itself.

She'd call her mother today. Just as soon as they had cell service again.

The sun was rising so fast now that the forest seemed to be constantly reinventing itself—first in browns and deep blues, then in rust and yellow-greens. Farther away, in a clearing, a blanket of purple-white fog whispered over the grass. *Screw it.* She had to go get her camera before this was gone forever, even if she woke up Alice and Summer in the process.

Tiernan usually hated nature photos. She preferred the edgier stuff, like the work of her all-time favorite photographer Diane Arbus. Arbus was big in the 1960s for her series of portraits of misfits and freaks—photos so raw and honest that Tiernan wondered if Arbus used some kind of magical lens that let her see beyond people's poses so that only their innermost selves shone through.

When Tiernan got back to the van, Alice was awake.

"You're alive!" Alice said, spitting a mouth full of toothpaste into the sink. The bed where they'd slept had already been folded away.

"What time is it?" Summer asked groggily, her hair cascading over the top bunk.

"Six fifty-three," Alice said. "I'm just going to wash my face, and then I think we should get going."

So much for the early-morning nature photography. Whatever. It was a stupid idea anyway. Every hack that owned a camera took boring nature shots.

Tiernan had only slathered one pit with deodorant when Alice started up the Pea Pod.

"It's seven o'clock," Alice announced, like it was a race and she'd won. "Let's get out of here."

Summer slid into shotgun before Tiernan had the chance. Evidently, snagging the top bunk last night hadn't been enough for Her Highness. Guess that meant Tiernan was flying coach.

"Wake me up when we get there," she said, flopping onto the bench seat and closing her eyes. Wherever "there" was.

Apparently, "there" was right here. Alice gunned the engine, but instead of moving forward, there was just the high-pitched squeal of spinning tires.

Tiernan opened her eyes just as Summer opened her door.

"Ruh-roh," Summer said, looking down.

For three people about to head off to college, they'd failed to remember a lesson they'd learned in preschool: Rain plus dirt equals mud.

They all piled out of the van, and this time Tiernan remembered to bring her camera. Her first picture was of Alice, standing in front of the Pea Pod, her face creased with worry. The tires were sunk under mud at least six inches deep.

Tiernan steeled herself for the impending bitch-slap from Summer and Alice. Sure, they'd given her a pass last night, but now that the van was stuck in sludge, who else did they have to blame but her? But, surprisingly, no one mentioned the fact that it had been Tiernan who'd convinced them to drive out here in the first place.

"You guys ready to push?" Alice asked.

Not really, Tiernan thought, but instead nodded yes. Why shouldn't she start off the day with a little backbreaking manual labor? It wasn't as if she didn't deserve it.

The Nikon went back in the Pea Pod, and Tiernan braced herself against the right headlight—knees bent, feet dug into the squishy earth—while Summer took the left.

"On the count of three," Alice shouted from the driver's seat. "One . . . two . . . *three!*"

Tiernan gave it everything she had. Wheels spun, and the engine whinnied like an injured horse. The tires were barely halfway up the deep divets—but they would go no farther. Alice killed the gas and the Pea Pod rolled right back down into the valley of mud.

"I know!" Alice said. "Maybe if one of us stood on top of the van, we'd be able to get cell service and call a tow truck?"

"And tell them to come get us *where*?" Summer held up her hands.

"Let's just give it another try," Tiernan said. She was the one who'd caused this, and she was going to be the one to fix it, too. "We were close. Close-*ish*."

This time Alice really floored it, and Tiernan and Summer hit the Pea Pod like linebackers taking out a player from the opposing team.

"Push, push, push, push, push!" Summer yelled as the tires spit out gritty clumps of mud all over them.

"We need better leverage," Tiernan said. She remembered all those arguments with her mother about how her C-plus in physics didn't matter because she'd never have to use physics in real life. The tree lying across the road was only three feet in front of the van, so driving forward wasn't an option.

"Why don't you try pushing from the sides?" Alice suggested. Of course, she'd aced physics.

Tiernan opened the sliding door and braced her hands against the frame as Summer moved to the driver's side door next to Alice. Through the inside of the van, Summer glanced over at Tiernan and gave her a nod. It was the same look she'd seen Luke give Travis and Ryan in concert, whenever they launched into a new song. But in that one tiny glance was a moment of connection—a quick *here we go, you ready?*—

before the music kicked in and they communicated only by song.

Summer looked a little surprised when Tiernan nodded back.

"One, two, three!" Alice yelled.

Tiernan took an even worse mud pelting than before, but this time the van was really digging in. The wheels snarled at Tiernan and Tiernan snarled back. She had mud in her eyes, in her hair, in her mouth. But she was not giving up. They had momentum. All they needed was another half inch.

"Give it more gas, Alice!" Summer cried, shooting Tiernan an imploring look.

Tiernan pushed harder, leaning all 103 pounds of herself into the doorframe as the engine's whine grew louder. *They were close, so close.* And then—pop!—the Pea Pod was free.

The bad news was, so was the sliding door. Tiernan had pushed so hard she'd ripped the damn thing off its hinges. It lay on the ground in a pile of mud and leaves as the Pea Pod slowly rumbled backward down the dirt road.

Summer was doubled over with laughter. "Alice is *so* gonna kick your butt," she said, wiping a giant streak of mud across her forehead.

Tiernan looked at the Pea Pod as it drove farther and farther away. Now that the van was actually moving, Alice wasn't about to stop.

"Well, you want to help me, or what?" Tiernan asked

Summer, who was just standing there giggling. "I can't lift this thing all by myself."

"I wouldn't be so sure about that," Summer said with a chuckle.

They each took an end and hurried after the Pea Pod, staggering under the awkward weight of the door in between them. It was a scene right out of an old silent movie. Except this film was in full Technicolor, between the shiny pea-green door, Tiernan's blue hair, and then Alice's face—crimson with anger.

"What the hell happened?" Alice scowled from the front seat as the Pea Pod idled on a dry patch of ground.

"Well, at least we're out of the mud, right?" Tiernan said, trying to stay positive. What else could she do? This trip had been utterly sucktastic from moment one, and most of it was all her fault. With Summer's help, they slid the door into the van through the open hole where the door should have been; then they were off.

The backseat was all breeze. Tiernan zipped up her hoodie to stay warm while she watched the trees whiz past. They were still in the woods, but her peaceful moment communing with nature seemed like a million miles away.

"Woo hoo!" Summer cheered when they finally hit pavement. Miraculously, the Pea Pod sailed out of the woods without a single wrong turn.

"So, where to, boss?" Tiernan asked, grabbing hold of the

map they'd made last night just as it was about to fly out the door. Or, rather, *lack of door*. Parts of the map were still sticky with glue. "According to this, we go through Kentucky next, which means snow cones are on the agenda."

"Well, before we do *anything* we need to get the door fixed," Alice said grumpily.

They found a garage a few miles up. At least it looked like it *used* to be a garage. It was a gray, perfectly square structure made from bare concrete blocks, the words CAR REPAIR painted on a piece of plywood leaning against it. A tan double-wide trailer sat no more than twenty feet away from it. The yard was a tangle of weeds, rusted out junk boxes, and assorted parts.

Alice gave the horn a quick double beep.

"You think this place is open?" Tiernan asked. It looked more likely that someone had died here years ago, their carcass probably still rotting away in their favorite armchair.

"It better be," Summer said. "I don't think it's legal to drive around without the door on, right?"

Summer Dalton, careful follower of rules, laws, and celebrity fashion trends.

Alice had just put the van into gear when a woman in a faded green nightgown emerged from the trailer. She was built like an oilcan, midfifties, with straggly silver hair held back with a rubber band.

"Better be an emergency at this time of day," the woman croaked.

It hadn't even occurred to Tiernan that it was only seven o'clock in the morning. Alice smiled apologetically, pointing to the other side of the Pea Pod.

"We had a little mishap," Alice explained.

The woman's face didn't register an expression. She merely stepped around the van and peered in through the hole.

"Hey," Tiernan said, waving a muddy hand. But the woman just touched the broken metal track and bit her tongue. Tiernan was pretty sure she was missing a tooth.

"I gotta get dressed and have my coffee first," she said, waddling back toward the trailer.

"Excuse me, ma'am?" Alice got out of the van. "About how much will it cost? To fix the door?"

The woman opened the metal screen door to the trailer, resting it on her shoulder as she squinted back at the Pea Pod. "Three hundred," she said. Then the door slapped shut and she disappeared inside.

Tiernan winced. Did Alice expect her to pay for part of it? *All of it?* Tiernan was willing to take the blame, but a three-hundred-dollars hit was another thing altogether.

"I think since we're splitting the cost of gas and hotels, we should probably split this, too," Alice said. "If you guys think that's fair."

"Sure." Tiernan silently breathed a sigh of relief.

"Maybe we should just find another garage," Summer said, tossing her hair in the direction of the used car graveyard.

"Or"—Alice's eyes were all lit up—"we could see if she'll barter with us."

Over lunch yesterday, Alice had subjected them to a lecture on the value of bartering and how it was a good way to "just say no" to consumerist culture.

"Barter what?" Summer asked.

"I don't know," Alice replied. "There's probably *something* she needs."

From what Tiernan could tell there was a lot the woman needed—a better house, a lawn mower, a new tooth.

If Tiernan were in charge, she would have greased the wheels a little (so to speak) before swooping in to ask about a barter. But as soon as the screen door squeaked open and the woman reappeared (now in dusty gray coveralls and holding a coffee mug that read "World's Greatest Nana"), Alice made her move.

"Ma'am, we were wondering . . ."

"Gert," the woman snarled.

"Gert," Alice went on, "we were wondering, if maybe there's something we could *do* around here to help you out, in exchange for you knocking down the price a bit?"

Gert snorted. "What don't this place need done?" She thought for a minute. "All right. I've got a barter for you. You girls have kudzu up in"—Gert glanced at the license plate on the Pea Pod—"Massachusetts?"

They shook their heads.

"Well, I got a shed out back that's covered in the stuff." Gert pointed to her jungle of a backyard. "You see it back there?"

At first Tiernan didn't see anything but a patch of tangled vines. Then, slowly, the outline of a shed emerged, the way a pointillist painting starts to make sense the farther you step away from it.

Every inch of the shed was covered in kudzu. It looked like something that belonged in a village from a children's fairy tale. It *was* a fairy tale—complete with its very own toothless old witch.

"You clear the shed, I'll make it one-fifty," Gert said.

Tiernan looked at Alice. Alice looked at Summer. Summer just shrugged.

They were idiots. Ignorant Yankee idiots who knew nothing about invasive Southern weeds. The kudzu was strong and thick and everywhere, and Tiernan was pretty sure that the harder she tugged at the stuff, the tighter it held on. So much for Tiernan's van-door-ripping Incredible Hulk superstrength of this morning.

Summer and Alice got the hedge clippers, cutting the roots at the base of the shed while Tiernan followed behind them, tearing out the remnants of the plants by hand. They worked like this for hours under the glaring midday sun. Tiernan normally despised doing yardwork of any sort, but part of her was happy they'd been tricked into doing such a thankless task. After all, if Gert was the bad guy, it meant

Alice and Summer were less likely to pin the blame on her.

"Photosynthesize *this*, you demonic weed!" Tiernan yelled at the nest of kudzu in her hand. Then the vine suddenly gave way and she toppled backward onto the ground.

"That's what you get for yelling at the vegetation," Summer said. "It's karma."

"More like *van*-ma," Alice added, which made Tiernan and Summer groan.

Two hours into it and they'd gotten giddy. Either that, or they all had heatstroke.

"Here sheddy, sheddy shed," Tiernan called in a bad Southern drawl. "Don't you go hiding on me, now." She tugged on a clump of kudzu, but it didn't even budge.

"Oh, won't you take me out in the sunshine? Won't you put your hand inside mine?" Ever since they'd finished with the groundwork, Summer had been randomly belting out the chorus to "The Great Outdoors" (the hit single off of Level3's last album).

Gert had lent them all "work shirts," all size XXXL. Alice got stuck with a mustard-yellow V-necked tent. Summer's was a plain white tee, covered in oil stains, but she'd looped a piece of kudzu around her waist, somehow making it look almost chic. Tiernan's was powder pink and hung to her knees. Between that and the pigtails she'd made to keep the hair out of her eyes, Alice had declared that she looked like the world's dirtiest baby.

"Either that or a cartoon character," Tiernan said, ripping

another handful of kudzu off the shed. "Like I should have my own show on *Adult Swim* or something."

Summer unlaced a vine that had weaved its way through the shutters. "You know who I think you look like?"

Tiernan shook her head. She wasn't sure she *wanted* to know.

"You look like *you*, back when we first met."

"Oh, my God!" Alice gasped. "Hair in ponytails, no makeup, soccer shirt two sizes too big . . ."

"*'Oh, won't you take me out in the sunshine? Won't you put your hand inside mine?'*" Tiernan sang it loud and a little off-key. It wasn't her favorite Level3 song, but she had to admit, it was catchy.

Next thing she knew they were all belting it out at the top of their lungs.

"*'I'll follow you, through the snow. I'll follow you, I won't let go. The air is cold, your hand is warm. So lift me out from my own storm. Oh, won't you take me out in the sunshine . . .'*"

A half hour later they had stripped the shed bare. It made Tiernan a little sad to see it like that. The kudzu had made the shed unique, almost magical. Now it was just a plain white shack, all of its imperfections glaringly exposed in the bright West Virginia sun. The paint was chipped, it was missing shutters, the roof was uneven and saggy.

Gert ambled over with a carton of lemonade and some plastic cups, standing next to the girls to admire their work.

"You done good," Gert pronounced as she poured their

drinks. "So good I decided I'm only gonna charge you a hundred bucks for the van."

"Thank you so much, Gert," Alice gushed.

"Thank you," Tiernan and Summer echoed.

"And if y'all want showers . . . you can just go inside the house and help yourselves."

They gulped down their lemonades, then Alice and Summer rushed off to the van to grab towels and clean clothes. But the only thing Tiernan took out of the Pea Pod was her camera. Gert was happy enough to pose in front of her newly unearthed shed. And despite the blank space where her tooth should have been, Gert smiled wide.

"SNOW CONE"

WHEN I WOKE UP
AND LOOKED OUT THE WINDOW
I DIDN'T BELIEVE IT
EVEN WHEN I SAW IT
WITH MY OWN TWO EYES

SO WE PUT ON OUR BOOTS
AND WE WANDERED IN THE YARD
WE CAUGHT SNOWFLAKES ON OUR TONGUES
WE WERE CAUGHT BY SURPRISE

I DIDN'T BELIEVE IT
TILL YOU POURED SUGAR ON SNOW
I DIDN'T KNOW
LIFE COULD BE SO SWEET

—*from Level3's second CD,* Rough & Tumble

Chapter Eleven

WHEN SUMMER OPENED HER EYES AND SAW THE STRIP MALL, FOR a second she thought she was back in Walford. There was a Radio Shack, a GameStop, a sketchy-looking Chinese takeout. Then she realized she was alone in the Pea Pod and they didn't have Piggly Wiggly supermarkets up north.

She was rubbing the sleep from her eyes when she noticed Alice and Tiernan walking toward her from across the parking lot, each of them swinging a white plastic Piggly Wiggly bag. Summer had always been fascinated by places like this—these ugly stretches of strip malls, fast-food joints, big-box stores. They were part of a game she played with herself to try to see through the current landscape and get a glimpse of how the land used to be. Sometimes it was impossible, but here she could make out the ghost of the farm that once was—cows in a lush grassy field over there, and, beyond it, a creaky red farmhouse.

In reality, the place looked identical to the one they'd passed yesterday back in West Virginia. Maybe the whole country looked like this.

"Where are we?" Summer asked as Alice opened the door.

"Welcome to Lucky Kentucky!" Tiernan said in a bad Southern drawl.

After they'd left Gert's, they all agreed that (a) West Virginia was cursed, and (b) no matter how much anyone had to pee, the Pea Pod would not pull over again until they'd crossed the border into a better state.

"Okay, ladies," Alice announced. "Which one of you is up first for your Pea Pod driving lesson?"

Summer stretched her arms and let out a long yawn. She vaguely remembered drifting off to sleep while Alice was in the middle of a tirade about how sick of driving she was.

"Not it!" Tiernan chirped before Summer could snap out of her yawn and answer.

"Okay, then you're making the sandwiches," Alice ordered.

Summer wasn't in the mood for a driving lesson—*she had barely woken up*—but once again, Tiernan and Alice had steamrolled her. *Classic.*

"You realize I don't even know how to drive a stick, right?" Summer asked.

"Well, you gotta learn sometime," Alice said, hopping into the passenger's seat. "Now, getting it into first is the hardest part."

Alice went on, detailing the basics of a manual transmission while Summer positioned herself behind the wheel.

"All you want to do is just give it the tiniest bit of gas," Alice instructed, "but make sure you wail on the clutch at the same time."

Well, here goes nothing. Summer took a deep breath and started up the Pea Pod. She could feel Alice's eyes on her as she gently pressed the gas pedal and shifted into gear. But the Pea Pod just jerked forward, then stalled out.

"You see what I mean?" Alice asked. "It's all about the timing."

When wasn't it about the timing? After all, if Jace hadn't dumped her, she wouldn't be stuck here in Alice's Auto School.

"Maybe it should be Tiernan's turn."

"You're doing fine; just give it another try," Alice said.

Clutch, shift, gas. Clutch, shift, gas. Summer repeated the order in her head as the van stalled out again, then a third time.

"Shoot!" Summer slammed her hands against the steering wheel as the Pea Pod stalled the fourth time in a row. "It's impossible."

"Don't wuss out now," Tiernan said with a mouth full of PB&J. "You're just getting started."

"Give it one more try," Alice pleaded.

Summer swept her hair out of her eyes and turned the key in the ignition. If Jace were here, he'd offer to take over for her. But at the moment, no one could get her out of first but herself.

Clutch, shift, gas . . .

"There you go!" Alice clapped excitedly as the Pea Pod chugged forward. "You did it!"

"Woo hoo!" Summer said sarcastically, but she couldn't

squelch the look of pride on her face if she tried. The Pea Pod was actually moving forward, and best of all, *she* was driving it. After Summer had circled the lot a few times, Tiernan placed a peanut butter and jelly sandwich on her lap. Grape jelly leaked through the crust onto her bare leg.

"Oh, no thanks," Summer, said handing the sandwich back. "I'll get myself something later."

"But I thought PB and J was your favorite," Alice said.

Summer caught Tiernan's eyes in the rearview mirror. "Not everyone can eat Hostess snack cakes all day long and manage to stay a size zero."

"Oy vey, don't tell me you're one of those . . ." Tiernan sighed. *One of what? The health-conscious? The non-obese?* No one Summer knew ate peanut butter anymore. A spoonful of the stuff practically had as much fat as a person was supposed to eat in an entire day. Not that anyone had consulted *her* on the sandwich choices.

Alice put her half-eaten sandwich on the dash. "What do you think, Summer? You ready to take it out on the open road?"

"That depends," Summer said. "Were you guys *hoping* to die today?"

"You'll do fine," Alice scoffed. "Just give yourself ten minutes to drive around the little roads before you take it on the highway."

Summer sighed and headed for the exit, shifting perfectly at the stop sign, then again when she pulled out onto the main drag.

"You do realize I have no clue where I'm going," she said.

"It doesn't matter," Alice said. "This is just for practice."

"But whatever you do," Tiernan warned, "make sure not to cross the West Virginia border."

Summer stalled out at the first set of stoplights, but she made it through the next two without a hitch. After a few more miles, it was hard to remember why the clutch had seemed so tricky in the first place. Kind of like her anger at Jace. Last night's crying jag seemed so far away. Today life didn't feel nearly as tragic.

"No freaking way!" Alice shouted excitedly. "Look!"

She pointed at a blue-and-white truck a few cars in front of them. On it was a cartoon painting of a snowman, dripping with all the colors of the rainbow. Above him were the words MR. FROSTY'S SNOW CONES.

Tiernan read the tagline aloud: "'If you want to be cool, come chill with Mr. Frosty!'"

"This is amazing!" Alice said. "It's totally a sign!" She held up the map they'd made last night, her finger on the collage of the snow cone smack dab in the middle of Kentucky.

Alice and her signs. As a girl, they'd all convinced themselves that they had some kind of "magical connection" with the band. It started in Strawberries Records at the Walford Mall while they were reading the liner notes off that first

Level3 CD (they'd all burned themselves copies by then) and noticed that track one was called "43," the same number as Tiernan's soccer jersey. Then they saw track four: "Skipper," the name of Alice's dog. Track eight was "Summertime Girl." Later, they'd gone online and learned that Level3 toured in a VW van that was just like the Pea Pod. The "Banana Boat" was the same year and everything—only school-bus yellow. Of course, the guys had ditched it for a real tour bus as soon as the band got big.

"Don't lose him; he's signaling!" Alice cried.

Summer followed Mr. Frosty down a side street. Two miles later, the landscape was all trees and farms.

"Don't you think we're getting a little far off track?" Summer asked.

"We're still on pavement," Tiernan said, her mouth full of peanut butter.

Alice looked out at the scenery. "Let's give it one more mile."

Exactly .9 miles later, Mr. Frosty turned into an elementary school parking lot. Alice and Tiernan were bouncing in their seats like a couple of two-year-olds, chanting, "Snow cone! Snow cone! Snow cone!"

At least snow cones were fat free.

The human Mr. Frosty was a bookish-looking guy in his thirties. All around the inside of the truck he'd taped pictures of a woman and a little boy. *Mrs. Frosty and Frosty Junior?*

Summer stared at the long list of flavors. *Cantaloupe, coffee, raspberry cheesecake*. There were so many to choose from, it was overwhelming.

"I'll have a purple plum, please," Alice said, stepping up to the counter.

"And I'll try a bubble gum–green apple combo," Tiernan added.

Summer reread the list. On the one hand, cream soda was a flavor you didn't see every day. But she was always a fan of anything banana.

"I don't want to rush you or anything," Mr. Frosty said, turning to her. "But just to give you a head's up: The rug rats are coming." He pointed over her shoulder to the playing field where a swarm of little kids, all in matching yellow T-shirts, had rounded the hill and were tearing across the grass toward his truck. Alice and Tiernan were already at a picnic table next to the school, digging in.

She handed Mr. Frosty a five. "I'll go with banana, then." It hadn't really been a decision as much as a response under pressure.

She made it to Alice and Tiernan's table just in time to avoid the munchkin stampede.

"Deliciousness," Tiernan said, slurping the juice from her waxy paper cup.

"Well, I think this proves our luck is starting to turn around, wouldn't you say?" Alice asked.

"Better than West Virginia," Tiernan agreed, shaking off a

case of the shivers. "That place is just plain scary."

Summer nodded as she nibbled the edges of her snow cone. It tasted okay, but she should have gotten cream soda.

"To Lucky Kentucky!" Alice said, holding up her cone for a toast.

"To Kentucky!" Summer raised her cone to join Alice's.

"*Salud!*" said Tiernan, giving each of their snow cones a gentle tap.

But when the toast was done, Summer lowered her cone back down a little too fast and the slushy mass of ice slid out of her cup, landing on the wood chips with a *squoosh*.

"Bummer," Alice said. She had already nibbled her snow cone flat.

"Just go ask them for another one," Tiernan said. "It's like the best unwritten law in the universe. Drop an ice-cream cone and you get a free replacement. It's a total do-over."

"Well, this isn't an ice-cream cone," Summer said, sounding more uptight than she'd meant to. "The policy might not be the same."

"Mr. Frosty's cool. He'll hook you up." Tiernan's lips were half-green, half-pink.

"That's okay. I'm fine." Summer shrugged. It wasn't like she needed all that sugar anyway.

"Oh, *please*," Tiernan shot back. "You barely even ate any of it. Look at you, sitting there with your little empty cup. It's tragic."

Summer glanced over at Mr. Frosty, and just seeing the painting of the snow cone on the side of his truck made her mouth start to water. If there was ever a perfect day for a snow cone, this was it—hot and muggy, and she'd probably burned three hundred calories with all that weed-pulling back at Gert's.

"I think the world would be a much better place if the free ice cream concept applied to everything, don't you think?" Alice asked, crunching on a chunk of ice.

"I'd get a new virginity," Tiernan announced, causing Alice to laugh so hard, she spit a mouthful of purple snow-cone juice onto the ground, which, of course, sent them all into complete hysterics.

Summer had always admired how uncensored Tiernan was. Sure, her lack of a filter got her into trouble sometimes, but it also got her what she wanted. Summer, on the other hand, spent so much effort *not* saying what she actually thought and denying herself the things she thought she "shouldn't" have that sometimes it was hard to remember what she really wanted in the first place.

But not this time.

"I'm going to get a new one," Summer declared, standing up. "A snow cone, that is," she clarified.

She took her place at the end of the long line behind a group of obnoxious ten- or eleven-year-old boys who were shoving each other and hocking loogies on the pavement. *Boys.* They didn't change all that much, did they?

Which reminded her she needed to call Jace.

"Hey, where've you been? Didn't you get my texts?" He sounded flustered, desperate.

"I got them," Summer answered slowly, trying not to give away too much about her feelings on the subject. Between last night and this morning he'd sent her about ten text messages— all of them sweet little apologies begging her to come home. The sad part was, his strategy worked. She was actually starting to miss him. But something about hearing his voice brought back those other, more complicated feelings. In text-message world, Jace was the perfect boyfriend. But in real life, Jace was still Jace.

"Come on, Summer, please." His voice was so low, she could barely hear him. "I said I'm sorry. You *know* I'm sorry. Just come home. I miss you."

"I miss you too," she whispered into the phone.

"If you get here by Friday morning, we could still leave for the Vineyard together. I'll even buy your plane ticket home, to make up for everything."

Summer's eyes flickered across the parking lot to Alice and Tiernan. "You mean, leave the trip before we even see the show?"

"Why not? You're not actually having fun, are you?" But Jace didn't wait for her answer. "Just tell me what town you're in, and I'll look up the closest airport."

Normally, Summer hated it when Jace flaunted his family's

money, but there was something romantic about the idea of having her boyfriend fly her back home because he couldn't live without her for another second. Then again, why should she come running just because he called?

"I don't know where I am," she finally answered.

"Well, do you see any signs?"

When Summer turned around to look, she saw Tiernan marching toward her.

"Jace, I'll call you back." She shut her phone and stuffed it in her pocket.

"Hey," Tiernan said. "I'm just coming to let you know Alice is going to give me my driving lesson while you wait. We didn't want you to think we were taking off without you or anything."

"Of course," Summer managed to sputter, even though two seconds ago she'd considered doing the very same thing.

"Wish me luck!" Tiernan called as she headed to the Pea Pod.

"Nice hay-er!" one of the little boys yelled at her back. But Tiernan just ignored him and climbed into the driver's seat.

Summer was still in shock. Until Jace's offer, it hadn't occurred to her that she could actually leave. That she still had a choice. Jace was trying to undo his mistake. And now he was giving Summer the chance to undo hers—coming on this trip. It would be like hitting the reset button.

Part of her was dying to go back to Walford, to be back

with her friends, curled up in the comfort of her very own bed. But if she let Jace pay for her plane ticket, that didn't just mean she was going back home, it meant she was going back to *him*.

The Pea Pod made a loud grinding noise as it lurched forward, then stalled out. At least she wasn't the only one.

"Bite me!" Tiernan yelled, forgetting about the open window.

"I'll bite ya!" shouted the same little boy. The rest of his gang howled with laughter. Then Summer noticed that one of the other boys had something in his hand. And whatever it was, he was aiming to throw it at the Pea Pod, which was now bucking along in spurts. Without even thinking, she reached out and grabbed the boy's wrist.

"You'd better not be throwing things at my friends." She glowered, like she was actually some kind of authority figure. She released the boy's wrist as he opened his hand. A golf-ball-size rock fell to the ground.

Her *friends*. The word left an aftertaste in her mouth. Were Alice and Tiernan really her friends, or had it just come out like that, out of habit? And, if so, was it possible she missed Jace out of habit too?

"These twerps bothering you?" asked a boy walking toward her. He appeared to be about her age, but he wore the same yellow T-shirt as the younger kids. And even though he wasn't very tall, he was strikingly handsome, with honey-blond hair and just the slightest hint of a double chin, suggesting a future as a frat boy, or a car salesman.

"I think I've got it under control," Summer said, shaking her hair off her shoulders.

"Twerps, if I find you acting out, y'all are gonna lose your snow-cone privileges," the boy warned. His voice had a twinge of Kentucky in it, but in a good way.

"Sorry 'bout that," he said to Summer. "These little hellions are mine for the next six weeks. Guess I got the short straw this year." He pointed to the word "counselor" just below the soccer-ball logo printed on his shirt, then smiled at the boys. His teeth were straight and white, with the clean familiar shape of someone who'd just gotten their braces off.

"I'm Finn." He held out his hand.

She took it. "Summer."

Then the Pea Pod's tires squealed so loudly that they both turned to look. At least Tiernan was actually moving.

"You with those girls, in the van?" Finn asked.

"Kind of," Summer said.

"Kind of?"

"Well, yeah. I'm currently with them."

Finn looked confused. "Y'all not getting along or something?"

Summer thought about it. "It's a long story," she finally said.

Finn smiled at her again. She was being enigmatic, but he seemed to be enjoying it. Most boys did.

"Camp's over in a couple of minutes." He pointed to the line of mothers waiting in their air-conditioned cars. "Then I'm going to take a swim in my pool. Maybe you and your 'kind of' friends want to come along?"

"Maybe," Summer said, smiling a little wider than she'd intended. *What was it with Southern boys and swimming?*

"Finn's got a girlfriend," one of the little boys sang out in the familiar teasing tune. They both pretended not to hear.

"Oh, shoot," Finn said. "I forgot that I took my morning run coming over here. If y'all do want to come over, maybe you could give me a lift back to my house? It's just up the main road about a mile."

Summer didn't mean to, but she laughed right in Finn's face. "I'll have to check with my *traveling companions* on that one."

"If y'all are headed back to the highway, it'll be right on your way."

Summer nodded back at Finn as she strode across the parking lot, soaring with renewed enthusiasm for the possibilities of the day. She'd call Jace later, when she'd figured everything out. There'd still be airports wherever they ended up tomorrow.

The Pea Pod cut through the steady stream of minivans now entering the parking lot, screeching to a stop right in front of her. Evidently Tiernan had gone from novice to stunt driver in five minutes.

"Summer has a boyfriend," Tiernan said in the exact same singsong voice as the little boy.

"His name is Finn," Summer said, looking past Tiernan to Alice. "And he invited us to go swimming with him. At his pool."

"Oh, good God!" said Tiernan indignantly. "Does anyone in the South do anything but swim?"

"Well, it is a million frigging degrees down here," Summer said, sweeping her hair off her neck. "Anyway, his house has to be pretty close by since he ran here this morning, so I figure if we want to go, we could give him a ride?"

Alice got that scrunched-up look on her face that she got every time she was about to get up on her high horse. "Well, not according to the rule *we* made . . ." She stared right at Summer on the word "we."

"Oh, come on, Alice. He's a camp counselor, for crying out loud. And a pool is way less sketchy than a swimming hole."

Tiernan gave her a snide grin.

"We've only driven three hours today," Alice said. "I'd like to make it at least as far as Lexington so we're not stuck with another huge day of driving."

"I'm down with that," Alice's sidekick agreed. Like Summer expected anything else.

Most of the time Summer went through life not knowing what she wanted. But every time she actually did manage to make a decsion, there was always someone there to question it, or make her feel like she was wrong. She stormed off in a huff, not even waving to Finn, who was staring at her from across the parking lot with a confused look on his face.

The line at Mr. Frosty had come and gone, so Summer marched right up to the window of the snow cone truck and slapped $2.50 on the counter.

"I'll have a cream soda, please."

As far as she knew, the free replacement rule only applied if you ordered the same flavor. But, for once, Summer was going to get what she wanted, even if it meant having to pay.

"LOST & FOUND"

I WAS LOOKING THROUGH THE LOST AND FOUND
FOR SOMETHING I COULDN'T DESCRIBE.
BUT THERE WAS ONLY ONE GLOVE,
AND IT WASN'T MY SIZE.

—*from Level3's second CD*, Rough & Tumble

Chapter Twelve

ALICE STRETCHED HER LEGS OUT AND GAVE A LOUD, ROARING yawn. If Summer wasn't driving fifty in a thirty-five zone, she might actually be able to close her eyes.

"Hey, Summer," Alice said as calmly as possible, "you mind easing up on the gas a bit?"

Summer answered by jamming on the brakes, sending Alice's purse careening off the counter next to the sink, half its contents skittering across the floor. Normally, she was the most laid-back of all three of them, like the season she was named for with its warm, carefree days and lazy, light-filled evenings. But occasionally Summer brought on brutal heat waves, and there was nothing anyone could do but wait for them to pass.

"In three hundred yards, turn left," Coach Quigley boomed.

"I wonder if this thing comes with a pirate voice." Tiernan snatched the GPS from the dashboard. "Turn starboard at three hundred paces! Argh!"

"We can't change Coach Quigley!" Alice protested, tossing her travel-size hand sanitizer back into her bag. "It'd be sacrilege."

Alice pulled her cell phone out from underneath the

passenger's seat. She hadn't looked at it once today, hadn't even remembered to turn it on. Now she had six messages since last night—four from her parents and two from a number she didn't recognize.

"Oh my God!" Alice gasped.

"What?" Tiernan turned to face her.

"I think"—Alice hit home on her speed dial—"this might be good news."

If Alice were a season she'd definitely be fall—all eagerness and schedules and brand-new back-to-school clothes.

Her mother answered on the third ring.

"Did I get a letter from Brown?" Alice asked breathlessly.

"What?" Her mom sounded confused. "Where are you? Didn't you get my messages?"

"No, I just turned my phone on. Why, is something wrong?" Her nervous excitement took a U-turn into just plain panic.

"I'm *fine* and Dad is *fine*. We've been trying to get a hold of Tiernan."

"Mom, is—?"

"Everyone's okay," her mother jumped in. "Except for the fact that we got a call from her mother at one a.m. last night asking if we'd seen her."

Alice looked up at Tiernan, who was still fiddling with the GPS.

"Alice." Her mother's tone was serious. "Did you know Tiernan didn't tell her mother she was going on the trip?"

"No, I had no idea."

"Well, she needs to call home right now. Judy was beside herself with worry last night. Thank goodness she thought to call us."

"Okay, Mom." Alice swallowed hard. "So, no letter from Brown?"

"No," said her mother sharply. "And I want you to call me back after Tiernan's talked to her mother, all right?"

"Okay," Alice said before she hit end.

Tiernan slipped off her shoes and put her bare feet up on the dash. If Tiernan was a season, it would be spring in New England—bitter cold one day, the next, a daffodil poking its head through the snow, and just when you thought winter was finally over, a blizzard would hit.

"So, what's the big news?"

"Apparently, *you* are," Alice said.

Tiernan smirked. "I take it Judy's called out a search party?"

"Can you blame her? You just took off without telling anyone where you were going."

"Chillax, Judy Number Two."

"Why should I?" Alice was fuming. "At least you could have had the courtesy of telling *me* you were running away."

"You guys—" Summer tried to interrupt.

"First of all," Tiernan spat, "I don't owe anyone an explanation of what I do or why."

"You don't *owe me* anything—"

"You guys!" Summer repeated, this time more forcefully. Alice looked at her, suddenly aware of the knocking sound coming from the engine. The van was barely moving as Summer pulled to the side of the road.

"I think we're out of gas."

"Well, so much for Lucky Kentucky," Tiernan said.

Alice could have kicked herself. First she'd forgotten to turn on her cell phone; now they'd run out of gas. Less than thirty-six hours on the road and she'd turned into a total flake.

"What should we do?" Summer asked.

"Well, we can't stay in here," Alice said. In this heat, the Pea Pod may as well have been an Easy-Bake Oven. Not that outside was much better.

Alice paced by the side of the road, trying to think of a plan.

"Look!" Tiernan said, holding up Coach Quigley. "According to this, there's a gas station four point two miles from here."

"*Four miles*," Alice whimpered. "There has to be something closer." Between the heat, last night's lack of sleep, and the backbreaking labor at Gert's, she wasn't sure she'd be able to walk another four feet.

"Maybe there's someone with a gallon of gas we can borrow," Summer suggested, pulling her ponytail through her pink Red Sox baseball cap. "Didn't we pass a house about a quarter mile back?"

Tiernan grabbed a bottle of water from the van. "Okay, let's go check it out."

HILARY WEISMAN GRAHAM

"Actually . . ." Alice gave Tiernan an apologetic smile. "I think someone should stay with the Pea Pod."

Tiernan's face went blank.

"Plus, I told my mom you'd call home right away."

"Well, I don't have a phone," Tiernan whined. "My mom confiscated mine when I got grounded, and it wasn't in any of her usual hiding spots."

Alice took her cell from her pocket and thrust it at Tiernan. Then she and Summer walked off, before Tiernan had a chance to argue.

"It's just rude!" Alice spat when they were finally out of earshot. "It's like she's using this trip as an excuse to run away from home."

"I just think it's typical," Summer said. "If Tiernan sees an opportunity, she takes it."

Alice was pissed off at Tiernan, but hearing Summer bad-mouth her wasn't making it better. It was like bitching about your mother—*you* were allowed to do it, but somebody else trash-talking your mom? Not so much. The only reason Alice had invited Summer and Tiernan on this trip was because she'd assumed enough time had passed to erase any weird leftover tension. Obviously, just another one of her naive hopes.

"I'm sorry this trip has been so crazy," Alice said. "Especially with everything you're going through." She sneaked a quick glance at Summer, afraid she might have stumbled into a conversational no-fly zone.

"I don't know *what* I'm going through," Summer said with a laugh.

Summer never talked about her feelings much, even back when they'd been close. Alice remembered how people who didn't know Summer very well often mistook her for being shallow. But that wasn't the case. Summer was smart, perceptive, and ridiculously creative—she was just very careful about who she let in. Alice had always respected that about her. A lot of girls seemed to just spill their guts to whoever happened to be in earshot. But when Summer opened up, it actually meant something.

Then, back in eighth grade, right around the same time boys started circling her like moths to a flame, Summer started to close that door. At least to Alice. It happened little by little, almost imperceptibly at first, until the night of the Winter Wonderland Dance when Summer slammed the door shut forever.

"It doesn't look like anyone's home," Summer said.

They had turned off the road and were traipsing across the lawn now—no lights on in the house, no cars in the driveway.

Alice knocked three times, but no one answered, so she moved on to the garage, standing on her tiptoes to peer in through the high windows. Normally, she wasn't the type to trespass, but all they needed was one measly gallon of gas. And somebody had to be proactive if they were ever going to get back on the road.

"Alice, what are you doing?" Summer asked.

HILARY WEISMAN GRAHAM

But Alice was too distracted by what she saw to answer. All the way in the back, wedged between a lawn mower and a dirt bike, was a shiny red gas can.

"Summer, I see one!" she said excitedly.

"So, what are we supposed to do? Break in and steal it?"

"Not *stealing*. Just . . . borrowing. We could even leave them five bucks."

Summer chewed her lower lip. "And if the door is locked, we walk away?"

"Of course." Alice said, already tugging on the handle.

The door was sticky, but it rose—its metallic springs knocking and clanging like some kind of homemade alarm system. Alice opened it just far enough to duck inside.

It was cool in the garage, and a shiver raced up Alice's spine—as much from the temperature drop as from the feeling of doing something illicit.

"You should come in!"she shouted. "It's so much cooler in here!"

"Cool enough to get arrested for breaking and entering?" Summer asked.

"Yes!" Alice shot back.

Summer poked her head in to verify Alice's claim. The rest of her quickly followed. For a moment they just stood there, enjoying the cold musty air and the exhilaration of being someplace they didn't belong.

"Boys live here," Summer pronounced, pointing her chin

toward a messy pile of lacrosse sticks and baseball bats.

It was a simple observation. Still, it was a level of noticing that always made Alice feel like a child next to Summer. Like it would take her years to understand all the things Summer already knew. Back in high school, Alice had watched Summer walk down the halls with at least a dozen different boys by her side. Meanwhile, Alice had never even dated anyone, unless she counted the slobbery make-out sessions she'd had behind the arts and crafts shed at camp with that kid Derek. Which she didn't.

"We should probably hurry, right?" Summer asked. The nice way of saying, *Snap out of it and move, girl.*

The garage floor was so cluttered Alice had to choose each step deliberately—careful not to slip on a stray golf ball, to avoid the booby trap of the perilously balanced bicycles.

"I feel like Indiana Jones," she called to Summer, just as her foot hit a soccer ball and sent it careening into a metal toolbox.

"Holy crap!" Summer gasped.

"Sorry," Alice said as she reached down and grabbed the gas can. Then she turned around and headed back across the clutter, the sound of the thin liquid sloshing through the can's open nozzle.

She was glad Summer was here for this little adventure. There was something bonding about the clandestineness of it all, as if the strangeness of their surroundings overshadowed the strangeness between the two of them.

Alice was almost back at the door when it flew up with such a terrifying thunder it made Summer scream.

First she saw Tiernan, her face bleached white with sunshine. Then a familiar blond-haired boy stepped out from behind her, his bright yellow T-shirt soaked through with sweat.

Finn nodded at Alice, then turned to Summer and shot her his trademark smile. "So, should I call the police, or does this mean y'all are taking me up on my invitation?"

"JACKIE NEEDS NEW GLASSES"

WE'LL LEAVE OUR GLASSES

ON THE NIGHTSTAND,

AND SEE EACH OTHER

AS WE TRULY ARE

AS I RELEARN LOVE

THROUGH YOUR EYES

WHILE YOU RELEARN IT

THROUGH MINE.

—from Level3's self-titled first CD

Chapter Thirteen

"STOP IT!" SUMMER SQUEALED AS FINN WRENCHED THE SUPER Soaker from her hands.

They'd been chasing each other around the shallow end of the pool for the last fifteen minutes—part water-gun battle, part lame excuse for groping each other's half-naked bodies.

"You are so dead!" Summer shrieked as Finn pelted water at the small of her back.

Alice figured she'd give Summer another ten minutes to satisfy her flirtation fix, then they'd head back on the road again. She hadn't wanted to delay their trip any further, but with the van now parked safely in Finn's driveway, Alice couldn't exactly use the excuse about not having their bathing suits. Plus, after walking back down that hot dusty road to gas up the Pea Pod, she'd actually been dying for a quick dip.

Alice sidestroked her way to the deep end just as Tiernan sprung off the diving board and did a midair somersault—*a double somersault? No.* Her legs hit the water with a slap.

"Well?" Tiernan asked when she'd surfaced.

"I'd give it an eight point two," Alice said. "You were close. Close-ish." Finn's swimming pool had cooled them off in more ways than one. Not that Alice ever stayed mad for very long.

She pushed herself off the edge and headed back toward the shallow end, thankfully empty since Summer and Finn's flirtation had evolved onto land. Finn still held the water gun, but now Summer had the garden hose, and she was merciless. Finn tried to dodge it, zigging and zagging across the lawn, then finally ducking behind the edge of the house to get out of range. Just then a boy on a bike came riding past him into the backyard, right in the line of fire.

"What the——?" The boy tried to veer away from the spray and fell off his bike.

Summer released the nozzle. "Oh my gosh, I'm so sorry."

"Don't worry about it," Finn said. "It's just my little brother, Quentin. Say hello to the ladies, Q-Tip."

"Hello, ladies," said Quentin.

With his tall, bony body, wire-rimmed glasses, and sardonic smile, Quentin didn't look anything like Finn. In the bike helmet, the effect was that of a human lollipop. And even though Finn had referred to him as his younger brother, there was something about Quentin's eyes that made him seem older.

"Where'd the sirens come from?" Quentin asked. He was staring right at Alice.

"What?" asked Finn.

Alice laughed. "Sirens, like in Homer's *Odyssey*," she explained, letting her gaze flicker across Quentin's before it made its way to Finn. "They sang to the sailors, drawing them in to shore with their voices."

"And making them shipwreck on the rocks," Quentin added with a grin.

"Tra-la-la-la!" Tiernan trilled, purposefully off-key. Then she hurled herself into the water like a wounded sailor.

Everyone but Quentin watched Tiernan's display. His eyes stayed on Alice. Suddenly she could feel the air on every inch of her bare skin, which was a lot, considering how she was just standing there in her bathing suit in knee-deep water with her blobby white thighs totally exposed. She did a quick dolphin dive into the deep end, hoping that the wedgie from her bathing suit had flashed by too quickly for anyone to notice. She swam underwater until her fingertips scraped against the concrete wall at the deep end. When she surfaced, Quentin was gone.

"Well, we should probably get going if we want to make it to Lexington before dark," Alice announced.

"Fine by me," Tiernan said.

Summer positioned herself on a float. "Ten more minutes?" she pleaded as Finn dragged her along by the ankles.

Alice was about to rattle off her list of reasons why it was important that they leave Right At This Very Moment when the back door of the house flung open, revealing Quentin—helmet- and glasses-free—wearing nothing but neon-green swim trunks. His floppy brown hair fell in his eyes, and his chest was lean, but muscular. He'd looked skinnier in clothes.

Quentin gave Alice a quick wink, then took off for the pool full tilt, sailing diagonally across the water, arms hugging his knees, heading *straight for her*. Too shocked to even think to swim away, Alice just stood where she was as Quentin's cannonball detonated two inches away, soaking her with its enormous splash.

She stared quizzically at Quentin as he surfaced, and Quentin stared right back at her, with a shameless self-satisfied grin. "Y'all are staying for dinner, right?"

"We thank thee, Lord, for happy hearts, for rain and sunny weather. We thank thee, Lord, for this food, and that we are together."

Alice wasn't a religious person, but she knew enough to recognize an unholy thought when it hit her. And when Quentin had taken his hand in hers for grace, *boy, had it hit her*. It was nothing like the feeling she'd had with Phred—his heavy arm weighing on her shoulder like a sandbag. Quentin's hand seemed to melt into hers in a way that made her whole body tingle.

"And we are also thankful to have you girls here with us tonight," Quentin's mother said. Mrs. Oldham was built like a pint-sized linebacker—broad shoulders like Finn, huge boobs, thin, almost spindly legs. Her hair was frosted blond, and she wore large gold hoop earrings and a matching gold cross around her neck.

HILARY WEISMAN GRAHAM

Mr. Oldham was an older, beer-bellied version of Quentin. He smiled kindly at the girls. "Well, with what y'all have been through, somebody 'round here needed to show you some Southern hospitality."

"Amen to that," Quentin said, giving Alice's hand an extra little squeeze. Then grace was officially over and, much to Alice's distress, Quentin wiggled his hand from hers. *Good Lord! Doesn't anyone at this table have something else to be thankful for?*

"Quey-yahn-tin!" Mrs. Oldham's Kentucky accent was as thick as the barbecue sauce Quentin licked off his fingers. "Use some manners, please. We have ladies around."

"Sorry, Mama." Quentin sheepishly wiped his hand on his napkin.

Mr. Oldham laughed. "I think my wife likes havin' you girls around as much as the boys do, what with bein' the only female in the house."

Mrs. Oldham threw her hands up in the air dramatically. "Sometimes I just go out of my mind with all this male energy around."

You can say that again, Alice thought. Twice since grace, Quentin's thigh had brushed against hers and it still felt electric.

"I just think y'all should stay here for the night," Mrs. Oldham continued as Quentin's knee bumped hers again— *accidentally?* "I'm sure your mothers wouldn't want you driving into some strange city after dark."

"We really need to make some more miles tonight," Tiernan said apologetically.

Alice shot Tiernan a look. If her leg wasn't already preoccupied, she might have kicked her. "We could just make it up tomorrow," Alice quickly added. "I mean, it's only a hundred miles, right?"

"Whatever." Tiernan smirked back at her. "Your call, boss."

"Well, we don't want to be an imposition," Alice said to Mrs. Oldham.

"No imposition at all." Mrs. Oldham smiled. "Guest room's already got clean sheets."

After dinner, Alice and Quentin teamed up in a cutthroat game of Monopoly, where they dominated all the other players, capping off their win with a duet of "We're in the Money." Then there was that moment in the den while they were all watching TV and Quentin leaned his back against her legs. The only thing that prevented it from being the most perfect night of Alice's life was having to witness Summer's reaction when Finn's girlfriend unexpectedly showed up.

But for once Alice wasn't obsessing about whether or not everyone else was having a good time. *She* was having an amazing time.

It was almost midnight when Mrs. Oldham came downstairs to tell them it was time to "get some shut-eye."

Quentin's mom had gone to a lot of effort to make them

HILARY WEISMAN GRAHAM

comfortable, setting up an air mattress next to the queen-size bed in the guest room, putting out fresh towels and bottles of water. But all Alice could think about was that Mrs. Oldham had whisked her away from Quentin before they'd gotten a chance to say a proper good night.

"So, did you kiss him?" Tiernan asked, plopping onto the air mattress.

"When could I do that?" Alice sighed, letting her body fall back against the frilly white bedspread. "We were never alone."

"Too bad." Summer climbed into bed next to her. "He seems really sweet. Unlike his poop-stain of a brother."

A knock on the door made Alice bolt upright. *If Mrs. Oldham had heard them talking about her sons . . .* Then Alice saw the note on the floor—a small square of white lined paper, meticulously folded. She sailed across the room and snatched it up, unfolding each layer carefully as her heartbeat thundered in her ears.

"Come on, Alice, spit it out. What does it say?" Tiernan bounced on the air mattress like a little kid.

The note had only three words, but Alice was almost too tongue-tied to say them. "You, me. P-Pod?"

Summer shrieked with delight. "At least someone's getting some tonight."

"Shhhh," Alice reprimanded her, though on the inside she was screaming. She loved everything about the note—the way he'd put "you" and "me" in the same sentence, the way he hadn't assumed anything by ending "P-Pod" with a question mark.

"You better take one of these." Tiernan rummaged through her toiletries bag and fished out a condom. "Just in case."

"Put that thing away, *please*," Alice cried.

"Don't listen to her," Summer said. "You don't want to sleep with him on the first date anyway."

"You guys, I am *not* having sex with him. I'm not even sure if he likes me."

"Oh my God." Tiernan collapsed dramatically, making the air mattress hiss.

"Alice," Summer said, nodding reassuringly, "*he likes you.*"

Alice quickly brushed her teeth, dabbed on a layer of strawberry lip gloss, then smoothed her hair with water. If only she'd remembered to put in some gel after swimming, she wouldn't look like she had a bird's nest on top of her head. Finally Summer jumped up and helped her pull her hair back in a French twist while Tiernan dug through Alice's wardrobe for something decent to wear.

"How about this?" Tiernan asked, holding up a plain black tank dress.

"Perfect." Summer nodded. "Sultry, yet understated."

Alice slipped on the dress, added her favorite dangly gold earrings, then gave her pits a quick sniff. A quick slather of deodorant and she was out the door.

"Wish me luck," she whispered while Summer and Tiernan waved and grinned like a couple of proud parents.

Alice padded down the squeaky wooden stairs, her breathing shallow and fast, like she'd just run a marathon. Then she took a deep breath and opened the front door.

The night air felt like a different world—warm, mysterious, sweet.

"Alice." Out of the dark Quentin whispered her name. She'd heard it a million times a day, every day of her life. But it sounded different coming from his mouth. Better. She could see him now, leaning against the van.

"Here I am," she said, suddenly feeling shy.

"I can see that," Quentin replied.

They stared at each other for a few beats in silence.

"So, you want to check out the van?" Alice asked, regretting the question as soon as it came out of her mouth. Could it sound any more like a cheesy pick-up line?

"Sure," Quentin said.

The side door rolled open quietly on its freshly oiled track, and Alice sent Gert a silent thank-you. Quentin climbed in first, stepping over her bathing suit, which had fallen from where she'd hung it to dry and was on the floor, inside out, its tan nylon crotch completely exposed. Alice scrambled in after him and quickly wadded the suit into a ball, tossing it in the sink. She left the door open a few inches, partly for the breeze and partly because the thought of closing it all the way made her nervous.

"So, is it like you expected?" she asked as Quentin looked around.

"Even better," Quentin said. "Though I try not to have expectations."

Alice sat down on the bench seat, tucking her bare feet underneath her. "How do you not have expectations? I mean, if you don't have expectations, how do you ever get what you want?" She hadn't imagined their conversation would get so deep right off the bat, which, she realized, was also an expectation.

"Well, I know one way to never get what you want is by trying to make it fit into your vision of how it should be." Quentin sat down next to her, close enough for her to feel his heat against her bare knee.

"You seem to have a lot of big ideas for a high school senior," Alice said. He was only five months younger than her, but a grade behind.

"Oh, I'm full of big ideas." Quentin smiled back. Alice stared at him until she felt herself blush. Then Quentin leaned forward to look at the collage taped to the cabinet below the sink. It wasn't one of their better works, but it was the only one they hadn't cut apart last night.

"This is cool." He pointed to a small cutout of her face— the center of a daisy made up of Level3 leaves. "Is that you?"

"When I was twelve." Alice rolled her eyes.

"You had a lot of artistic talent for a twelve-year-old."

"I didn't make it alone. Summer and Tiernan, they're really the creative ones in the group. But making collages, well . . . it used to be kind of our *thing*."

"So were you *friends* before you became groupies, or were you *groupies* before you were friends?"

"First of all, we're *not* groupies," Alice corrected him. "Groupies are fanatical, plus they usually sleep with the band." She'd been alone with Quentin for ten whole seconds and already she'd brought up sex. *Smooth.* "And, yes, we were friends first. I mean, *before*."

"Before what?"

"Before we stopped being friends."

Quentin looked confused. "So what are you now?"

Alice paused, exhaling through her nose. "The only reason we're all together is to go see Level3, because we have that history. But back in the real world, we don't even hang out."

"Isn't this the real world?" Quentin asked.

Alice laughed. It certainly didn't feel like the real world, sitting here in the Pea Pod in the middle of the night with a cute boy.

But Quentin wasn't letting it go. "Doesn't it bother you? Hanging out with people who aren't your friends anymore?"

"Well, I wouldn't say they *aren't* my friends," Alice said. "I mean, it's cordial; it's not a big deal, really." She turned to face him. "Can we talk about *you* for a while?"

Quentin nodded. "Well, I'm seventeen, I'm a Virgo, my brother once broke my nose with a baseball bat—*supposedly an accident*—and that's why it's crooked. And in two more weeks, I'm getting the *hey-yell* out of this backward, godforsaken town to spend a month up north at a summer art program."

"Where?" Alice asked, her heartbeat swishing in her ears.

"At RISD. Rhode Island School of Design. That's near Massachusetts, right?"

RISD was in Providence, practically right down the street from Brown. "Mm-hmm." Alice nodded, trying to act casual. "So, you're an artist?"

Quentin shrugged. "I try to be. If things go well at the summer program, it'll help my chances of getting in when I apply to go to school there next year."

Alice felt a flutter of hope beating its wings inside her chest. *What if she was at Brown and Quentin was at RISD?* It was almost too good to be true. Wait a minute. It *was* too good to be true.

"Why are you laughing?" Quentin asked.

"Oh, nothing," Alice said. "I'm just amused by my own failure to not have expectations."

They talked like this for hours, until the black sky brightened to cobalt blue, until they were yawning as much as talking. They were both lying on the floor now, the door closed all the way to keep out the chill of the predawn air. Their bodies were millimeters away from each other, but not touching.

"We should probably go back up," Alice said, even though it was the last thing she wanted to do.

"Okay," Quentin said, turning to face her, his mouth so close she could feel his breath on her chin.

Suddenly Alice's brain was seized by the list of things she'd messed up today—how she'd forgotten to turn on her cell phone, to get gas for the van, how she hadn't called her mother back, forgotten to even check whether or not Tiernan had called *her* mother. Of course, they'd never made it to Lexington.

"How do you not have expectations?" she asked, suddenly jumping back into their old conversation. "If you don't anticipate certain outcomes, how do you ever plan where you'll end up?"

Quentin smiled at her, then reached out and put his palm on her cheek. "Maybe you'll end up right here."

Then, he leaned in and kissed her—her cheek still in his hand as if he were holding on to something precious. Alice had kissed boys before, but never like this. Their kiss was a thing of their own invention—like a river flowing through every cell in her body, then out into the universe.

He pulled her in closer and she devoured his smell—a mix of pool chlorine and sweat that might have seemed unpleasant to anyone else in the world, but to Alice, it was delicious. His lips wandered down to her ear, her neck.

She let out a little moan, unintentionally, but she didn't even think to be embarrassed until she felt him pull away. Had her noise freaked him out? What other reason could there possibly be for him to interrupt this perfect moment? But when Alice opened her eyes, she saw the reason right in front of her, looking in through the window of the van. And her name was Mrs. Oldham.

"TOMFOOLERY"

I WANT TO LIVE LIFE LIKE VACATION
I WANT TO RUIN MY REPUTATION

GET OUT OF MY CAR
IF YOU DON'T LIKE THE STATION
ON MY RADIO.
BUT I DON'T WANT YOU TO GO.

—from Level3's self-titled first CD

Chapter Fourteen

made a rasping sound, then stalled out. *Again.* Tiernan glanced at the clock. She'd been trying to make her "quick getaway" for the last three minutes. Not that getting the Pea Pod into gear was easy under normal conditions, let alone with an angry Southern Baptist giving her the stink-eye.

"Do you need me to drive?" Summer asked.

On the front porch, Mrs. Oldham scowled at them, sunlight glinting ominously off the gold cross at her neck.

"Look at her, glaring at us like we're a bunch of Yankee hussies," Tiernan whispered as she restarted the van. "It was just Alice!" she pretended to shout to Mrs. Oldham. Then she ever-so-gently hit the gas, and the van conked out with a spasmic sigh.

"Could you skip the commentary and just get us out of here?" Alice hissed from her hiding spot in the back. Only ten minutes had passed since she'd burst into the guest bedroom babbling incoherently and yanked Tiernan and Summer out of bed.

"All I'm saying is that the woman has anger management issues." Tiernan paused to restart the van. "I can see the headline now: Tennessee Mother Kills Three over Hickey."

"We're in Kentucky, bonehead," Summer pointed out.

"And it wasn't a hickey," Alice chimed in.

Without knowing exactly how it happened, Tiernan realized she was moving, so she seized the momentum, gunning the Pea Pod turbo-speed down the Oldhams' driveway and whipping it onto the road *Dukes of Hazzard* style.

"Thanks for your hospitality!" She waved liked Miss America out the window as the Pea Pod bucked and lurched down the street.

"Oh. My. God!" Alice screamed. "That was the most embarrassing thing that's ever happened to me!"

"Think of how Quentin must feel," Summer offered. "She's *his* mother."

Tiernan cringed. "Can you imagine getting caught with a boner in front of your own mom?"

"Not really," Summer said.

Then all three of them busted out in silent hysterics. Tiernan was laughing so hard, she had to wipe her eyes to see the road.

"Do you even know where you're going?" Alice asked, gasping for air.

Tiernan looked at the unfamiliar landscape, suddenly aware that she was driving. If Alice and Summer were in their usual moods, they probably would have yelled at her. But this morning, her cluelessness just triggered another round of laughter.

"I may not know where I'm going," Tiernan began, her words coming out in snorts, "but I know where *you're* going, Alice Miller—straight to *hay-ell!*"

"Ay-a-may-en," Summer said in a bad Southern accent.

"Turn around when possible," Coach Quigley offered.

Eventually they made it to civilization—or in this case, a Waffle House, which was about as close to civilization as things got in these parts. Over weak coffee and soggy bacon, they charted their course for the day. The plan was to drive until they made it to Nashville, Tennessee, and then chill out in the nicest hotel they could find. For under one hundred fifty dollars. With a pool.

"What about this one?" Summer asked, holding up her phone. "It has a spa, a fitness center, three swimming pools, and an indoor waterfall. . . ."

Since Alice seemed to be stuck in a permanent state of la-la land (at the moment, smiling at her French toast like she was about to French kiss it) Tiernan looked at the website first.

"You wanna stay at *the Gaywether?*" Tiernan blurted out, louder than she'd intended. "Summer . . . is there something you'd like to tell us?"

"Oh, calm down." Summer snatched her phone back. "We don't have to stay here. I'm just saying it looks pretty nice, and it's not that expensive, considering."

"What?" Alice looked up from her breakfast as though she'd just arrived on Planet Earth.

"This hotel Summer wants to stay at." Tiernan raised her eyebrows. "It's called *the Gaywether.*"

Summer handed her phone to Alice. "Check it out—they have this whole indoor garden area with a waterfall and a river."

"Hotel, or Epcot? You be the judge," Tiernan said.

"What's wrong with Epcot?" Summer asked.

"Nothing, if you like that kind of sanitized, generic family entertainment."

In Tiernan's opinion, *real* fun didn't happen by going to places like Disney World. Real fun was something you stumbled into, by accident.

Alice scrolled through the website. "I think this looks nice. I mean, why not splurge a little? Maybe we'll even be able to get a little R and R for once."

"Okay. I'll make the reservation right now," Summer said, taking her phone back.

Alice turned her attention to Tiernan. "Hey, I meant to ask you . . . how did the conversation with your mom go?"

Tiernan pushed a bite of waffle around her plate, mopping up the leftover syrup. Could Alice just give it a rest already? It wasn't like she was in any hurry to dial up *her* mom and give her the play-by-play of last night's spit-swapping session.

"She wasn't around," Tiernan lied, licking syrup off her fork. No need to ruin the girl's post-make-out euphoria.

"So, did you leave her a message?"

Tiernan shook her head in what she hoped was a remorseful way. "I'll try her again today, okay?"

Three hundred and twelve miles later, Alice was zonked out in the back (drooling all over the upholstery) and Tiernan still hadn't made the call. Although as penance for *not* making it (a habit from the Catholic side of her family) she'd kept Alice's cell phone in her front pocket so that it dug uncomfortably into her hip bone.

The weird thing was, Tiernan wasn't sure why she *wasn't* calling. Yeah, Judy was going to be tweaked. But a watered-down phone version of Judy's bitch-slap was better than facing the real thing. And unless Judy was planning to track her down bounty-hunter style, Tiernan had another week before she had to face whatever punishment Judy was cooking up (though the heaping side order of guilt trip could probably be delivered via telephone).

"Okay, I have a good one for you," Summer said. They'd been talking in stops and starts like this for the last five hours. At first, Tiernan figured it was just a way to pass the time while Alice slept, but somewhere in southern Kentucky, she'd actually started to enjoy their little trips down memory lane.

"Remember the time we ran away?"

"Of course." Tiernan smiled. "We were such rebels back then."

Their infamous running-away episode had happened at

Tiernan's house at a play date. (That's how young they were—their hangouts were still called play dates.) Something her mother had done set her off; Tiernan couldn't remember what. Maybe they'd been caught watching an R-rated movie on Showtime, or maybe she'd decided to lead a revolt against Judy's tyrannical two-Popsicle limit. Whatever the nature of the injustice du jour, nine-year-old Tiernan had the solution: running away.

Naturally, Alice and Summer had joined her in solidarity, loading up Tiernan's little red wagon with canned goods (for nourishment), blankets (for warmth), and a dictionary (so they could continue their education on the road). Then, the three fourth-graders set out into the cold, cruel world. Cut to one hour later when Tiernan's dad spotted them while mowing the lawn. They had made it as far as the next-door neighbor's azalea bush.

"I love how we even remembered to bring a can opener," Summer said.

Tiernan laughed. "As I recall, we actually ate an entire can of green beans."

"With our hands," Summer added.

The whole thing seemed pretty pathetic in retrospect. Then again, was it really any less pathetic than what Tiernan was doing right now?

She stuck her hand out the window, cupping the air with her palm so that it rose and fell with the wind. She was more than one thousand miles from home—her most successful run-away attempt to date.

"I'm just so happy for Alice," Summer said. "She and Quentin were so cute together."

"I know." Tiernan nodded. "She totally deserves it."

"It was total love at first sight," Summer went on.

Tiernan shrugged. "If you believe in things like that."

"And you don't?"

"I just think that most people do such a bad job making *themselves* happy, it's completely ridiculous to think anyone else can do it for you."

"So, you're saying that you don't believe in love?"

"Oh, I believe in love, all right," Tiernan clarified. "But only as a temporary condition. Like insanity."

Summer laughed. "Wow. That's optimistic."

"I think being in love's the best feeling in the world. But that feeling never lasts."

"Sometimes it does," Summer said defensively.

"I guess it depends how much you're willing to delude yourself," Tiernan said, sounding harsher than she'd intended.

Tiernan wished she could take back that last part, but it was too late. She could already see Summer slipping into that distant mood she got in every time her cell phone rang, like a black-and-white print left in the developer too long—its details fading away until the entire sheet went dark. And once a photo was overexposed, it was too late to get it back.

Suddenly Tiernan was hit with this crazy urge to spill her guts to Summer right here and now. To finally tell her the truth about that night at the winter dance and just deal with the consequences. But the funny thing was, you needed guts to be able to spill your guts.

Anyway, Tiernan had missed her big chance. Coach Quigley was already barking instructions to turn off the highway, which had woken Alice up. And before Alice had fully opened her eyes, she was busy adjusting the stereo, cranking up the Level3 tune "Dinosaur," the song that had brought them to Nashville.

. . . IF THERE'S ONE THING WE LEARNED FROM
JURASSIC PARK
IT'S THAT THE PAST CAN EAT YOU ALIVE

BUT I SWEAR,
JEFF GOLDBLUM'S ALIVE AND WELL
AND LIVING IN NASHVILLE . . .

Tiernan had been so quick to write off this album back when it first came out, but once you got beyond the catchy melody and poppy beat, there was actually something much darker underneath. Pain, longing, regret. Jeff Goldblum. Her shoulders wiggled from an involuntary shiver when she thought about seeing Level3 play Friday night.

"Can you believe they actually got back together and

we're seeing them play in two nights?" Summer asked.

"Crazy," Alice said.

Tiernan nodded. "I was just thinking the exact same thing."

They valeted the Pea Pod at the Gaywether's grand entrance. Ah, the Gaywether. The name alone was worth the $163 a night.

The woman at reception told them they had an hour to kill before check-in, so they wandered off to explore "Li'l Miss," one of the Gaywether's two enormous glass-covered atriums.

Other than the fact that it smelled like her cousin's iguana cage, Tiernan thought the Li'l Miss lived up to its name—a mini replica of the Mississippi River delta, complete with flowing river—yet at the same time offering all the comforts of air-conditioning. The place was crawling with fat Southern tourists strolling about in families or pairs—window shopping in Li'l Miss's tacky stores, grazing like cattle at the all-you-can-eat buffet, cruising along the indoor river on actual miniature riverboats.

"I know there are already Seven Wonders of the World but I vote this place as number eight," Tiernan said, snapping a photo of a portly middle-aged couple, their matching Dollywood T-shirts stretched taut over their matching beer guts.

"At least it's cool in here," Summer said.

"Seriously," Tiernan said. "I say we cover the entire southern half of the country in a giant glass bubble."

"What about the ozone layer?" Alice asked.

"Slap that baby in a bubble, too."

Summer watched as a boat cruised by. "Oooh! Let's take a riverboat ride!"

"Sweet." Tiernan high-fived Summer. "I'm in."

"I don't know." Alice shook her head. "It's probably expensive."

"Oh, pleeease, Alice. We have to. Those boat rides are the pièce de résistance of this whole craptacular place!"

"I'm being serious," Summer said. "I think it looks like fun."

"And I'm agreeing with you," Tiernan shot back.

"Not really." Summer sighed. "You want to have air-quotes fun. I just want to have regular fun."

"Is there a difference?" Tiernan asked. Summer rolled her eyes.

"*Girls.*" Alice's voice sounded worn, like an exasperated mother disciplining two cranky toddlers. "You both want to go on the boat ride, right?"

Summer and Tiernan nodded.

"Then shut the *hey-yell* up!" Alice yelled in a bad Southern accent, silencing them for a beat before Tiernan and Summer both had to laugh.

Except for one elderly couple, they were the only non-family and non-obese people on the boat. The faux Mississippi smelled even swampier up close.

"Instead of a flat boat, they should have called it a *fat* boat," Tiernan whispered.

"Be nice, T-Bird," Summer scolded, even though she was laughing.

"If it makes you happy, *Sunny-D*," Tiernan shot back. Then she pretended to take a picture of the river, when she was really taking a shot of the elderly couple, or more specifically, the tube socks they'd pulled up over their flabby spider-veined calves. She showed the back of the camera to Alice.

"Look. That could be you and Quentin, sixty years from now."

Alice pursed her lips, pretending to act grumpy.

"Come on, A-Plus. You know you want to have his grandchildren," Tiernan taunted.

Alice let out a yelp. "Don't call me that."

"Sorry, but Sunny's the one who started it," Tiernan countered.

Alice giggled. "Those nicknames were dorky even back in middle school."

"Embrace your inner dork, A-Plus!" Tiernan said, snapping a picture of Alice, then immediately looking at the shot. "Nope, not enough dorkitude," she said, shaking her head, disappointed.

"Take one of me." Summer straightened her posture and placed an index finger under her chin, letting her gaze defocus somewhere in the middle distance, as if she were deep in thought.

"Now that's what I'm talking about!" Tiernan crowed, as

she snapped the shot. "This belongs on the back of your book jacket." She showed the picture to Summer.

"Did I write a book?" Summer asked.

"The Dork's Guide to Cheesy Tourist Destinations. Volume One."

"Look, pulled-pork sandwiches!" Alice pointed to a sign at a "riverside" smokehouse. "Can we get those for dinner?"

"Speaking of pork sandwiches . . ." Tiernan shot Alice a lascivious smile. "You never told us about last night."

Alice nearly spit out the sip of water she'd just taken. "Ew! There were no 'pork sandwiches,' thank you very much."

Summer leaned in, her voice dropping to that low register people use for talking about sex. "Well . . . how was it?"

Alice took another drink of water, then let out a dreamy sigh. "It was . . . thirst quenching," she said dramatically.

Summer squealed and clapped her hands, causing the people sitting in front of them to turn around and sneer.

"You guys . . ." Alice kept her voice low, so Tiernan and Summer huddled in close. "I think Quentin might be the coolest guy I've ever met."

Tiernan laughed, wondering exactly how many guys Alice had actually "met" other than the nerdlingers from yearbook. But she enjoyed listening to Alice gush about Quentin's intelligence and creativity, his likes (collecting vinyl) and dislikes (fondue restaurants). Alice was only halfway through a detailed description of Quentin's hair when Summer wrinkled her nose and pulled herself away from their powwow.

"Did someone forget to brush their teeth today?" she asked, staring at Tiernan accusingly.

Tiernan cupped her hands over her mouth and nose and breathed into the enclosed space. "Holy halitosis, Batgirl! Sorry 'bout that."

"I thought that was you." Summer smiled apologetically. "I'd remember that bad breath anywhere."

"Still gives me nightmares." Alice nodded in consensus.

"We were in a rush this morning," Tiernan whined. "Who had time to brush?"

"I did!" Summer and Alice said simultaneously, and they all laughed.

"For your information, ladies, my stank mouth is very sought after." Tiernan held up her index finger like a teacher giving an important lecture. "They might even make it into a body spray."

"I can see it now," Alice said. "Bad Hygiene by Calvin Klein."

"Or how about Morning Breath?" Summer chimed in. "By the makers of Poison."

Tiernan never minded a good laugh at her own expense, and in a strange way it felt kind of comforting to know that after all these years, a detail they were probably dying to forget had snagged a place in Alice's and Summer's memories.

It was like when Tiernan had noticed Alice's fingernails—or lack thereof—while they were yanking weeds back at Gert's.

It wasn't as though she was *glad* Alice was still a pathological nail biter, but something about it was oddly reassuring, like no matter how much time had passed, she was still an expert on Alice's and Summer's meaningless details, and they were still experts on hers.

They continued with the bad-breath jokes way past the point they were funny anymore, laughing twice as hard at the stinkers (ha!) as they did at the witty ones. Tiernan wasn't exactly sure when the boat ride had changed from "fun" to fun. But, for once in her life, she could actually tell the difference.

"SAD SONGS"

WHY ARE ALL THE SONGS I SING THE SAD SONGS?
WHY ARE ALL THE GIRLS I LOVE THE MAD ONES?

I SAID I WALK LIKE THIS
BECAUSE I SHOT MYSELF
IN THE FOOT

AND I LIVE IN MY HEAD
BECAUSE THE REAL WORLD
ISN'T SO GOOD

—*from Level3's third CD,* Natural Causes

Chapter Fifteen

"I CALL THE BED BY THE WINDOW!" SUMMER SAID, POUNCING onto the pastel floral comforter.

Alice dove onto the other bed. "I call this one!"

Tiernan sauntered in the doorway like a cowboy ready to shoot up the saloon. "Well, I hate to be the bearer of bad news, but one of you lucky ladies is getting a bed buddy tonight."

"Oooh, is it Robert Pattinson?" Summer asked. Then she and Alice shared a laugh. Summer had been feeling punchy ever since the boat ride.

"Laugh it up, bed hogs, but either you two decide, or I will," Tiernan threatened.

"Not it!" Summer and Alice shouted simultaneously, which incited another round of giggles, during which Alice accidentally cut one. Of course, that really got them howling. Summer lay on the bed in the fetal position, her cheeks sore from smiling.

Tiernan staggered over. "I guess I'll be bunking with you, Sunny-D," she sputtered between laughs.

"Don't worry." Summer wiped her tears with the back of her hand. "This is a fart-free zone."

"It's not my fault!" Alice's face was pink, her cheeks wet with tears. "It was the pulled-pork sandwich!"

It took Summer a second to recognize the pulsing feeling in her back pocket was her cell phone. But she didn't have to check caller ID to know who it was. She'd been steering clear of Jace's calls all day, but she couldn't avoid him forever.

"Hello?" She giggled into the phone.

"So you're alive." Jace sounded mad that she was happy.

Summer held up a finger and mouthed the words *Be right back* to Alice and Tiernan. But after seeing the disappointed looks on their faces, Summer made sure to avoid their eyes as she headed to the door. Who were they to judge her, anyway? They didn't understand her relationship with Jace. It was complicated.

"I'm sorry," Summer whispered into the phone as she trudged down the long carpeted hall. "Things have been crazy since yesterday."

"Things have been crazy?" Jace said accusingly. "How do you think *I* feel? My parents keep asking if you're coming, and I don't know what to tell them. It's embarrassing."

He went on like this down three flights of stairs. *The Vineyardhaven ferry will sell out,* he scolded as she tromped through the lobby. *You're acting childish,* he accused as she entered the the Falls Atrium.

Just like the Li'l Miss, the Falls Atrium was buzzing with people, and Summer had to turn up the volume of her phone to hear Jace over the noise of the massive waterfall the room was named for and the annoying country music piped in overhead.

"Where *are* you?" Jace asked.

"I'm going to the big waterfall." Summer didn't feel like giving much more of an explanation.

"Well, are you going to explain yourself?"

"It's part of the hotel," she answered flatly.

"I *meant* are you going to explain why you've been avoiding me?"

Summer paused, waiting for the words to form.

"I guess," she started tentatively, "I'm just wondering . . . why you want me back?"

Even through the racket she could hear Jace's impatient huff. "I told you, Summer. I made a mistake. It was totally immature and stupid and I should never have done it."

"I didn't ask why you broke up with me," she said, loud enough for people to hear. "I asked why you wanted me back."

By now she could see the forty-foot waterfall in the distance, a crowd of people admiring it from the far side of the greenish-gray lagoon, tossing in pennies and making wishes.

If her life were a movie, this would be the scene where Jace would bust out with some ultraromantic line, like "You had me at hello," and then—*somehow*—her cell would be on speakerphone and the crowd by the waterfall would listen in, swooning over Jace's heartfelt confession of love, tears in their eyes. There might even be applause.

Instead, she got a laundry list.

"Well . . . you're smart, and you're nice, and you're funny. And you've got an incredible smile. Not to mention an amazing ass," he said with a chuckle.

Summer didn't know exactly what she'd wanted Jace to say, but she knew it wasn't this. She wanted him to tell her she was special, even if she was only special to him. Even if it came out in plain old Jace kind of words.

That was one of the things she liked best about poetry—the way ordinary words, if you used them right, turned magical. How the whole became greater than the sum of its parts. But there was no magic in Jace's inventory of compliments. And "Uh . . . my parents really like you" definitely wasn't poetry.

When he was done Summer was silent.

"You know what I think is going on with you?" Jace said accusingly. "I think you're holding a grudge."

Summer bit the inside of her cheek. If she was hotheaded and impetuous like Tiernan, she might have chucked her cell phone right into the waterfall. *That ought to be worth something in the wish-making department.*

"Yeah, that's it," he said, sounding more sure of himself. "You're the master of holding grudges."

Summer rode the wave of anger flooding though her body. "*You're* the one who dumped *me* because you wanted to add some notches to your belt with a bunch of meaningless hookups. I think I'm allowed to feel a little resentful."

That got him quiet. When Jace finally spoke, his voice was so soft she could barely hear him. "I got scared," he confessed. "Everything's changing, Summer. You're going away to school in the fall—"

"Thirty minutes away!"

"I don't care if it's five minutes away. *I'll* still be right here." He paused again. "You keep talking about moving on and finding a new life. And I'm afraid . . . that you'll end up leaving me behind."

Summer's eyes welled with tears. Other than the time Jace cried when his dog got hit by a car, she'd never actually heard him share such honest emotion. Even the way he said "I love you" always reminded Summer of one of those guys from some cheesy daytime soap. But his fear of being abandoned was real. She could tell it was, because it was her fear too.

"Jace." She said his name to soothe him. "It's okay."

There was nothing more irresistible than a man who was broken. It was kind of a messed-up thing to admit, but it was true. Summer always had a thing for boys who were a little off, boys who, on the surface, seemed impervious to pain but had a layer of sadness underneath. Like Travis Wyland. Alice and Tiernan used to think her crush on Travis was all about his looks, but Summer was just as attracted to his suffering. Even before his brother had died, she could feel Travis's pain in every song he wrote.

"I guess I am holding a pretty big grudge against you," she admitted.

"Well, you got over your grudge with that Tiernan chick. Maybe you could do the same for me?"

Summer scoffed. *Had* she gotten over her grudge against Tiernan, or had she just forgotten about it for the time being? Forgive and forget. Summer understood the forgetting part, but she never really knew what the deal was with forgiveness. Were you supposed to just go around pretending as though it didn't matter that someone had done something really horrible to you? And, if so, why not forgive all the murderers, too? Just open up the jail cells and let them roam free.

No. Tiernan had betrayed her, and nothing could ever take that away. It didn't matter if it happened four or four hundred years ago. Tiernan had taken what Summer had told her in confidence and used it against her. Even worse, she'd twisted her words. Not that Alice had been any better, embarrassing her with a huge public scene.

Even now, thinking about that night at the Winter Wonderland Dance made the anger rush out of Summer with such force her whole body trembled. And the worst part was, Summer had just let herself fall in with them all over again, as if none of this nastiness had ever happened. Like a little giggling on some ridiculous road trip could just magically make it all go away.

"So, what am I supposed to do, Jace? Just forgive and forget?"

"If you want to," Jace said softly.

Summer was close enough to the waterfall now that she could feel its mist settling on her bare skin.

Part of her *did* want to trust Jace again. Graduation day aside, he was one of the steadiest, most reliable people she knew. Even his football game was like that—solid, dependable. He didn't have a lot of dazzling moments on the field, but you could always count on Jace to play well, to be consistent.

Tiernan, on the other hand, was a wild card. One minute, she was a normal fourteen-year-old girl, a friend. The next, she was a Goth-punk backstabber. But unlike her dyed hair and combat boots, betrayal didn't look good on anyone.

"There's a computer room here, at the hotel," Summer said. "I'll go look at flights."

"Call me when you've found something," Jace said. "And Summer . . . I love you," he added, like an afterthought.

"Me too," she said absently. But her mind was already someplace else. A new poem was flowing out of her so fast and loud that, for a second, she couldn't even hear the waterfall. She pulled her journal from her purse, scrawling furiously.

The Collage

You can take all the snapshots you
want,

but you will not capture me.

I have already been torn to pieces

by you,

and pasted myself together again.

I may just be an amateur

But I have found what it takes to

make me whole

And it turns out, the only things I

need

Are time, a little glue, and a

design of my own.

The Gaywether Hotel business center rented computers for
fifty cents a minute, so Summer handed the man her ID and
plunked herself in front of a machine in the corner. The least
expensive flight was out of New Orleans at six a.m. on Friday.
It would time out perfectly. Tomorrow they'd hit the road early
and head down to New Orleans. All she had to do was make
it through her the night on the town with Alice and Tiernan,

HILARY WEISMAN GRAHAM

then they could drop her off at the airport and Jace would pick her up in Boston on his way to the Cape on Friday morning.

Summer used the credit card number Jace had given her to purchase the tickets. She could already see the tragic look on Alice's face when she broke the news about leaving. It was hard to say if it would be more or less painful than Tiernan's inevitable shrug of cool indifference.

Whatever. She didn't owe them anything, least of all loyalty. The reason they were all here had nothing to do with personal stuff anyway. They were here because they all liked Level3. That was the only real bummer—that she wouldn't get to see the show.

Summer ran to catch the elevator up to the third floor, but just as she got there, the brass double doors started to close and she found herself glaring at her own reflection, the seam in the doors splitting her face in two.

Thankfully, the next elevator was empty. Summer could use a minute alone to practice how she'd deliver the news. *Hey, you guys, when we get to New Orleans, I was wondering if you could . . .?* Then she noticed the music in the elevator, or more precisely, Muzak. It was Level3. Not that Level3 Muzak was shocking in and of itself—sadly, they were popular enough to suffer the indignity of being turned into easy listening. The weird thing was hearing Level3 at the Gaywether Hotel in Nashville, Tennessee. Down here they force-fed you country music until your ears bled. And yet, there it was—"Sad Songs," the power ballad off of *Natural Causes*, being piped into the elevator for her listening pleasure.

Summer hurried back to their room. She couldn't wait to tell Alice and Tiernan about "Sad Songs." But as she dug out her key card, her heart sank a little. How could she burst into the room all excited about the coincidence of some dumb elevator music when she had bigger news to deliver?

Tiernan and Alice were both on Alice's bed, huddled on a mountain of pillows, watching TV.

"Oh my God, you have to see this!" Alice gushed, pointing to the TV. "It's the Level3 *True Hollywood Story!*"

Tiernan smiled, a Twizzler hanging limply from her mouth.

Summer sat down on the edge of the bed and watched with them. She had come back just in time for the heartbreaking part.

"*. . . Then, as Level3 was preparing to go into the studio to record their second album . . . tragedy struck.*" The narrator had one of those melodramatic movie trailer voices. "*Travis Wyland's twenty-four-year-old brother Dean was rushed to the hospital due to complications from Duchenne muscular dystrophy. Three days later, Dean was dead. . . .*"

"God!" Tiernan laughed. "Do they have to use those awful sound effects? Do they think we won't get that it's sad if they don't put in a *bump-bump-buuuuum* at the end?"

Summer got up off the bed so Alice and Tiernan wouldn't see the tears in her eyes. She'd probably feel much better once the show ended and she could just tell them she was leaving.

HILARY WEISMAN GRAHAM

Even if Alice got upset, chances were it would be more about someone disrupting her plans as opposed to actually caring whether Summer left or stayed.

Tiernan offered her a Twizzler and she took it. After everything she'd eaten on this trip, a few more grams of high fructose corn syrup couldn't hurt. She watched the rest of the *E! True Hollywood Story* from the corner of the desk, riveted. It was weird how she could be that into a story when she already knew the ending.

Summer knew the ending to the three of them, too. She would leave the trip tomorrow. Back home, they'd be Facebook friends, at best. Then in the fall, they'd each head off for college. And maybe—*maybe*—they'd see each other again at their ten-year high school reunion.

The show ended with "Sad Songs" over the credits. A funny fluke, to be sure, but life was full of stuff like that.

"So, you guys . . . ," Summer began, keeping her eyes on the TV. "About New Orleans tomorrow—"

But a knock at the door cut her off.

Alice shot Tiernan a look. "Tell me you didn't order room service."

"Dude, I don't have that kind of cash. But maybe it's turn-down service! Score!"

"What's turn-down service?" Summer asked. Her family stayed in *mo*tels, not *ho*tels. That is, if they went anywhere at all.

Tiernan leaped off the bed. "It's when the hotel maids come

in to fold down your covers and put a chocolate on your pillow!" she said, flinging open the door like she was expecting to see a truckload of M&M's in the hallway.

Instead, what Tiernan found waiting for her on the other side of the door lacked the ability to melt in either her mouth *or* her hands (and was definitely a whole lot less sweet). Her mother.

"UNDERGROUND"

THE EARTHWORMS

WELL, THEY LIKE TO KEEP IT SIMPLE.

THEY SLEEP IN DIRT

AND THEY EAT IT, TOO.

BUT, THERE'S SOMETHING TO BE SAID

FOR HAVING LUNCH IN BED.

THEY'LL NEVER GO HUNGRY

AND THEY'RE ALWAYS RIGHT AT HOME.

—*from Level3's third CD,* Natural Causes

Chapter Sixteen

"TIERNAN, GIRLS. MAY I COME IN?" HER MOTHER ASKED, THOUGH it wasn't really a question. And even if it was, Tiernan had no voice to answer it, the air had been sucked from her lungs into the black hole that was Judy Horowitz.

Judy wore a red silk blouse, black slacks, and heels—half corporate lawyer, half matador dressed for a bullfight. Her makeup was perfect.

"You girls wouldn't mind giving us a little privacy, would you?" she asked, smiling at Alice and Summer. Her voice had that soothing tone she used to coax their cat into its travel box for a trip to the vet. The cat always made a break for it. Tiernan fought off the urge.

"Sure, not a problem," Alice said, practically falling over herself to get out the door.

Summer heaved her massive purse onto her shoulder. "We'll be back . . . later."

Then the door slammed shut and it was just Tiernan and her mother, mano a mano at the Gaywether Hotel. It had all the makings of a pay-per-view special.

With a flick of her manicured fingernail, Judy turned off

the TV so that the only sound left was the hum of the white noise machine. Hotels used white noise machines to drown out sounds from adjoining rooms—voices, the television, the moans and groans of the newlyweds next door. Judy had one at her law firm to protect her clients' privacy. Her own daughter's privacy was clearly less of a concern.

"How did you find me?" Tiernan asked. If her mother was a matador, Tiernan was the bull bucking in its pen before the match.

"The Millers," Judy said, kicking off her heels. "They called me after they spoke to Alice yesterday telling me to expect a call from you." Her eyes bore into Tiernan. "But that call never came."

"Mom, I was going to call you, but I—"

Her mother cut her off with a *talk to the hand* move. "Stop, Tiernan. Just stop." Judy sat down on the corner of the bed. Now that Tiernan got a good look at her face, she seemed tired and worn, like she'd come looking for a nap rather than a fight.

"You know, I was really, really angry when I found that note. And I was still angry when I got on the plane to come down here." Judy took a deep breath. "But now that I'm here, I'm just . . . happy to see you're okay."

Cue violins here. This little performance was about to go down in the Jewish Mother Guilt Trip Hall of Fame.

"So, are you girls having a nice time?" her mother asked (and not in a sarcastic way). Strangely, Judy's eyes looked wet.

Tears weren't part of her mother's usual MO. Unless this

wasn't a guilt trip. But what else could it be? A head injury?

"I don't know." Tiernan stopped pacing. "Kind of. I guess."

"Well, that's good. I always thought Alice and Summer were a good fit for you." Judy pulled her feet up under her. With her size-two frame, she looked small, like a little kid.

Tiernan knew what to do with a ranting and raving Judy Horowitz—the Judy Horowitz who confiscated cell phones and bought drug-testing kits from CVS like they were Tic Tacs. But what the hell was she supposed to do with this?

"Mom, is this some kind of reverse psychology thing?"

Her mother smiled. "Why? Is it working?"

Tiernan snorted disdainfully, but it didn't quite hide her smile.

"Come, sit next to me." Judy patted the bed and Tiernan sat. As if there was another choice. On her mother's right foot, her big toe poked through a hole in her stocking.

"I was hoping we could just talk for a minute, like two adults."

"Well, we can give it a shot," Tiernan said. She could still run. She was faster than Judy. She had shoes on.

"I want you to know how scared I was, Tiernan. How hurt I felt when I found your note . . . those hours I spent not knowing where you were."

Tiernan's stomach tightened. Her mother's voice had a hollow sound to it, as it had in those weeks after Tiernan's dad had moved out.

"I was so frantic to find you, I even called Dustin."

Tiernan winced. Dustin was the boy she'd dated junior year. It hadn't ended well.

"He's at his parents' lake house in New Hampshire for the summer. He said to say hi."

"Hi," said Tiernan.

"Anyway, on my way down here, something happened."

You bumped your head on the airplane's overhead compartment? You converted to Hare Krishna at the airport?

"I realized that *this* right here"—she gestured to the room— "is not about your anger at me for grounding you, or for confiscating that alcohol, or for any of the squabbles we've had in recent times. This is old stuff between us."

Her mother reached out and put her hand around Tiernan's clenched fist, gripping it so tightly, Tiernan could feel the throb of her own pulse, as if Judy were holding her actual beating heart.

Her normal response to maternal affection was to pull away but, for some reason, she didn't. This time, Tiernan relaxed her fist and held her mother's hand back.

"Tiernan, we've both made mistakes and done things we regret. . . ." Judy's voice trailed off. "But if we want to try to work it out—instead of doing what we've been doing over and over again for the past four years—then we need to go all the way back to the start."

Tiernan gave her mother a wry smile as she fought back tears. "How long do you have?"

"As long as it takes," Judy said.

They sat like that in silence for what seemed like ages while Tiernan's mind reeled back through the past few years. What was there left to talk about? The divorce was old news. Her parents did the best they could to make it as painless as possible for Tiernan and her older brother, Todd—sat them down for the mandatory "it's not your fault" lecture, as if they were a couple of kindergartners, even though Tiernan was fourteen at the time and Todd was about three weeks away from leaving for college. *The lucky bastard.*

But life wasn't fair. And marriages were no different from anything else in the world—eventually it all turned to crap. It's not like it didn't bother Tiernan that her father had cheated on her mom and moved to Colorado with his new girlfriend, but it wasn't as if there was anything she could actually do about it.

"Tiernan," her mother began, "I'm going to tell you something I've been afraid to say for a really long time."

Tiernan's stomach tightened as if she were readying herself for a punch in the gut.

"I feel like—" Judy's voice quavered. "I feel like I've let you down. That I haven't been the mother I wanted to be. The mother you deserved."

So Judy guilt-tripped herself as much as she guilt-tripped everyone else? Interesting.

"I was so sad when Dad left, so consumed with my own problems, that when you started acting up and getting into

HILARY WEISMAN GRAHAM

trouble at school, it just felt like, like too much to take. It's no excuse. It's a horrible excuse. And I know you were only acting out because you were upset about the divorce, about Dad leaving. But at the time, I could barely manage my marriage falling apart." Judy paused while a single tear rolled down her cheek and plopped onto the bedspread. "And I didn't give you the attention you needed because it was easier . . ." Judy bit her lip and shook her head.

Tiernan wanted to tell her mom that she didn't have to finish the sentence, but she couldn't bring herself to speak.

"It was easier . . ." Judy sucked in a breath as more tears came. "It was easier to let you push me away."

Tiernan sat perfectly still while the weight of her mother's words settled over her. Part of her wanted to scream at her mother, to throw things against the walls and watch them smash. Her own mother, the one person in the world who *had to* love her and instead had abandoned her. Just like her father. Just when she'd needed her most.

"But I'm not going to do that anymore." Judy sniffled. "And I know in two more months you'll be off at college . . . but I'd rather spend the rest of our lives slogging through the mud together than to just sit back and watch you drift away."

Tiernan hugged her knees into her chest, listening to the sound of her mother cry. She hated her father for running off to Colorado with his girlfriend—for lying to them, for leaving. But the truth was, she hated Judy even more. Judy, who was *right there with her the whole time* in the same house, and until this moment had never seemed to notice Tiernan was good for anything other than yelling at or punishing.

Judy slid her arms around Tiernan's back and held tight. If she hadn't felt so weak, she would have flung her mother off right then and there. Just busted out of her embrace and taken off into the night. *Stop pretending we're a normal mother and daughter!* Tiernan wanted to scream. *It's too late for that. Way too late.* But for some reason she couldn't move a muscle. It took everything in Tiernan's power to hold back her own waterworks.

"You and I build walls to protect ourselves," Judy whispered as she stroked Tiernan's hair. "It's what we do. I put on my war paint and my suit and my heels every day, and I go to court and I fight, fight, fight. And everyone always says to me, 'Judy, you're so strong.'" Her mother sniffled. "But you know, Tiernan, a person can't be strong every minute of her life."

Suddenly all the tears Tiernan had been trying so hard to keep down rose up in her throat and she was sobbing hard, her head pressed into her mother's chest.

She couldn't remember the last time she'd let loose and cried like this, but now that the well of pain had opened up inside her, there seemed to be no stopping it, and the more Tiernan tried fighting it off, the deeper she fell—down, down, down into the darkness. If her mother really loved her, why did she push her away? *Who else did Judy think Tiernan had during the divorce?* Her father was gone. Her brother was off at college. She'd already shipped her off to boarding school, tearing her away from Alice and Summer, the only people who really knew her back then, the only people who'd truly cared. They *had* cared, even though Tiernan's insecurities had made her doubt it.

No, Judy was wrong. Being strong was what protected her from being like this—a pathetic, sniveling mess. And given the choice, she'd rather end up a soulless stone-cold bitch than have to deal with this kind of pain. *Wouldn't she?*

All at once the answer came to her, and Tiernan pulled herself free from her mother's grasp just far enough away to look Judy in the eye. Tears had left her mother's makeup a mess—streaks of blush and mascara in all the wrong places, her lipstick faded and smeared—like a watercolor painting left out in the rain. It was a wild look, but at the same time, Tiernan was comforted to see her impeccably dressed, buttoned-down mom looking so imperfect.

"I love you, Tiernan," Judy continued. "More than you'll ever know. But I'm still making mistakes and finding my way in the world, just like you are. That's the big secret about being a grown-up—you're never actually done growing up at all."

Fresh streams of tears spilled down Tiernan's cheeks.

"And I know what I said isn't what you wanted to hear. It isn't what any daughter should *have to* hear." Judy rested a hand on hers. "But if we're ever going to get back to that place of trust and respect, of closeness—closeness I miss so much—then we have to start by being honest. With each other, and with ourselves."

Tiernan used the back of her hand to wipe her nose and took a deep breath. She didn't know what she wanted to say exactly, just that something in her needed to finally put words to all the feelings that for years had been bottled up inside. Feelings that, for better or worse, were begging to be set free.

"Want to know why I dyed my hair black that first time?" Her voice sounded nasally, from crying.

Judy nodded.

"I did it . . ." Tiernan's tears began again in full. "I did it so I wouldn't be a redhead like Dad. So you wouldn't look at me and be reminded of . . ." Her sentence trailed off under her blubbering while her mother's arms surrounded her.

"But then you hated it." Tiernan continued through her sobs. "You'd just look at me with pure hatred in your eyes."

Judy lifted Tiernan's chin and held it, so that they were eye to eye. "You're my daughter, Tiernan." Her voice was steady and firm. "I would *never, never* look at you with hatred."

Tiernan nodded like a guilty child. Judy's mouth eased into a smile.

"No matter how much I despise the color of your hair."

Tiernan inhaled a short laugh, sucking the tears from her lip.

"Sorry," Judy said. "That's another way I try to protect myself. With the wisecracking."

You mean, we, Tiernan thought. But instead, she reached for her mother's hand. "Do you know how mad at you I was when you sent me off to New Jew freshman year?" she asked.

"Yes." Judy sighed. "I think you made that pretty clear."

"I know you thought the reason I kept getting into trouble was to punish you for sending me there."

"The thought had crossed my mind," Judy admitted.

Tiernan paused to blow her nose. "But it wasn't. I just felt like messing things up. Like ruining stuff was the only thing that made me feel better."

Judy nodded. "Was that what happened with Alice and Summer? I never really understood what went wrong between you girls."

Tiernan had never thought of it like that before, but maybe there *was* some part of her that had wanted to ruin their friendship. A part of her that *wanted* to drive Alice and Summer away before they wised up and decided to leave *her*. The thought made Tiernan shudder. But even more frightening was the realization that maybe she was more like her mother than she dared to admit—pushing away the people who mattered most.

"I never even *tried* to make any friends at New Jew," Tiernan admitted. "Making friends takes effort, but pissing people off"—she snapped her fingers—"piece of cake."

"Oh, you pissed people off, all right," Judy said, rolling her eyes. "Especially the administration."

Tiernan smiled. "Hey, if I were on the swim team, I would

have been psyched to swim in a pool of grape Jell-O."

"*Tiernan.*" Judy pursed her lips.

"Seriously, Mom. Don't you think it was a little harsh that they expelled me over that? I mean, it didn't even congeal!"

"They had to drain the entire pool," her mother said disapprovingly. "Not to mention the fact"—a small smile peeked through Judy's scowl—"that you didn't even . . ." Now her mother was trying hard to keep a straight face. "That you didn't even use kosher Jell-O," she managed to sputter as they both erupted with laughter.

"So does this mean I'm not grounded anymore?" Tiernan asked through her giggles.

"That depends," Judy began. "I think you still might have some work to do on this trip. And I'll consider letting you stay, but only if you're staying for the right reasons."

The right reasons. Ha. When had Tiernan ever made *that* part of the equation? She'd always been more of a fly-by-the-seat-of-her-pants kind of gal. The type of person who leaped before she looked. That is, if she bothered to look at all.

And what kind of work did Judy think she needed to do, anyway? Was she supposed to sit down with Summer and Alice for some big heart-to-heart like in one of those schmaltzy Lifetime original movies? And if so, just how many soul-rending conversations could a girl be expected to have in one week?

The truth was, Tiernan had no clue what the "right" reasons for staying were, only that running away had been the wrong one. And that was a pretty good start, wasn't it? The rest she could figure out as she went along.

"So, what do you think?" Judy asked, breaking their silence.

Tiernan was skeptical. "You're honestly giving me a choice in the matter?"

Judy nodded.

"Well, in that case. . ." Tiernan inhaled a deep breath. "I guess I'm going to stay."

"FASTER"

THEY TELL ME ROME WASN'T BUILT IN A DAY,

BUT WHEN I MET YOU, I KNEW RIGHT AWAY.

AND WE WERE MOVING FAST

BUT TIME WAS GOING SLOW

YOU SAID LET'S MAKE IT LAST

AND WATCH THE FLOWERS GROW

BUT I WANNA GO FASTER

I WANNA GO FASTER

A GORGEOUS DISASTER

WE WATCH IN SLOW-MO.

—*from Level3's second CD,* Rough & Tumble

Chapter Seventeen

ALICE HATED THE GARDEN CONSERVATORY. SHE HATED THE WET, greenhouse smell that overpowered the scent of Quentin's sweat on her shirt collar. She hated the little plastic signs that identified each flower, shrub, and tree by family and species, while her own brain was cluttered with so many things unknown.

"Do you think we can go back up yet?" Summer asked for the third time.

Even though it was the smallest of the hotel's atriums, they'd been wandering around the Garden for hours. At least it felt like hours. In purgatory, one tended to lose all sense of time.

"Let's give it ten more minutes," Alice said, stabbing her straw into her frozen lemonade, trying to cleave the glacier it had become.

Until a few hours ago, Alice had floated through the day living inside a bubble of bliss—replaying her sweet memories of last night with Quentin, laughing over nothing with Summer and Tiernan. Then Mrs. Horowitz had shown up and popped it.

Now that Tiernan was leaving, everything felt different, fragile. Even Alice's daydreams of last night were losing their euphoric quality, eclipsed by the dark shadows of her anxious thoughts. She'd been psychically willing Quentin to call for the last two hours while simultaneously trying to keep her expectations in check.

"What if his mother confiscated his cell phone? Tiernan's mom did that."

"*He'll call*, Alice. Just be patient."

Patience. Hah. She took a sip from her lemonade, but all she got was a mouthful of lemon-tinged water. If she couldn't even be patient with a slushy, how could she be patient with a guy she liked? But Alice could never seem to stop herself from sucking up the sweet part first.

He should have called her by now. Or at least texted, right?

What if the reason Quentin wasn't calling was that he had a girlfriend, like Finn did? What if they were both just a couple of players, and they were in their basement, laughing about her right now? *No.* She pushed the thought from her brain. But that just let a new image in—it was an airport, and Judy was dragging Tiernan through security on a leash.

"Do you think Mrs. Horowitz will let her say good-bye to us? I mean, if she's not already on a plane flying out of here."

"Maybe." Summer put her finger over the end of her straw and gave her lemonade a shake.

"It's just so weird," Alice said. "I thought this trip was just going to be me and Tiernan, and then you showed up . . . and now it's just going to be me and you."

"Mm-hmm," Summer said, bending down to run her fingers along a flower, its red petals so tall and waxy, they looked plastic, fake.

It wasn't that Alice had a problem being alone with Summer. The truth was, it was easier to make decisions with two people rather than three. But it wasn't the way things were supposed to go. They were supposed to be together—all three of them—having fun, like they had this afternoon. Sheesh, she was really failing miserably at this "no expectations" thing.

Of course, Alice had made the transition from three to two before, back when she'd gone from being best friends with Summer and Tiernan to being best friends with MJ. In many ways, two was the more logical number for a friendship. Marriages were built for two. So were kayaks and buddy movies. And just how many people could squeeze in to your innermost circle anyway?

Even during the glory days of her friendship with Summer and Tiernan, it was a rare moment when all three were equally close. There were always shifting allegiances, always an odd one out. It wasn't like any of them did it on purpose. It was just part of the package deal with a three-person friendship. That, and the fact that if only two of you were together, chances were you'd talk about the third. Nothing you wouldn't say to her face (at least that was the unwritten rule).

Alice tossed her lemonade in the trash. She could hear the chunk of crushed ice breaking apart on impact.

"I have a weird question for you," she started. "What did you and Tiernan used to talk about, when you talked about me?"

Summer looked at her strangely.

"You know, when I wasn't there?"

"When weren't you there?" Summer asked with a smile.

"I don't know. When I was at piano lessons. Or sick, or on vacation . . ."

Summer took a sip of lemonade, then chucked it in the trash even though it was still halfway full. "We talked about how you would look better if you wore your shirts tucked out," she said, with a self-deprecating eye roll. "Are you mad?"

"Nah." Alice laughed. "The tucked-in look was never really working in my favor. You know, with my thick waist issues."

"Not anymore," Summer said.

"Please." Alice pinched her stomach as evidence.

"That's called skin, Alice. Anyway, I think you look great."

Alice shook her head like she was trying to shake off the compliment. But Summer wasn't one of those people who said something just to make you feel good. In fact, she spoke so honestly, some people thought it made her a bitch.

"What about me?" Summer asked. "What did you and Tiernan used to say about me, back when we were kids?"

The first thing that jumped into Alice's mind were all the times during middle school that she and Tiernan had talked about Summer and boys. How Summer seemed to crave attention from the opposite sex like most people craved food and water. Not that she was about to admit to that.

Plus, it wasn't as if she and Tiernan said those things to disparage Summer. They were just concerned she might be selling herself short. Or did their triangular friendship have sharper edges than she remembered?

"Remember your essay from Mrs. Howe's class in seventh grade?" Alice finally said, relieved to come up with a safer topic. "The one where we had to write about our role models?"

Summer nodded. She had written about Alice and Tiernan.

"Well, after school that day, you had a dentist appointment, so you didn't come over to hang out in the Pea Pod. Tiernan and I talked about your essay all afternoon. It made us cry."

Alice looked at Summer's face, trying to read it, but her nose was buried in a fuzzy purple flower. "Who did you write your essay on?" Summer asked, changing the subject.

"Nelson Mandela," Alice said with a laugh. "It was total BS. I mean, nothing against the man who ended apartheid, but . . . he wasn't really *my* role model, you know what I mean?"

Summer stood up and faced her. "You should have done it on your parents."

Never in a million years would Alice's seventh-grade self have considered her parents role models. But now that she was older, she could almost see it. Sure, they smothered her a bit, but that was part of the package as an only child. And she'd rather have too much attention than too little, like Summer, who, between her five other siblings, was barely on her parents' radar.

"I always loved going to your house," Summer continued. "All those old books your parents kept around. And I loved staring at the African masks in your living room, and those Guatemalan tapestries."

Growing up, Alice always assumed that everyone fit into their families as well as she did, but when she thought about the Daltons, she realized that wasn't the case. It wasn't as if anything tragic was going on at Summer's house. Her parents loved her and fed her and shelled out for new sneakers twice a year. They just didn't really *get* her. Even Tiernan, who seemed to argue with her mother even in her sleep, was at least *like* her mother. Maybe even too much.

"Remember how your mom used to make homemade banana bread and serve it to us warm with sweet cream butter?"

Alice nodded. "But your parents always got Dunkin' Donuts on Sunday mornings."

"They still do," Summer said disdainfully. "And the TV's always on."

Alice remembered how the Daltons ate all their meals around the television, and not even all together as a family, just whenever they felt like it. No wonder Summer liked all the attention from boys. She probably just wanted attention, *period*.

They walked in silence all the way to the elevators, each of them checking their cell phones for messages. Summer read through a few texts. Alice's inbox was empty.

"You mind if we take the stairs?" Summer asked.

Alice followed her up the concrete stairwell, listening to the sound of their footsteps echo off the walls. She wanted to say something to Summer, to admit that maybe she hadn't always been the most loyal friend. But if she started digging through the past now, who knew what else she might unearth?

Maybe it was a good thing Mrs. Horowitz had shown up and saved them from going down that road. After all, if Summer hadn't gotten over the incident freshman year, she wouldn't have bothered to come on this trip. Would she?

Alice had replayed that scene at the Winter Wonderland Dance in her mind a million times. It was ugly, yes. But it wasn't like she was the only one at fault. Summer had lied to her, plain and simple. All Alice had done was respond to that.

When she'd bought the Level3 tickets, Alice had assumed that enough time had passed since that horrible night. But now that she was actually with Summer and Tiernan again, it was almost as if she could actually feel the wounds of their past festering below the surface, like a cut trapped under a Band-Aid when what it really needs to heal is just light and fresh air.

If Alice were a braver person, she'd bring it up right now. Just go ahead and get the whole thing out in the open once and for all. In her mind, she always thought of herself as someone who wasn't afraid to speak the truth. But the *real* truth was that Alice hated to talk about unhappy stuff. And why should she bother to bring up that ridiculous night when the subject could just as easily be avoided? Especially now, when they were finally getting along so well.

Summer fumbled through her purse for her room key, then opened the door. The room was dark, curtains drawn, and Level3 blared from the stereo.

I DUG A HOLE

YOU BROUGHT YOUR FLASHLIGHT

YOU WERE AFRAID OF THE DARK

I WAS AFRAID OF DAYLIGHT

"Don't turn on the light," Tiernan called out as Alice reached for the switch. She stopped her hand just in time while Tiernan and her mother giggled from the shadows. When Alice's eyes adjusted, she could see them, lying on their backs on the bed by the window. *What the—?*

"We're trying to chill," Mrs. Horowitz's silhouette explained.

Alice stifled a laugh. Either Dr. Phil had made a housecall while they were away or Mrs. Horowitz had smoked something funny. Alice followed Summer to the other bed and sat down, melting into the darkness.

"Guess what?" Tiernan asked when the song switched to an instrumental part. "My mom says I can stay."

Alice lay back on the bed, smiling to herself as she took in this unexpected news. So Tiernan didn't just come on this trip to escape from her mother? She actually *wanted* to be here. Even if it was only to see Level3.

"So what exactly happened in the last two hours?" Summer asked, never one to mince words.

Tiernan and her mother laughed.

"I guess you can say that we finally had it out," Mrs. Horowitz said.

"*All* of it," Tiernan added, her laughter dissolving into the music as the song swelled to its chorus.

I WAS HIDING FROM YOU BUT YOU FOUND ME
IN THE LAST PLACE I WAS SUPPOSED TO BE
THERE I WAS (MUD IN MY FINGERNAILS)
THERE I WAS (TEARS IN MY EYES)
OH, THERE I WAS,
THERE I WAS.

"SUNBURN"

IN YOUR PARENTS' BATHROOM
I RUB ALOE ON YOUR BACK
WHITE STREAKS LEFT BY MY HAND
DISAPPEAR IN YOUR RED SKIN
YOU SHIVER AND YOU SWEAR,
NEVER AGAIN, OH, NEVER AGAIN.
YOU CURSE THE SUN, YOU WANTED
TO CHANGE YOUR SKIN.

—from Level3's self-titled first CD

Chapter Eighteen

"I SWEAR," TIERNAN SAID. "WE JUST TALKED ABOUT STUFF, THEN SHE gave me a choice of whether I wanted to stay or go."

It was too bad Judy was already on a plane back to Boston. As a lawyer, her mother would have been proud of the cross-examination Alice and Summer had been giving her for the past hour and a half.

"But you didn't tell her *everything*, did you?" Alice was an eyes-on-the-road kind of driver, but her curiosity about Tiernan and Judy's tête-à-tête had sent them swerving into the breakdown lane more than once.

"I told her I tried E."

Summer gasped from the backseat. "You did not!"

Tiernan nodded. So, she hadn't told Judy exactly how *many* times she'd tried it, but it was the PG version.

"I'm serious. It was like she *liked* hearing about all the bad stuff I did."

"You should have made things up," Alice joked.

"Trust me, I didn't have to."

"That doesn't sound like the Judy I remember," Summer chimed in from the back.

"I know," Tiernan said. "But if you're thinking she's gone soft 'cause she's dying of a terminal illness, she's not. I asked."

On a normal day with less than six hours' sleep, Tiernan would be crashing hard right about now. But this morning she was wide-awake. Level3 was on the stereo, and her foot, with its freshly painted lime-green toenails (Judy had sprung for all four of them to get pedis at the hotel spa), was up in its preferred spot on the dash, tapping along to the beat.

It wasn't as if she had any delusions about this new lovey-dovey phase with her mom. It would wear off over time. No doubt things would flare up and get ugly. But at the moment it seemed like a good thing Judy had tracked her down. Like their big Moment of Truth couldn't have happened if they were still back in Walford, in their normal environment.

Tiernan picked their map up off the floor, admiring the New Orleans collage she'd created that night in the woods, based on the song "Drink it Up." It was a giant martini glass made up of pictures of Luke, Ryan, and Travis—half of Luke's snare drum garnishing the Level3 cocktail like a lemon wedge.

"I am so psyched to go out in New Orleans tonight!" The music was cranked so loud Tiernan had to shout. "I've heard there are tons of places that don't even card."

"I thought you were on the up-and-up now," Alice said.

"I didn't have a personality transplant."

"So your mother's okay with you drinking?" Summer

HILARY WEISMAN GRAHAM

asked, turning down the stereo's volume a smidge.

"She doesn't have to be. We have a new thing going. What's the phrase she used? Oh, yeah, we're 'keeping it real.'"

This sent Summer and Alice into hysterics.

"Oh, shut up," Tiernan said, but even she was laughing. Ever since her conversation with Judy, Tiernan felt a weight had lifted. Every horrible confession had lightened her until she felt giddy and clear, as if she'd inflated her brain with helium. There was only one ugly memory Tiernan was still too scared to touch, and it didn't have anything to do with family stuff.

She thought about what her mother had said about wanting to slog through the mud *with* her as opposed to just letting Tiernan drift away. But friends played by different rules than parents. Not that Alice and Summer even considered her their friend. And what was the point of unburdening herself with something they'd never forgive her for anyway?

No, now was not the time for true confessions. Not as long as they were having fun. Tiernan reached back and turned up the music full blast, and soon they were all singing along.

AND TOGETHER WE WILL WALK
DOWN THE MIDDLE OF THE STREET
AND THE CARS, THEY MAY CURSE US
BUT THEY WON'T MAKE US RETREAT

Reunited

SHOULDER TO SHOULDER, HAND IN HAND

HEART TO HEART, FEET TO FEET

WE HAVE COME SO FAR

WE HAVE COME SO VERY FAR

Tiernan hadn't found the energy of a city in Nashville (actually, she hadn't even left the hotel), which made entering New Orleans at dusk seem all the more dazzling, like crossing the border into a foreign country.

"I wonder how it's changed, post-Katrina," Summer wondered as the Pea Pod snaked its way through the French Quarter, bumping along the cobblestone streets.

Tiernan looked around for signs, but how could she tell if anything was different in a place she'd never been before? The city was so alive, it was hard to know where to look first, so Tiernan took out her camera and just started snapping. First, a saxophonist bebopping away on the street corner. Then, a group of roly-poly fifty-something women peering through the tinted windows of a strip joint. Above it, the delicate wrought-iron balconies with their tidy flower boxes seemed completely out of place.

"The whole city's like a jazz song," Summer said.

Tiernan nodded. It always surprised her when Summer came out with stuff like this, even though she'd been this way for as long as Tiernan could remember. Maybe it was Summer's looks that threw her off, as if wearing a ponytail and an Aeropostale

T-shirt meant a person couldn't be smart or perceptive.

They checked into their hotel room, which was small, generic, and worn. Not that it mattered where they slept—they'd probably be out half the night partying anyway.

"Let's pick up the pace, people!" Tiernan said, slipping on her Doc Martens. "Those frozen drink machines are calling our names."

"It seems so radical that they actually let people drink in the middle of the street," Alice said.

"Radically *awesome*," Tiernan countered.

But Summer just sat on the bed, writing in her journal. She'd been strangely quiet ever since they'd checked in, and she didn't seem to be in too big of a hurry to change into any of the ten thousand flouncy dresses she'd brought along in her duffel bag.

"What up with you, Sunny-D?" Tiernan asked. "You going out in that?"

"I think I'm gonna stay in tonight and write."

"What are you talking about? We're in New Orleans!"

"I know where we are," Summer said.

Alice put down her mascara. "Come on, Summer, look at all the places we can go." She held up at least a dozen brochures she'd snagged from the lobby. There were piano bars, a vampire tour, and three separate restaurants that claimed to serve the city's best gumbo.

"Fro-zen drinks! Fro-zen drinks!" Tiernan chanted.

"Okay, stop." Summer closed her notebook and looked at the clock. Tiernan could tell she was cracking.

"You have to come out with us," Alice begged. "It's the only night we've had so far with just the three of us together."

"Pleeeeaasse," Tiernan whined. It wasn't like she needed Summer with them to have fun, but the thought of her moping around by herself in their dumpy hotel room while she and Alice partied on Bourbon Street was too lame for words.

Summer rolled her eyes and got up off the bed. "Fine." She unzipped her duffel bag. "I'll go out for one drink."

"And together we will walk, down the middle of the street . . ."

Four bars later, they were all arm-in-arm shrieking Level3 lyrics as they stumbled down Bourbon Street. Tiernan knew it was obnoxious, immature, and a total drunken cliché, but *damn*, it was fun. She could barely believe that less than twenty-four hours from now, they'd actually be seeing Level3 in concert.

"'. . . and the people, they may curse us, but they won't make us retreat!'"

"Good evenin', songbirds!" an old man called to them from the sidewalk. He held a plastic paint bucket filled with red roses that he swung as he walked. "Where're your boyfriends at?"

"Away," Alice answered. Tiernan wouldn't have answered at all.

"Those boys is askin' for trouble, lettin' pretty girls like you come down here, all alone." The man's voice sounded hoarse,

HILARY WEISMAN GRAHAM

probably from shouting at strange women. "So, whaddya say, pretty ladies?" He pulled out a single rose. "Five dollars each, three for ten."

"No thanks," Tiernan said, pulling Alice by the arm.

They kept walking, but the man still followed them.

"You're modern girls, I can tell. Well, then you just buy your own roses. Show those boyfriends you don't need 'em."

"Persistent little bugger," Tiernan whispered to Summer, who was busy fishing around in her bag. When Summer pulled out her hand, there was a ten-dollar bill in it.

"Here you go," she said, handing it to the man. "Three, please."

The man looked as surprised as Tiernan felt, then quickly plucked three roses from his bucket. "You're some lucky girls to have a friend like that."

Tiernan begrudgingly took her rose. In her opinion, "friends" didn't make you interact with creepy old street vendors.

"Oh, when your boyfriends see this, it'll make 'em sooooo jealous." Even though their sale was complete, the rose guy was still following them.

"Come on," Tiernan whispered, veering off the street and leading them into a hole-in-the-wall bar.

The place was one of those classic New Orleans dives where everything was served in Styrofoam cups and no one seemed too concerned with checking ID. Behind the bar, instead of

shelves of alcohol, twenty frozen drink machines swirled hyp-
notically in every color of the rainbow, like some kind of psy-
chedelic Laundromat.

"What can I get for you?" the bartender asked, sweeping the
bangs out of his eyes. His question seemed to imply a plural
"you," though he only made eye contact with Summer.

Tiernan sneered at him openly (a benefit of not being
attractive enough to be on his radar). He was one of those gym
rat types who probably spent about an hour on his hair each
morning, as if steroids and a handful of mousse could make up
for the acne scars all over his face.

Summer—who had some theory about not mixing hard
liquors—was sticking with Hurricanes (though why they
served a drink called a Hurricane down here was beyond
Tiernan's comprehension). Alice ordered a Blue Hawaiian (a
rookie drink if there ever was one). Tiernan picked her liba-
tions like she picked her nail polish—*by name*—and ordered a
Calm Before the Storm.

"I bet he works the second shift at Chippendales," she whispered as the bartender made his way down the row of drink
machines, their Styrofoam cups bending inside his meaty hands.

When Chippendale delivered their beverages, he told only
Summer to "enjoy."

"These drinks don't separate like normal slushies do,"
Alice said, cupping her Blue Hawaiian with both hands. "Did
you ever notice that?" Tiernan couldn't help but smile as she

watched Alice, hunched over her drink, slurping it up with intensity. She'd always admired the way Alice remained firmly in Alice World, no matter who she was with or what the surroundings.

On the barstool next to her, Summer bopped along to a cheesy techno song, her blond hair flying as she swiveled around in a perfect 360-degree turn. If Tiernan squinted (and their drinks were replaced with Fribbles) this could have been an afternoon at the Friendly's in Walford Center, back in fifth grade.

A year ago—even *a month* ago—Tiernan would have never believed a moment like this could exist—the three of them together on a road trip, *having fun.* But the truth was, she liked being in this dumpy bar even with its d-bag bartender and sticky floors. Sure, the place was super sketchy, but it wasn't trying to be anything other than it was. It was "keeping it real." She'd have to send Judy a postcard.

Tiernan pulled her camera from her bag. She wanted to capture this feeling. Whatever it was.

"Hey." Tiernan held her camera up to the bartender. "You mind taking a picture of us?"

Chippendale gave her a rude little grunt and took the camera. "Squeeze in," he directed, pressing his back against the whirling drink machines.

Tiernan and Summer each leaned toward Alice and she slung her arms around their shoulders.

"Say Bourbon Street!"

Tiernan smiled the way she usually did for photos. It was a pose she'd practiced many times, alone in the mirror—chin down, lips pursed, eyebrows raised in a mix of sultriness and irony. Her "picture face," her friend Melissa called it. It was the way she looked the best. But it wasn't the way she really looked.

Chippendale was already pulling the camera strap over his head—a feat that took some time since he was trying to do it without messing up his male stripper hairdo.

"Hey, wait." Tiernan stopped him. "You mind taking another one?"

He gave her a slightly annoyed head flick, but stepped back into position.

"Ready? In one, two . . ."

"Level3!" Alice blurted out as he snapped the shot.

When Tiernan got her camera back the difference between the two photos was striking. In the first one, the girls wore well-rehearsed (if slightly tipsy) smiles. In the second, Alice had a double chin going, Summer was all nostrils, and Tiernan's smile was so wide she looked like the Joker from *Batman*. To a stranger, their picture would look like three friends having fun. But was it possible to actually *be* a friend to people she'd lied to for all these years?

"Aren't you glad you came out with us?" Alice slurred as she leaned in to Summer.

Summer nodded. "I had no idea you guys were actually this fun."

"Thanks," Tiernan said, giving Summer's arm a playful slap.

Part of her wanted to just blurt it out and get it over with right here and now, even if it ruined the moment. Even if they hated her forever. The later it got (and the more Tiernan drank), the more she felt her secret from freshman year scratching and clawing away at her insides, like the squirrel digging his way out of his grave. And if she didn't do something about it soon, Tiernan was afraid that the truth about that night might just bust its way out all on its own.

"Oh my God!" Alice screamed. Then she jumped off her barstool, searching the floor frantically. "My purse! Have you guys seen my purse?"

"Where did you put it?" Tiernan asked, still trying to make sense of what was happening.

"I thought I put it on the bar, right in front of me. But then I went to pay the bill and ..."

Tiernan just stood there, taking it all in, as Summer immediately sprang into action—dropping to her hands and knees and rummaging beneath every barstool in the place as if Alice's purse might have fallen down and then hopped away on its own.

"Well, one of you needs to take care of this." Chippendale waved their bill in his hand, unconcerned by their crisis.

Tiernan slapped twenty-five bucks on the bar. No compassion, no tip, *dink-weed*.

Summer made her way back to them from the end of the

bar, looking resigned. "Nothing," she said sadly.

"That's 'cause it's not here!" Alice said.

"When do you last remember seeing it?" Tiernan asked in her calmest voice.

Alice's eyes looked wild. "I don't know!" she cried, throwing her hands in the air.

"Well, let's just take a breath and try to retrace our steps," Tiernan instructed. She didn't know how she was managing to keep her composure. Just that someone needed to do it.

They all held hands as they ran back down Bourbon Street plowing their way through the mob, dodging the people who looked even wobblier than the three of them.

Finally, they got to the place they'd been last, an obnoxious Mexican-themed chain restaurant so strict with ID that Tiernan had resorted to begging some lonely middle-aged loser to order their drinks. A half hour ago the place was packed to the point of being uncomfortable. Now, it was just ridiculous.

"We were right here!" Alice shouted over the crowd, sounding a lot more sober than she had ten minutes ago.

"Did you use the ladies' room?" Summer asked.

Alice nodded and dashed off to the back of the bar.

"This totally sucks," Tiernan said, as a waitress holding a tray of margaritas squeezed in front of her.

Summer exhaled through her nose. "We shouldn't have let her get that drunk."

"*We* didn't *let her* do anything," Tiernan said.

HILARY WEISMAN GRAHAM

"And who was pushing the frozen drinks on her for hours?" Summer asked.

As if this were all Tiernan's fault, when Summer was drinking all night too. Not to mention that it was Alice who had lost her purse, all on her own.

"I didn't find it," Alice said, emerging from the crowd. Her face looked so shiny and pale Tiernan was sure she was about to get puke on her shoes.

"You guys . . ." Alice spoke haltingly, as if the words themselves tasted of bile. "Our tickets were in there."

"THE NEW, NEW THING"

I WANTED A NEW THING

I WANTED A NEW, NEW THING

DON'T WE ALL? DON'T WE ALL? DON'T WE ALL?

I WANTED A NEW THING

I WANTED A NEW, NEW THING

BUT THE OLD THING

TURNED OUT TO BE BETTER

THAN NOTHING AT ALL

—*from Level3's second CD,* Rough & Tumble

Chapter Nineteen

AS FAR AS SUMMER COULD TELL, SOMETIME AROUND MIDNIGHT
Bourbon Street turned into a total free-for-all—sweaty tourists
packed in like a kitchen at a keg party, a different tune wafting
from the door of each bar they passed. Yet Alice's voice managed to rise above the din—the runaway trumpet in a jazz solo
gone wrong.

"I know you think going to the police is pointless. So, what
am I supposed to do, Tiernan? Nothing?"

It wasn't the first time Summer had witnessed an Alice
freak-out. There was the episode in sixth grade when Alice got
assigned to do a presentation on the excretory system in front
of the whole class, while Summer and Tiernan got to work
together on a circulatory system diorama. There was the time
she left her brand-new pink cleats at the Andover soccer field.
And, of course, her swan song: the Winter Wonderland Dance.
The main difference about tonight was that this time, Alice's
tantrum was fueled with rum.

"Just don't be delusional." Tiernan's voice rose to meet
Alice's. "You think the New Orleans police don't have anything better to do than to look for some girl's purse?"

"Can you guys keep it down!" Summer yelled. Yes, she was shouting about shouting.

"Fine! If you guys don't want to go with me, I'll go by myself!" Alice marched off in a huff.

Tiernan grabbed Summer by the arm. "Come on, help me talk some sense into her."

For some reason, Summer let herself get dragged along. The path of least resistance. Of course, there was an even easier option. She could leave. Just flag down a cab and go to the airport right now, before this night completely spiraled out of control. But she couldn't walk away in the middle of this crisis.

Tiernan yanked Summer's wrist, slamming her straight into two middle-aged guys in business suits.

"Yo, blondie," one of them called out drunkenly.

She pulled herself loose from Tiernan's grasp. "I can walk on my own, okay?"

"Well, hurry up. We don't want to lose her."

Summer's head was throbbing, like she'd gone straight from buzzed to hungover.

"Alice!" Tiernan screamed blindly into the crowd. But Summer had several inches on her and she could see Alice's frizzy mass of hair just fine, ten feet ahead.

"Calm down, she's right up there."

"You need to talk to her," Tiernan said. "She'll listen to you."

Ah, yes. The same person who just let herself get peer-pressured into drinking four Hurricanes, the person who was gallivanting around in a strange city at two in the morning, the person too chicken to break the news that she was leaving in a few hours, was now the voice of maturity and reason.

"Alice!" Summer yelled when they were finally close enough. Shockingly, Alice stopped, moving over to the side-walk where the flow of human traffic was slightly less intense.

"I think we should go back to the hotel room and talk," Summer said. "We need to get out of here."

"I don't want to go back." Alice pouted. "I want to find my purse."

Summer stifled a sigh. "Your purse is gone. You just need to accept it."

"I don't need to accept anything!" Alice shot back. "I'm not like *you*, I don't just drift along letting whatever happens happen. I make things happen for myself!"

Summer felt the blood rush to her cheeks. Here she was, trying to help, and once again Alice was treating her like a second-class citizen.

"Yeah, you *do* make things happen. Like this wonderful trip we're on." The words flew out of her mouth before she could stop them.

Alice just stood there, her face cycling through emotions so fast it was hard for Summer to tell if Alice was about to slap her or burst into tears.

"Guys . . ." Tiernan tried to butt in, but Alice shouted over her.

"You chose to come on this trip! No one twisted your arm."

"I did . . ." Summer swallowed hard. "And now . . . I'm choosing to leave it."

And with that she turned and walked away. She didn't need to deal with this. She hadn't even wanted to go out tonight in the first place.

"Wait up." Tiernan was right at her heels. "Where are you gonna go?"

Summer paused just long enough for Alice to catch up. "Home," she said quietly. "Jace bought me a ticket. My flight leaves in a couple hours."

Alice's eyes had a million questions, but all she managed was a quiet "Oh."

"So, how long have you known you were bailing?" Tiernan asked.

"Since yesterday, at the hotel. It's not like I'm trying to ditch you guys. It's just . . . Jace and I had plans to go the Vineyard together, and I thought they were canceled, but then . . ." Summer couldn't think of the right way to sum up just what had happened between her and Jace. "Anyway, I'm gonna head back to the room to get my bags, if you want to come with." She tried to sound casual, as if by ignoring the angry words she and Alice had exchanged, she could pretend it hadn't happened.

"I brought a key," Tiernan said, making eye contact.

Summer dug through her wallet and handed Alice a fifty. "Here's some money for the ticket. When I get back home, I'll send you a check for the rest if that's okay with—"

"He's cheating on you," Alice said, her eyes locked on the bill in her hand.

Summer felt her body stiffen. For a second the world seemed to move in slow motion.

"He's cheating on you," Alice repeated, this time staring at her with such intensity, Summer actually stumbled back a step.

Tiernan's gaze flew from Alice to Summer, then back again.

Summer opened her mouth to refute this claim. But when she went to speak, nothing came out. Her body seemed to know the truth before her brain did.

"With that sophomore girl, Debbie Davis—" Alice continued.

Tiernan held up her hand like a stop sign. "Alice, just—"

"Everyone knows they've been hooking up forever."

Summer's last phone call with Jace flashed through her mind, all of his texts. All the times he swore up and down "nothing happened" now made it seem so glaringly obvious that something had. And what about Melanie and Jocelyn and the rest of her friends? If *everyone* knew . . .

"You know, Alice . . ." Summer's voice quavered. ". . . if I thought you were telling me this out of kindness, that would be one thing. But you're not."

The fear in Alice's eyes made Summer's voice grow stronger.

"I think the only reason you're telling me this is to try to get me to stay on this stupid trip. And if you think, after all these years, that I'm still your little puppet, that you can control what

Reunited

I think and what I do, then you must be even drunker than I thought."

Alice started to speak, but Summer didn't let her. There were still so many things she wanted to say. Hurtful things.

"Maz was right. You're obsessed with me—with *us*. But there is no 'us.'"

Now there were tears in Alice's eyes.

"You think the three of us could still be friends after what the two of you did to me? After what you're still doing to me?" The words came out of her mouth like bullets.

"How naive are you, anyway? Wait—don't answer that. I know exactly how naive you are. It's late June, and you still think Brown is going to let you in."

Summer shut her mouth so Alice could absorb the full impact of her words.

"That was low," Tiernan whispered, almost to herself.

"And you'd know all about that, wouldn't you?" Summer shot back. "Tiernan O'Leary, the paragon of truth and integrity herself."

Then Summer turned and ran. She could feel her blood pulsing through every corner of her body as she threaded a path through the swell of people. It was the same feeling she'd had at the freshman winter dance when Alice had caused that ridiculous scene, while Tiernan, her other supposed "best friend," just stood there doing nothing. Summer could still hear the sound of Alice screeching her name as she entered the gym—like she was happy she had the power to hurt Summer, to shame her, in front of the whole school.

Summer kept running even after she'd made it past the crowd. No more "drifting along" for her, no way. For once in her life, she was taking action, even if it just meant going home.

Back at the hotel, her bag was basically still packed, so all she needed to do was leave her key on the bed and hail a cab.

Twenty minutes later, her taxi pulled up to the curb at the New Orleans airport. It seemed almost too easy.

Even though Summer hadn't traveled much, she'd always imagined airports were busy at all hours, like hospitals. But surprisingly, nearly all of the shops were dark, their metal chainlink gates shut. She had some time to kill before her flight boarded, so she wandered into the only open café she could find and bought an oversize chocolate chip muffin.

"You haddagit time in N'awlins?" the man at the counter asked, his Cajun accent so thick it took Summer a second to realize he was speaking English.

She nodded. "Mm-hmm." Whatever. The truth was, she actually *had* been having fun in New Orleans. Up until Alice's freak-out.

Summer took her thousand-calorie muffin and sat down among the other lost souls scattered about the café. In the corner, a TV hung from the ceiling playing CNN on mute. The closed captioning was on, full of typos and cut-off sentences, further confirming Summer's theory that the world was conspiring to mangle the truth. Not *one* of her friends back home had had the guts to tell her about Jace and that girl. *Not one of them.*

Summer was angrier with her friends than she was with Jace himself. Everyone knows boyfriends cheat. But her girlfriends, they were supposed to have her back, no matter what. And yet, the only person who'd actually told her the truth was Alice.

Summer took a huge bite of the muffin, wincing from the crunch of the oversize sugar crystals against her teeth. She wished she could just sprawl out on the carpet and go to sleep, like those two backpackers she'd seen in the hallway. But she'd never been comfortable sleeping in public. Anyway, that's what airplanes were for, weren't they? She didn't really know. The only other time she'd taken a plane was when her family had gone to Disney when she was ten. That was one good thing about this trip. At least she'd gotten out of Walford.

Summer pulled out her phone and composed a text to Jace. She'd be damned if she had to see his lying face waiting for her at the gate back in Boston.

"Won't be there tomorrow. Think you know why."

She pressed the send button and laughed out loud. Okay, so she was still a little tipsy. But who cared if all the random weirdos in here thought she was crazy. She *felt* crazy, being in an airport in the middle of the night all by herself. It was too bad she was only going home and not jetting off to someplace foreign and glamorous, like in the silly make-believe world she'd cooked up for herself as a kid.

HILARY WEISMAN GRAHAM

Summer was the one who'd started their fantasies about the boys from Level3, the one who'd always begged them to play pretend. And to Alice and Tiernan's credit, they'd always indulged her.

But the weird thing was, even now, at age eighteen, Summer still had just as many daydreams. Only, instead of imagining herself walking the red carpet at the MTV Awards as Mrs. Travis Wyland, she was strolling through Harvard Square, where her award-winning book of poems was featured in the window of the Grolier Poetry Shop. *Probably just as unlikely as marrying a rock star, truth be told.*

Summer opened her journal, flipping through the dozens of pages she'd filled in her four short days on this trip—proof that pain and suffering were a writer's greatest source of inspiration. Her eyes went right to two lines:

> You steal my joy,
> And now you give it back to me.

She'd written that after her phone call with Jace—the first time he'd tried to woo her back. They were uninspired lines at best, but right now it wasn't the poetry (or lack thereof) that jumped out at her. It was the way the words were phrased, as if Jace were actually capable of stealing *her* joy. As if she didn't have anything to do with it.

After all, she wouldn't even be in this position if she'd just dumped his sorry ass months ago, back when she realized she didn't love him. But instead she'd let herself drift along, waiting for things to change, as if she had no control over it. As if waiting wasn't a choice in and of itself.

In a way, Summer figured she should be *thankful* Jace had cheated on her, or knowing her, she probably would've ended up marrying the guy. Summer laughed out loud again, this time relishing the stares of the other customers.

She turned to a fresh page in her journal. For once in her life, she wanted to make a choice, even if it was the wrong one. At the top she wrote:

What do I want?

Back in her Pea Pod glory days, anything seemed possible. Alice and Tiernan never questioned her daydreams, no matter how wildly unrealistic they were. Maybe that was as good a place to start as any—to just own up to wanting all the crazy things she wanted, even if they never had a chance of coming true. In the left-hand margin Summer wrote the numbers one through ten.

1. To be able to eat whatever I want without getting fat
2. To know what I want

Three through ten were blank. Summer stared at her list until sunlight started slanting through the airport's glass doors, then she closed her journal and tossed it in her purse. She was going home. Not making a choice was kind of a choice, too, right?

But as she stood up to leave the café, an image on the television caught her eye. She didn't need to read the horribly misspelled closed captioning to see that it was Level3. There was a "rdiocpntest in Huustn, TX." At five thirty a.m., people were already lined up around the block for a chance to compete for front row "tckeets to tonigh'sshiw."

Seeing all those excited Level3 fans on TV made Summer realize just how bummed she really was to be missing the concert. She'd just been too consumed with Alice's hysteria to realize it. Oh, well. It was too late now.

The line at security was long and Summer stood in the back reading a sign that informed her exactly how many ounces of liquid she could bring in her carry-on.

"You need to check your luggage with your airline first," the man behind her said, pointing to her duffel bag. He looked like a frequent flyer, gray suit, laptop case, freshly shaven.

"Thanks," Summer said, stepping out of the line and lugging her bag toward the ticketing desks. She glanced back at the man. She swore she'd seen him earlier that night on Bourbon Street, making drunken catcalls at girls half his age. Now he looked totally professional, chatting with a woman in a business suit, a completely different person than he'd been the night before.

Summer stepped onto a moving walkway to save her the trouble of hauling her bag the entire way. She stood to the right, letting the expert travelers zoom past her on the left with their little wheeled suitcases. Even the people who weren't on the moving walkway seemed to be going faster than she was—the businessmen, the parents with their strollers and babies in backpacks, a rowdy group of middle school girls in matching red Riverdale Junior High Volleyball shirts.

The volleyball girls were way too loud for five in the morning—singing, shouting, busting the occasional dance move, the beads on their cornrows swinging to and fro, clattering in their hair. Even in identical outfits it was easy to pick out the leader of the girls. Her hair was the longest, the beads on the ends of her braids the most intricate. There was something about the way she strutted in her flip-flops that caught Summer's eye. It was a walk of sheer confidence—like she didn't need to look where she was going or think about her next step, knowing she had a buffer of friends to safely guide her wherever she was headed. She was the leader of the group, and yet, her hangers-on were the ones paving the way.

Summer was so entranced by these middle school girls she hadn't noticed that her free ride on the walkway had come to an end until her right foot hit the metal ridge, sending her face-forward onto the scratchy blue carpet. Of course, the volleyball team exploded with laughter. Summer's face flushed red, her chin raw from rug-burn. And yet she found herself laughing too—deep, forceful laughs so intense people inched away from her instead of stopping to ask if she was all right. Robert Frost chose the road less traveled. Summer Dalton chose a moving walkway. And this is where it landed her—flat on her face.

Summer pulled her journal from her bag, right there on the airport floor. Let the people step around her. She had something to add to her list and she needed to do it right now, before she changed her mind.

3. To see Levels play tonight.

By the time Summer looked up, the volleyball girls had moved on. And on the flat-screen TV on the wall, in front of an outdoor stage in Houston, Texas, the sun was just beginning to rise.

"CHRISTMAS IN JULY"
THE VERY THING THAT I WANTED
WAS TO GET
EVERYTHING I WANTED

THEN IT ALL CAME TRUE
THAT'S WHEN I KNEW
SURPRISE, SURPRISE

—*from Level3's third CD,* Natural Causes

Chapter Twenty

ALICE OPENED HER EYES AND STARED UP AT THE BROWN WATER-
stained ring on the ceiling above her bed. Her tongue felt dry,
like she'd slept with her mouth open. The sharp details of last
night stabbed at her head.

She remembered a blurry taxi ride, stumbling into the hotel
room, Tiernan putting her to bed. The rest she didn't want to
remember.

It was 6:06 a.m. The same time she'd woken up every
Monday through Friday for the last four years. Hangover or
not, Alice was a morning person and her internal clock was
strong.

A strange vibration made her sit up so fast her brain seemed
to flip inside her skull, as if it were trapped in one of those
frozen drink machines. Then she realized she'd slept with her
phone in her back pocket, in her entire outfit from last night,
earrings and all.

It was Quentin. *Finally, Quentin.* Thank God her phone had
been in her pocket and not her purse. She needed someone to
tell her everything would be okay, that she wasn't a horrible
person. Even if it wasn't true.

But when she opened his message, all she saw were two little words:

```
I can't
```

A wave of nausea traveled from her belly to her eyebrows. She made it to the toilet just in time.

The last time Alice puked was after the eighth grade beach day when she'd gotten sun poisoning. Summer had rubbed her back while Tiernan assembled a cold pack for her neck out of a facecloth and a bag of frozen peas. She hadn't deserved their kindness.

Tiernan rapped at the door. "You okay in there?"

"No," Alice moaned.

Tiernan came in anyway, last-night's makeup smeared across her cheeks, and puffy owl eyes.

"You want something to hold back your hair?"

Alice shook her head, her knees digging in to the cold tile floor. "I just need to be alone."

Tiernan closed the door, and Alice retched the last of it into the bowl. It was all gone. Everything was gone—*Summer, the Level3 tickets, her dignity*. And yet she kept on heaving like her body had more to give.

When it was finally done, she scrubbed her hands with the hottest water she could stand, the smell of the hotel's soap so perfumey, she thought she might get sick again. She brushed her teeth, washed her face until it was squeaky and raw, then stared at her reflection for a solid five minutes. *Who was this girl underneath the pink skin?* Her mirror self seemed to answer more honestly than the real Alice was capable of. It frightened her.

When she came out of the bathroom, Tiernan was back in bed.

"You asleep?" Alice asked.

"Uh-uh," Tiernan answered groggily. "You feel better?"

"A little," Alice said. She sat down on the edge of her bed. Standing took too much energy.

Tiernan gave her a weak smile. "We could still get tickets from scalpers."

"I can't afford to pay those prices," Alice snapped, harsher than she'd intended.

"So, what are we supposed to do?"

"Well, I guess we just give up," Alice said. What else was there? It was done. Game over.

Tiernan was silent for a few seconds, then she hauled herself out of bed, angrily gathering last night's outfit from where she'd scattered it around the floor. *Great. A fight with Tiernan.* The perfect capper to a perfectly wretched morning.

"Tiernan, don't be mad. You know how much scalpers charge," Alice reasoned. Using her loud voice made the room start to spin.

Tiernan rolled her miniskirt into a ball and chucked it into her suitcase.

"I thought you were done with this trip, anyway," Alice said, sounding curt. "I saw you last night, deleting those pictures."

The last thing Alice remembered before falling asleep was seeing Tiernan, over in the armchair by the window, going through her camera and deleting her photos one by one. A colorful shot of the frozen drink machines—gone. A picture of the three of them at the bar, smiling—poof—right in the digital trash can. If only Alice's memories of last night could be so easily wiped clean.

"I was hurt," Tiernan said.

Right, Alice thought. *Since when did Little Miss Hipper Than Thou start having feelings?* "Hurt about what?" Alice asked. She raised her eyebrows in disbelief, but it only made her headache worse.

"Forget it," Tiernan said, tossing her backpack over her shoulder. "I'm gonna go find someplace to get a coffee."

And with that Alice was alone again, having driven away not just Summer but now Tiernan, too, exactly like she'd done freshman year.

Alice rubbed her forehead and sighed. Less than twelve hours ago, she'd actually believed the three of them could be friends again. Had *wanted* them to be friends again, if she was perfectly honest. Why couldn't she just get over it? Why couldn't she be like a normal person and just shake off the bad stuff and move on without even looking back?

Alice knew history repeated itself, but up until this moment she never realized why. Now it seemed obvious: Human beings weren't capable of learning from their mistakes, even if they wanted to. They were just doomed to repeat the same awful patterns over and over, no matter how hurtful or stupid they were. *That* was the universe's brilliant master plan—to put the song on repeat.

Freshman year, she'd blamed everything on Tiernan and Summer. After all, it wasn't Alice who'd decided she wasn't cool enough for Tiernan anymore, or popular enough for Summer. At least that was the story Alice told herself. But now she could finally see the truth. It wasn't them, it was *her*, all along. Alice's neediness was the thing that had sent them running. *She* was the one who didn't want anything to change, the one who wanted to keep hanging out in the Pea Pod even after high school started, to keep Summer and Tiernan all to herself, doors closed off to the rest of world.

No doubt her neediness had sent Quentin running too. Boys had a way of sensing desperation. Or so she'd been told.

Alice quickly packed her bags, then went down to the reception desk and returned all three keys. Outside the hotel, she gave the valet her ticket and waited for Tiernan to get back from her coffee run. That is, if she even *was* coming back.

The early-morning air made Alice shiver. It was the first time she'd had a chill since they'd been down South and it made her homesick for New England. Oh, well. She'd be back there soon enough. By October in Vermont, they'd probably have snow.

She leaned back against the hotel's cool granite exterior, listening to the hypnotic pulse of a bass line in the distance. The noise grew louder and louder, until a neon blue ghetto glider cruised around the corner. *Thump, thump. A-thump, a-thump, a-thump, thump.* This car was the real deal—wheels tricked out with spinning chrome hubcaps, a lightning flash painted along the side in electric yellow. It was still too far away to make out the song, but Alice could feel the bass traveling right up her spine. *Thump, thump. A-thump, a-thump, a-thump, thump.* The car crept closer, the music distorting as it bounced between the tall gray buildings, her head throbbing along with the beat. Then she heard it. Of course, it was the one hip-hop song that sampled Level3.

IF YOU WANT TO SEE THE LIGHT OF DAY
YOU CAN'T BE AFRAID OF THE DARK.
IF YOU WANT TO SEE THE LIGHT OF DAY
YOU CAN'T BE AFRAID . . .

Yesterday she would have taken it as a sign. Today the idea of believing in signs seemed simple and selfish, as if this vast, incomprehensible universe would ever bother with someone as trivial as little Alice Miller. If hearing this song meant anything at all, it was only as proof that there was nothing new in the world, nothing was fresh. It was just the same old stuff going around and around and around.

The Pea Pod arrived, and she tipped the valet two dollars and climbed inside. The last place she wanted to be. In her hasty departure, Summer had forgotten to grab Coach Quigley, so Alice started the van and turned him on. The real Coach Quigley had a team motto he made them chant before each game: "Never Give Up! Never Say Die!" But the GPS version was happy enough to just navigate their way home. The drive to Walford was 1,532 miles. If they did it nonstop they could make it in a day. No. She wouldn't plan it. They'd drive each day only as far as Tiernan wanted to go. For once, Alice would keep her big mouth shut and just go along for the ride.

A minute later Tiernan appeared around the corner, bouncing along in cutoff jean short-shorts and a hot pink tank top, an oversize iced coffee in hand.

"Hey," she said quietly as she slipped into the passenger's seat. Alice waited to hear Tiernan's seat belt click before pulling away from the hotel.

The sun was so bright in the middle of the street, she had to drive slowly to let her eyes adjust. Even so, she would never have seen the girl running along the shaded sidewalk if it weren't for the flash of green from her duffel bag as it swung through a patch of light. *It couldn't be. . . .* Alice stomped on the brakes just as Summer stepped out of the shadows, her skin glowing white, like an apparition of herself, still in her clothes from last night.

Half in shock, Alice yanked the keys from the ignition while the van was still in gear. Next to her, Tiernan's jaw appeared to be swinging in the breeze. Summer waved to them casually, then headed toward the van. *Was it a wave of forgiveness?* More likely, it was a tail-between-the-legs kind of wave because she'd missed her flight.

But even in Alice's bewildered state, she could feel a small seed of hope growing inside of her. She did her best to fight it off, but the closer Summer walked, the bigger it grew. Maybe, in spite of the miserable mess she'd made of everything, even with the shame and regret she felt about what had happened last night, there was a tiny part of her that held on to the crazy idea that she could somehow fix this. That she could redeem herself and make things good between them. That she still wanted to.

"Did you miss your flight?" Alice asked when Summer opened the van's sliding door.

"No." Summer shook her head. "I remembered our dance."

Their dance. Like all seventh-grade girls throughout the history of time, Alice, Summer, and Tiernan spent many a sleepover choreographing dance routines to their favorite songs. They'd created lots of different numbers over the years, but their dance to Level3's "Parade" was far and away their best. They'd performed it for Alice's parents in her den at a quarter a ticket. A few hours from now, they'd perform it in front of hundreds of strangers in Houston, Texas, to try to win tickets to the Level3 show.

It was a long shot, and they all knew it. But like last night's fiasco, no one brought it up. Right now they were all business.

"So the contest is in *Houston*, not in Austin where the show is?" Alice was confused.

"They give you a limo ride to Austin if you win," Summer explained. "I think it's only two or three hours away."

"Tell us exactly what you saw on the news segment," Tiernan said. "What are other people doing?"

"We can't think about what other people are doing," Summer spoke with authority. "This dance is what *we're* doing. It's all we have."

Normally, Alice would have tried to come up with a better solution. Their old dance routine was kind of goofy and not all that original. But this was Summer's plan, not hers. Plus, their dance was something they'd created together. Maybe it was all they had left.

Coach Quigley said it would take them five hours and thirty-seven minutes from New Orleans to Houston. That meant they'd arrive at the contest twenty minutes before it ended at noon. But the real Coach Quigley voice, the one inside Alice's head, said: *Never give up. Never say die. Screw the speed limit.*

"How are we gonna practice?" Tiernan asked.

Reunited

"Two of us can rehearse in the back while the other one drives," Summer said.

"But we can't pop the top while we're driving," Alice pointed out, flying past an eighteen-wheeler. "We'll have to dance all hunched over."

"We'll do what we have to," Summer said, unbuckling her seat belt. "Okay, T, you're up."

"Parade" filled the Pea Pod as Alice moved into the left lane to pass a granny going sixty.

AND TOGETHER WE WILL WALK
DOWN THE MIDDLE OF THE STREET
AND THE CARS, THEY MAY CURSE US
BUT THEY WON'T MAKE US RETREAT

She couldn't get the full picture from the rearview mirror, but from the glimpses she caught, Summer and Tiernan looked like two Beyoncé wannabes with osteoporosis. Their first run-through got as far as the bit with the scissor jump; then Tiernan hit her head on the roof and fell to her knees, doubled over in hysterics.

"Is there a prize for worst act?" she gasped from the floor.

"Stop laughing!" Summer commanded. "We have work to do."

Two hours later, necks and backs sore from bending, they had it down. At a pee break, they made the switch—Tiernan at the wheel, Alice in the back.

So, maybe dancing in a moving van wasn't the wisest idea, considering that Alice's stomach felt like it was eating itself and even sitting down made her dizzy, but what choice did she have? Summer was back. They were moving forward. At least the Texas highway was flat.

"No, no, no," Summer coached from the bench seat. "The head bob comes after the part where you bring your hands together in prayer."

Alice was pretty sure she remembered it the other way around, but now was not the time to question Summer's memory.

Summer clapped to the beat. "And feet together, jump back, side-to-side, kick and turn. You got it! Nice!"

When she was young, Alice had loved coming up with new routines. She was probably the worst dancer of the group, but that never seemed to matter to Summer and Tiernan. The magic was never in the individual dance moves anyway. The thing that made their routines good was that they performed them together, in perfect synchronicity. Or at least it *seemed* perfect to them.

"Does it worry you guys that we won't get a chance to practice all together?" Alice asked. She wasn't feeling very optimistic about their chances of winning, but she wasn't about to mention it when they were still on such shaky ground. Literally. They'd been driving for hours now, and no one had dared to breathe a word about last night.

"It'll work," Summer said confidently. "We just have to trust it."

They were only fifteen miles outside of Houston now, thirty minutes ahead of schedule. Except for the shoulder shimmy (which, according to Summer, Alice performed like she was having an epileptic seizure) she'd perfected her part.

"Hey, check it out!" Tiernan called from the front. She cranked up the radio, and out of the static two voices emerged, stretched taut with exaggerated DJ happiness.

"Welcome back to WKID. This is Kai Kidman . . ."

". . . and Laura G."

"And we're coming to you live from the Freedom Stage at Houston's one and only Liberty Park on this very, very hot June morning with our Level3 Super-Fan Challenge."

Through the hiss of the radio, the crowd erupted in high-pitched hysteria.

"Okay, here's a question for our Level3 fans. Which do you guys think is hotter—Travis, or the summer in Houston?"

"Travis!" the crowd screamed.

Laura G.'s voice was scolding. "Getting back to the contest, Kai . . ."

"Oh, right, right. The contest." Some forced chuckling on Kai's part.

"Well, next up," Laura continued. "We have a couple of young ladies who've just graduated from our very own Rice University where they say their majors were Travis Wyland and

Ryan Hale." More fake laughter from the DJs. "No, seriously, though—you girls are mechanical engineers?"

There were two nervous "mm-hmms," then Kai jumped back in, his crazy DJ voice working overtime. "I don't even know what that *is*."

"Me neither. But I know it means they're smarter than we are."

"That's not too hard," Kai added. Laughter from the crowd.

"Holy crap." Tiernan sighed. "If their performance is as bad as these DJs, we're totally gonna win."

Summer shushed her. "I want to hear."

"Ladies and gentlemen, we present to you the lovely Molly and Priyanka, who'll be singing a duet of 'Little Me.'"

"THERE WAS A TIME, YEARS AGO,
WHEN WE DIDN'T KNOW WHAT WE DIDN'T KNOW . . ."

"*American Idol* wannabes," Summer proclaimed.

Tiernan shook her head disparagingly. "Basement karaoke at best."

Alice felt her heart start to race. There was that hope again, that need. *We could win this. At least we have a shot.*

"In eight-hundred yards, exit right," Coach Quigley said.

Two more mediocre songs and a dog act that didn't translate well over radio, and they pulled up to the station. Alice's cell phone said it was 11:11. Normally, that meant it was time to make a wish. But Alice wasn't making wishes anymore.

"THE METRIC SYSTEM"

WE LIVE IN THE ONLY COUNTRY
THAT DOESN'T USE THE METRIC SYSTEM
WE KEEP OUR FEET IN OUR YARDS
WE GET THERE IN MILES.

AND I'D LIKE TO LEAD THE REVOLUTION
TO OVERTHROW OUR RULERS,
I THINK THE WORLD WOULD APPROVE
MAYBE EVEN BUY ME A LITER OF BEER

DESPERATE TIMES
CALL FOR DESPERATE MEASURES
OUR NUMBERS ARE DIFFERENT,
OUR DISTANCE THE SAME

IF ONLY WE COULD SEE IT LIKE THAT
IF ONLY WE COULD SEE IT LIKE THAT

—from Level3's second CD, Rough & Tumble

Chapter Twenty-One

OKAY, SO IT WASN'T HER BEST PARKING JOB. BUT IF ALICE WASN'T saying anything about the wheel up on the curb, Tiernan wasn't about to bring it up. The rules were different today anyway. Alice had been eerily quiet and easygoing for the entire drive to Houston—rehearsing her dance without even one suggestion of a "better idea."

In a way, Tiernan was relieved Alice wasn't barking orders per usual, but there was something unsettling about a mellow Alice Miller, like drinking flat Coke. She'd only seen Alice like this once before, freshman year, right after Summer had officially dumped them as friends. But if anything could make Alice happy, it was the fact that they were about to perform their dweebie seventh grade dance routine.

Tiernan smoothed her hair in the rearview mirror, shoved some quarters into the meter, and the three of them took off down the street. They didn't need to speak. All they needed to do was get there in time. Then they needed to win.

By the time they reached the end of the block, she could hear "Parade" reverberating across the field at Liberty Park.

"What the duck?" Tiernan gasped.

Alice looked stricken. "Someone's singing our song!"

"It doesn't matter," said Summer. "We have our own thing going. We just have to believe in that."

Easy for her to say. Her long strawberry blond hair and perfect bone structure had unlocked so many doors for her, it was as though she expected them to just fly open whenever she approached. Of course, they usually did. Not a bad thing if you managed to squeeze yourself in along with her.

The entrance to the Freedom Stage (barf) was flanked by two black WKID vans with giant speakers on top. Next to them, a couple of radio station lackeys handed out free bumper stickers and neon green wristbands. As Tiernan put on her admission bracelet, a group of four women in their twenties exited through the gates, laughing and talking animatedly as they passed. One of them wore a giant poofy wedding gown, the other three had on tacky pink bridesmaids' dresses. Tiernan had listened to Kai and Laura G.'s play-by-play of what was apparently a staggeringly awful dance routine the women had performed to "Always a Bridesmaid" about a half hour back. Now they looked like they were about to pee themselves, they were laughing so hard.

"Too bad we don't still have matching outfits," Summer said as they made their way onto the field. Tiernan laughed. Back in sixth grade they had this thing where they dressed identically every Friday—blue cords, tan Uggs, Level3 baseball shirts. *Oh yeah, they were chic.* But Tiernan had loved getting dressed for school on Friday mornings. It was the first time she could remember being part of something bigger than herself. Until right now, she'd never even realized she'd missed that feeling.

The field inside the stadium was crawling with Level3 fans—emo dudes in skinny jeans, punk chicks with skin the color of paste, your standard variety high school kids, college kids who looked like older, grubbier versions of the high school kids, and, of course, the prerequisite teenybopper girls with someone's mom lurking ten feet behind. The festiveness of it all put Tiernan on edge.

Onstage, a dude in his early twenties played an instrumental version of "Snow Cone" on clarinet. The fact that it wasn't half bad made Tiernan's whole body seize up with an overwhelming desire to run.

"He's good," Alice said.

Tiernan nodded. "We can still bail if you want."

"No. We can't," Summer snapped. She'd been all "Eye of the Tiger" ever since her big comeback.

Tiernan tried to shake off her nerves. She didn't really want to bail, but she didn't want to lose, either. If she was going to put herself out there for the entire world to see, then Summer and Alice better be ready to bring their A game.

"Chillax, Sunny-D. I was just kidding."

"Can you not call me that?"

Tiernan shrugged. "Sorry. I thought you liked it."

"You think I like having a nickname that compares me to a sickeningly sweet fake orange juice concoction?"

Tiernan wanted to tell Summer that she never meant it like that. Not to mention that she actually *liked* SunnyD. But Alice jumped in before she had the chance.

"You guys," Alice commanded. "We need to focus."

A guy in a WKID T-shirt directed them to the end of the line of performers and handed Alice a registration sheet to fill out. In front of them were three college-age girls, each holding a Paris Hilton–style rat-dog dressed up in miniature human clothes.

"Look!" Summer said, pointing to the handwritten names on their little dog collars. "They're supposed to be Travis, Ryan, and Luke."

The dog dressed as Luke wore mini-Wayfarer nerd glasses. "I'm making an anonymous phone call to PETA," Tiernan whispered.

"Do we have a group name?" Alice asked. Having a clipboard in her hand was bringing her back to life—the order, the control—like a shot of booze for an alcoholic.

The Ex–Best Friends? The Extremely Awkward Road Trip Trio? Yesterday Tiernan could have suggested these as a joke. But today they had a contest to win.

Or maybe it was about more than just the contest. Back home, Tiernan and her friends were always insulting one another with a constant flow of quick-witted banter. But with

Alice and Summer, it was different. She was still her usual sarcastic self, but around them, she didn't feel the need to be "on" all the time. She didn't have to blurt out some mean ironic joke, just so she could do it first.

Sometimes it seemed like her friends back home were secretly in some silent competition with one another to see who could be the cleverest or who knew the hippest bands. But at the end of the day, who really cared? Summer probably liked Top 40, but that didn't take away from the fact she was probably ten times more original than half of Tiernan's friends pretended to be. And no one Tiernan had ever met even came close to being as shamelessly genuine as Alice.

"What about the Pea Pod Experience?" Alice offered, answering her own question. She'd always been good at this type of stuff, with or without a hangover.

"Well, it's definitely been an *ex*perience," Summer said. *Emphasis on the* ex.

The radio station intern came back to collect their clipboard. "I'm not quite finished yet," Alice said.

"Actually, I just got word from my producer that we don't have time to see any more acts today," he said, glancing at his watch. "I'm sorry."

"What do you mean?" Tiernan snapped. "We drove five and a half hours to get here." She hated peons like this who thought a stupid VIP badge around their necks made them superior.

"I'm sorry, but they need to wrap up the morning show

by noon." He pointed to the DJs at the side of the stage.

Tiernan's legs felt twitchy, like she needed to run, or kick someone. Preferably the weasel with the clipboard.

"Sir, we came all the way from Massachusetts." Summer pouted. "We practiced our dance in a moving van, for God's sake!"

"It's not up to me, ma'am," the man said, then walked away.

Alice just stood there, catatonic.

"No, they're not going to deny us," Tiernan said. "They *can't*."

"I don't think we really have a choice," Alice replied. She looked like she was fighting off tears.

"This is bull," Summer said. "They *have* to give us a chance. After everything we've been through."

"Wow, that was wonderful," Laura G.'s voice boomed out over the PA when the clarinet kid was done.

"Do your lips get sore playing that thing?" Kai asked. His bouncy DJ voice didn't match his scruffy, middle-aged body.

"I guess we should just go," Alice said. "I don't really feel like sticking around this place, do you?"

Summer shook her head.

"Hang on," Tiernan said.

Even though it was hell here, Tiernan didn't want to leave. She didn't want it to end like this—shut down by some radio station d-bag. It wasn't that she was in love with the idea of shaking her booty in front of hundreds of strangers—that part she could do without. But they'd come too far not to perform. They'd endured too much to just sit around and let this happen. Tiernan had messed things up for them in the past; that was true. And there was nothing she could do to change that. But she *could* do something about the present. At least she had to try. And if her plan worked, if she could convince the DJs to let them perform, then maybe, just maybe, she could finally make things right between them.

"Give me a minute," Tiernan said, then she ran off into the crowd. She didn't know what she was going to say to Kai and Laura G. (if she could even get through to them) but she needed to say something. Her impulsiveness got them into that whole mess freshman year, and it just might get them out of this one.

The front of the stage was lined with more radio station minions with VIP badges, and behind them, a row of big dudes in orange "Security" T-shirts. There was no way Tiernan was getting through without getting arrested. *But maybe . . .*

The van wasn't far. The keys, still in her pocket. Tiernan took off across the field past a group of emo boys whose dramatic sideswept bangs seemed to point her toward the gate as if to say *Go for it. Run.*

So she ran—down the entrance to Liberty Park, across the street, up the sidewalk, her blue bob bouncing against her cheeks, fanning her face from the midday Texas heat. Back in Massachusetts, she would have been sweating buckets on a day this hot, but here, the air was so dry it sucked the sweat right off her face before it had a chance to collect.

Carefully, she opened the van's sliding door, grabbing a pen from the glove box and peeling their map-collage-spectacular off of its designated spot on the wall. Then she speed-walked back to the contest, writing as she went. Being raised Jewish, she'd never written a letter to Santa before, but she imagined it was pretty much like this—hopeful, demanding, and naive all at the same time. Kind of like Alice.

Dear WKID bigwigs,
I'm writing this letter to ask you—no, to beg you—to give us the chance to perform today . . .

Tiernan waved her wristband at the security guys as she tore through the gate. A paper airplane could work, if it didn't veer horribly off course. Or she could just ball the collage up and chuck it onstage—but security might think she was some kind of deranged fan trying to blow up the DJs. The third option was to give it to someone who could deliver it to Kai and Laura G.

The security guards were all total Neanderthals. And the people in the WKID T-shirts looked like lowly interns who'd probably be too afraid of pissing off their bosses to take a chance. Then Tiernan saw him—a dude in his early thirties with a hipster's handlebar mustache, black cowboy hat, and an all-access press badge. In his hands he held a camera with a lens as big as a loaf of bread. He was a photojournalist, and photojournalists were always looking for stories, weren't they?

"Hey, camera guy."

The man turned around.

"I was wondering if you might do me a favor?"

She handed him the collage, rolled up like a sacred scroll and secured with a hot pink hair elastic. He reached for it skeptically, as if she were handing him a pipe bomb or a love note.

"Can you give this to Kai and Laura for me?"

"I don't work for the radio station—" he started.

But Tiernan had already run off, leaving him stuck with it. Now he could make a choice—perform a random act of kindness for a total stranger or do nothing. She wondered what she would have done. The better version of herself would have delivered the note. The thoughtless, selfish version of herself would have blown it off, tossed it in the trash, and pushed the memory away.

When she got back, Alice and Summer were lying on the grass in a patch of shade. "Hair of the Dog" was blaring from the speakers. Naturally, the dog act was onstage.

"Where were you?" Summer asked.

"Just trying to help our cause," Tiernan said enigmatically. "Trust me." Alice opened her eyes just wide enough to reveal the doubt in her expression. It took a lot to make a cynic out of Alice Miller, but leave it to Tiernan to have found a way. Up on stage, the smallest of the miniature dogs pranced about on his hind legs.

Tiernan wanted to tell them about giving the DJs her note written on the back of the collage. But what if that photographer hadn't given it to Kai and Laura G.? Or what if he had and they just didn't care? And if Tiernan had given away the collage for nothing, there's no telling what Alice might do. It wouldn't matter that she'd done it for them, for all the right reasons. She'd told herself that exact same thing the night of the Winter Wonderland Dance, hadn't she?

"Can we just go?" Alice sat up. "This is too painful to watch."

"Let's just wait a few more minutes," Tiernan said. Onstage, Canine Luke marked his turf on the leg of the judge's table.

"Okay, I think we've seen enough," Kai's voice boomed out across the field as he leaped from his chair.

The audience laughed.

"Seriously, kids," Kai said to the dogs' owners. "We're gonna have to stop here. We're calling it off."

"You mean, we're calling it *arf*," Laura G. corrected.

The audience let out a collective "Awwwww."

"Oh, give me a break. You guys like dog pee on you?" Kai shot back.

The sound effects guy played a Wolverine-like growl.

The only thing more torturous than this radio schtick was the anxious feeling in Tiernan's stomach. If her letter hadn't worked, it would all end here.

"Okay, then." The plastic voice was back. "We're going to

tabulate the scores for today's performances, and we'll be back with the results after this message."

"Crap," Tiernan said.

The radio station cut to commercial. That was it. Her plan hadn't worked. Of course it hadn't. What had she been thinking? That she could actually save the day and be a hero? And what were the odds that their stupid little dance would win them the contest anyway? Even if it did, what was the point? Two months from now, they'd all be away at college and she'd probably never see Alice and Summer again.

"So what now?" Summer asked.

Alice just shrugged. She looked tired, older.

An ad for an all-you-can-eat Chinese buffet played over the loudspeakers while Kai fired WKID T-shirts into the crowd out of a T-shirt cannon. You'd think he was shooting out nuggets of solid gold the way people clamored for them—screaming and elbowing each other, like some crappy T-shirts could make up for the fact that none of them had tickets for tonight's show.

Tiernan tugged at the green bracelet at her wrist, hurrying along the back of the field, skirting around the crowd.

"Slow down," Alice called out.

But Tiernan kept on walking. As long as she was moving forward, she could pretend that she didn't care about failing to get them into the contest, that missing the Level3 show meant nothing to her at all. Whatever happened between here and the van, Tiernan wouldn't let herself even *glance* at Alice's and

Summer's faces. She had too much disappointment of her own to deal with to even begin to tackle theirs.

Next thing she knew, something hit her shoulder, knocking her flat on the ground. Frantically, Tiernan looked around for the person who had thrown the sucker punch. But when she saw the T-shirt lying next to her, she realized she'd suffered a more humiliating injury—popped in a drive-by T-shirt shooting.

Already Alice and Summer were on their knees next to her, their faces a mixture of shock and concern.

"Sorry, my bad," Kai said over the loudspeakers, his voice not even approximating genuine concern.

"Are you okay?" Alice asked.

Tiernan nodded. Her shoulder stung, but she was fine. Which was more than she could say for the brainless crowd of rubberneckers gathered around her.

"Do you mind?" Summer asked, glaring at them. Tiernan had always loved the way Summer could just shut people down with a word or a look. Tiernan could piss people off, but Summer made them wither.

"What the hell?" Tiernan asked, picking up the T-shirt. It was rolled into a tight little cylinder, like a giant cotton-poly-ester-blend bullet. "WKID, Houston - For the kid in all of us."

"I fricking hate WKID," Alice spat.

Tiernan squeezed her shoulder in her hand. At least a big nasty bruise might buy her some sympathy later when Alice discovered she'd given away their Level3 map. The radio station theme song blasted out onto the field. Their signal to keep moving.

"We are back on the air at the Level3 Super-Fan Challenge, and this is Kai—and Laura G.—coming to you live from the Freedom Stage at Liberty Park. As you know, we are in the final moments of this contest where four lucky fans will win front-row tickets to tonight's Level3 concert in Austin, complete with a limo ride to and from the show."

The crowd hooted and screamed on cue.

"Well, Kai, I've got some good news and some bad news," Laura G. said.

"Uh-oh."

"Well, the bad news, *you* already know. But for those of you who aren't actually here with us at the Liberty Park Freedom Stage, during our commercial break Kai accidentally shot a girl with our WKID T-shirt gun."

"Who needs two eyes anyway?" Kai laughed at his own joke. "Really, though—what's the good news?"

"The good news is that I've been handed a note from our producer telling me that we have time for one more act," Laura G. said.

The crowd cheered. Tiernan slowed as she exited the gate, her stomach felt like clay.

"Is there a Pea Pod Experience in the house?"

Before she had time to absorb the meaning of Kai's words, Tiernan was running—charging through the crowd toward the stage, Alice and Summer at her heels.

"It's step, step, turn together, jump back, right leg kick . . ." The sudden change of plans had snapped Alice from her coma and right back into cruise director mode.

"Just pretend we're back in the basement," Summer whispered as the security guards examined their wristbands, then motioned for them to head up the stairs. Tiernan quickly smoothed her hair, wishing she had more time to make herself look presentable, but a radio station employee already had her by the elbow, whisking her out to center stage, the sun beating down on her from straight overhead, the audience staring.

"Now, my producer tells me earlier today he was handed a very special note," Laura G. said, holding up the collage. "What would you call this? A collage?"

Tiernan nodded. She could feel Alice's and Summer's eyes on her but she couldn't bring herself to meet them.

"It's very intricate piece of artwork here," Kai explained to the audience. "Lots of old photos of Level3, and some pictures of these girls, too. And it also appears to be a map?"

"Mmm-hmm," Tiernan said, nodding. It had never crossed her mind this might involve public speaking.

"So, tell me if I got this right." Laura G. took over. "You girls drove here all the way from Massachusetts to see the Level3 show tonight, but then your tickets were *stolen*?"

A radio station employee held a microphone in front of the three of them.

"That's right," Alice answered, confused.

Looking at the audience made Tiernan's stomach tighten like a fist so she brought her gaze back to Laura and Kai. *This is just a conversation between us and them. We're the only ones here. Just keep looking at the DJs.*

"And the name of your group—The Pea Pod Experience—it has a special meaning?"

"Well . . ." Alice gave the DJs a brief history of their friendship, conveniently skipping over the part where it ended.

"Wow," Kai said. "So, you girls have been best friends for eight years?"

Tiernan's neck and face muscles tightened from nervousness so that she smiled involuntarily, like a crazy person. For a few seconds nobody spoke.

"It's kind of a long story," Alice said.

The audience gave a collective laugh.

"Well, I think we want to hear this story, right?" Kai asked the crowd. Naturally, the crowd answered with a roaring "Yes!"

This time Tiernan knew it was her turn to reach for the mic. It didn't matter that her stage fright made it feel like there were a million tiny knives stabbing her in the gut. She knew what she had to do, and it had to be done right here, right now, no matter how terrifying it felt.

"Freshman year, I did something . . . bad," Tiernan began, her voice quivering. "I told a lie, and I never told them about it." The crowd fell quiet. She could feel thousands of eyes staring up at her, waiting. "And because of it, things got all messed up between us."

Somehow Tiernan found the nerve to look at Alice and Summer. She hadn't brought her camera, though later she would remember these moments like a series of photographs—Alice's and Summer's surprise, Laura G. smiling with genuine sympathy, and the lens of the man with the handlebar mustache focused just on her. She was exposed, overexposed—spilling her guts in front of hundreds of strangers—thousands more listening at home or in their cars.

"Freshman year, I went to a different high school than Alice and Summer, so I didn't get to see them as much as I did before, and it felt like we were starting to drift apart. Especially me, since I wasn't around. So I decided to come home for the weekend, so we could all sleep over my house, just like we used to, just the three of us."

Instantly Tiernan was transported back to that night. How she'd called Summer from the train station, all excited, to figure out what movie they'd rent, when Summer dropped the bomb that she'd been asked to the Winter Wonderland Dance by some meathead junior from the basketball team. She still wanted to have the sleepover, Summer assured Tiernan, only she thought they should all go to the dance first.

"What about Alice?" Tiernan had asked. "What does *she* want to do?"

"I haven't told her yet," Summer admitted. "I'm not sure

how well she'll get along with Tom's friends, you know what I mean? And Tom's bringing beers for us to drink in the parking lot before. Anyway, if you don't want to go, that's fine; I can always meet up with you guys later."

It was a tiny thing, really. A minor little delay to their weekend of fun. But it hit Tiernan right where it hurt. She'd come all the way home to see them, and here Summer was, throwing her under the bus for some boy.

"Let me talk to Alice and call you back," she said, as Judy pulled up in Tiernan's dad's old Land Rover.

The entire ride home, Tiernan only managed to give one-syllable answers to Judy's questions, her anger over Summer's change of plans—over being interrogated by her mother, over *everything*—building by the second. What was so wrong with her that made everybody want to leave? What had she done that was so awful?

When she got home, Tiernan stormed down to the basement without another word to Judy and called Alice from her cell.

"We can stop by the dance for a while, can't we?" Alice asked meekly.

Tiernan couldn't believe it. She'd thought Alice, *of all people*, would be on her side.

"Why would I want to go to some lame-ass Snowball Dance?" Tiernan hissed. "I don't even go to WHS."

"First of all, it's called the Winter Wonderland Dance," Alice corrected. "And second, it's just a dance. Who cares whether or not you go to school here?"

Tiernan knew that Alice didn't mean it the way it sounded, but still. *Who cares?* The words had a ring that seemed to resonate through Tiernan's entire body.

"Don't you know what Summer is doing?" Tiernan spat. The words seemed to fly out from someplace dark, perfectly aimed at Alice's heart.

"She doesn't *really* want us to go, Alice. She thinks we'll embarrass her. Plus, she basically told me her new friends don't like you anyway."

Tiernan could actually feel the sting of Alice's hurt on the other end of the line, as if the phone's fiber optics could silently transmit another person's pain.

Sadly, the audience in Houston was not so silent. Some people in the crowd actually hissed and booed. Not that Tiernan didn't deserve it.

"I made it up because I was jealous." Tiernan wiped a tear with the back of her hand and looked at Summer. "I was jealous that you two got to go to school together while I was off by myself, missing everything. I was jealous that every time I talked to Alice, all she could talk about was what *you* were doing, and how you were making other friends. Like you were the only one who mattered. Like I didn't matter at all."

Tiernan looked to Alice next. "And I lied to you, Alice, because I *wanted* you to be as angry at Summer as I was. But then, when you were, I felt so guilty that I could barely talk to you. I didn't want to answer your calls."

Tiernan could still remember that ugly night in perfect detail—chasing Alice through the halls of Walford High, like she was actually trying to stop her instead of just fanning the flames of the fire she'd started. Hell, she'd brought the kindling and the lighter fluid, too. By the time they made it to the cafeteria, Alice was moving so fast, the giant paper snowflakes that hung from the ceiling swayed in her breeze.

Tiernan could have still stopped it then, that moment before Alice found Summer in the crowd, her eyes narrowing like a cat's when it sees a bird. Summer didn't even see them coming, sitting on a windowsill next to Tom and his friends and laughing—*not even dancing*, Tiernan had noted—even though Level3 was on.

It was our heyday, hey day, hey . . .

"Sorry to interrupt your little date," Alice began. The match to the wood.

The microphone crackled, snapping Tiernan back to the present. "Alice, that night . . . I just made up all that crap Summer said about you because I was afraid . . ." She looked down at the dusty stage floor. "I was afraid you liked her better than me. That you'd *always* liked her better than me." If this was the mud her mother was talking about slogging through, Tiernan was up to her neck in it now.

"I know I acted like it didn't bother me that the three of us were drifting apart." Tiernan brought her gaze back to Alice and Summer, relieved to see tears welling in their eyes. "But I did care . . . I *do* care."

For a moment they all just stared at one another.

"Hey, kids, I don't want to interrupt your tender reconciliation . . ." Kai's voice broke the silence. ". . . but we're a bit short on time."

The audience laughed. Tiernan laughed with them.

"Sorry."

"Well, on that note," Laura G. jumped in. "You girls ready to dance, or what?"

"ENCORE"

CALL ME OUT, AGAIN

AND I'LL PLAY YOUR FAVORITE SONG

IT'S NOT MUCH TO REPEAT

OUR GREATEST HITS,

IF YOU'RE SINGING ALONG

SO WHY DID I PRETEND

I WAS DONE WITH THE SHOW?

AND THEY'RE CALLING ME OUT AGAIN

BRAVO, BRAVO, BRAVO, BRAVO.

—from Level3's third CD, Natural Causes

Chapter Twenty-Two

confession. *Hands on hips. Chin over right shoulder.* There was so much she needed to process, so many story lines to rearrange in her head. But there wasn't time for that now.

The song kicked in and off she went—marching forward eight beats, heads up, gaze straight ahead, the feeling of someone shuffling a deck of cards inside her chest. The opening of "Parade" was all percussion, an actual recording of the marching band at Travis, Luke, and Ryan's old high school. Summer had spent the last four years listening to drums like these from the bleachers of the Walford High football field as they inspired the team to victory. This time, it was her turn.

Stomp, hip swivel, jump left, jump right, stomp. The steps were so deeply etched in her subconscious that they seemed to come without memory.

DON'T TELL ME I'M GONNA BE LATE
YOUR P-P-PARADE WILL JUST HAVE TO WAIT,
OR MAYBE IT WON'T, BUT I'M STILL GONNA BE THERE
RIGHT ON TIME . . .

Summer twirled just as the zap of the electric guitar broke through the steady drumbeat, like that first frenzied breath after surfacing from underwater. Out of the corner of her eye she saw Alice's ponytail slip from its holder, her mane of tangled hair flying in all directions.

At least now she knew. Not that Summer was ready to instantly forgive Alice and Tiernan, but she was ready to let it go. She *needed* to let it go. How many times had she relived that awful night in her mind, repeating all of the vile things Alice had said until she'd actually started believing them?

Summer's eyes brushed past Tiernan's, and the three of them moved seamlessly into the Britney Spears hip-grind stomp, like three sexy babies throwing tantrums. As mad as she was, Summer always loved watching Tiernan do this part—the way she could come off as strong, fearless, and sultry in equal measure. *Fricking Tiernan.* How was it possible that a girl with so much confidence could actually be jealous of *her*? Or was her confidence just an act? And if so, why had Summer bought into it—even *envied* Tiernan for it?

UP AHEAD, THE BAND PLAYS THE FIGHT SONG,
BEHIND US, THE BEAUTY QUEEN SMILES
AND WE'RE WALKING HERE TOGETHER
WE'VE BEEN WALKING HERE FOR MILES . . .

Reunited

They were almost at the part where Summer always blew it. She'd make the mistake of following Alice, who'd inevitably start with her right foot instead of her left, and then Summer's whole series of knee-lifts would be off. But today Summer wasn't following anyone's lead. Today the music was her only guide.

. . . BUT IN THIS PARADE
I'M GONNA MARCH TO MY OWN TIME . . .

Without even thinking about the steps, Summer nailed them. She felt like that girl back at the bonfire in West Virginia. *Dancing only for herself.* Maybe that was the key to staying together—letting Alice and Tiernan make their own mistakes and just dance her own part of the dance as well as she could.

After all, the only person Summer was in charge of was herself. She couldn't control what Alice and Tiernan did onstage (or off it, for that matter). But what she *could* do was make a choice. She could let anger take the lead—just like she'd always done. *Or* she could choose to let it go.

Letting go. Maybe that's all forgiveness really was.

Summer marched in place as the routine circled back to where it had started—three girls in a row, arms raised in triumph, eyes straight ahead. She stayed like that as the melody faded and the drums came back in again, letting the applause rush over her while rivers of sweat collected in the corners of her mouth.

"Holy dance routines, Batman! Those girls know how to

boogie," Laura G.'s voice boomed. The crowd responded with the appropriate whistles and catcalls.

Summer dropped her arms and looked over at her dance partners. Alice was all dimples and teeth. Tiernan's eyes sparkled— half joy, half tears. Summer had so much to be angry at them for, so many questions left unanswered, but all she wanted was to enjoy the moment. The funny thing was, the choice didn't belong to anyone but herself.

Summer smiled wide as applause thundered all around her. Not that she needed the affirmation. The feeling of victory was already shining inside of her, and it felt like freedom, right here on the Freedom Stage.

"So, how long have you girls been rehearsing this number?" Kai asked.

This time Summer reached for the microphone. "We haven't practiced all together for a while." Her breath came hard. "But it was easy. We knew it all by heart."

She stole a glance at Alice and Tiernan, and they looked back at her, their eyes shining. For someone who loved the English language as much Summer, she realized that some of her favorite moments in life came when words were superfluous. The silent exchanges, those were the real-life poetry.

"My producer has just handed me the tabulated scores," Kai announced. "And it appears as if we have a tie." Kai paused to create suspense. "Geoff Newman, could you come out here, please?"

A droopy-faced man walked onstage holding a clarinet. It took Summer a second to recognize him as the same guy who'd played that great instrumental version of "Snow Cone."

"Geoff, *Pea Pod Experience*"—Kai said their name with a heavy dose of sarcasm—"one of you will be going to Level3 tonight!"

The audience screamed and cheered. Alice grasped Summer's hand and squeezed it hard. "And we'll find out who right after this break."

The radio station sound effects blared out of the speakers, and Summer could feel the floorboards trembling under her feet. Or maybe she was the one trembling. But before she could figure it out, the microphone boy was herding them offstage to a holding area in the wings.

Summer practically dove into the cooler of complimentary energy drinks. Not that an overcaffeinated soda was likely to help with her shaking. Tiernan chugged hers down in one gulp. Alice sipped from one drink while holding another ice-cold can against the back of her neck. For a long time, no one said a word. There was so much to say, it was hard to know where to begin.

"So, what do you think they'll have us do?" Alice asked, breaking their silence. "You know, for the final showdown."

It hadn't occurred to Summer that they might actually have to *do* something else. What did they have left?

"It doesn't matter," Summer whispered. "We're going to win this thing."

HILARY WEISMAN GRAHAM

"Mmm-hmm." Tiernan nodded. "It's *beshert*."

Alice smiled. "I thought you guys didn't believe in fate anymore."

"Things happen for a reason," Summer said. "And maybe it doesn't have anything to do with this contest or even with Level3 . . . Maybe it's just about the three of us, being here, together, and finally, you know, having things out."

Alice's eyes locked on Summer. Tiernan fiddled with the metal tab on her can.

"I'm not saying that I'm over it," Summer added quickly. "What you guys did to me was awful. You don't know what it's like to feel publicly humiliated like that."

"I'm sorry." Alice's eyes welled with tears. "I know it was wrong. But when Tiernan told me how you said I embarrassed you—"

"*Which was a lie*," Tiernan cut in.

"An exaggeration," Summer corrected, surprising herself with her own admission.

Alice wiped her eyes. "Even if it wasn't exactly the truth, it felt like it was . . . like you were abandoning me for all of your new 'popular' friends, who didn't like me and Tiernan. Like suddenly Tiernan and I weren't good enough for you anymore."

Summer always assumed Alice didn't care what people thought of her. That she didn't have the same insecurities regular people did. Just another fiction she'd convinced herself was true.

"The three of us were best friends since the fourth grade. Did you think I just turned into some cold, heartless jerk?"

Summer went on. "I know part of it was my fault. I *did* blow you guys off for my new friends freshman year. I'd be lying if I said I didn't. But all I wanted was a little space to do my own thing, for once in my life. You guys were always doing exciting stuff like going off to summer camp or jetting off to New York City to go shopping for the weekend. You always had so many opinions about things. Sometimes stuff I'd never even heard about. But all I had was you." Summer could feel her anger rising up again. "And I didn't deserve to be treated like that."

It would be so easy to just let the angry feelings take over again, whereas letting go felt like a constant effort. More proof that doing the right thing isn't always necessarily the easiest path.

"I know." Alice nodded guiltily. "You didn't deserve it."

"You were hurt, and you lashed out," Summer said. "But a lot of what you said was true. Just like it was true about Jace."

Alice shook her head. "I'm sorry. I shouldn't have told you like that—"

"Don't be sorry." Summer cut her off. "You told me. That's the main thing."

"Well, whatever either of you did or didn't do, I think we can all agree that I'm the *real* a-hole here," Tiernan said.

"That's true." Summer smirked. Then she gave Tiernan a playful elbow to the gut. "Come on, that was a joke."

Tiernan forced a smile.

"What I'm trying to say is . . ." Summer took a deep breath. "No single one of us is completely innocent for what happened. And no one is completely to blame."

"So, we all suck?" Tiernan asked.

"I think we've all been hurt." Summer swallowed the rest of her drink as if washing down her words. "And I think it would probably take the rest of our lives to figure out all of the messed-up reasons we did what we did."

Summer shivered from the chill of the ice-cold liquid in her stomach. It felt surreal admitting these things out loud. To be here, in Houston, Texas, rehashing the past with her ex-best friends, who, as it turned out, still happened to be two of the people who knew her the best—Alice, all wide-eyed and eager; Tiernan, who looked so uncomfortable talking about "feelings," she probably would have jumped into her soda can if she fit.

They were both so different from her. And yet, Summer had spent the last four years hanging out with people who all looked alike and dressed alike and acted alike. But the only thing her Walford friends really seemed to have in common was the fact they were too afraid to actually be themselves.

"As mad as I am at you," Summer said to Tiernan, "and I *am* still mad at you, I think it was very brave doing what you did out there."

"Psh." Tiernan shook her head. "I had to stop being a wuss sometime, didn't I?" She lifted her soda and took a large swig.

"Just don't tell my mom about it, or she might think I've actually learned some kind of 'lesson.'"

"Oh, that would be tragic," Alice joked.

Summer stared at Tiernan. She could relate to feeling scared. Maybe that was forgiveness, too. Understanding.

"Welcome back to the Level3 Super-Fan Challenge!" Kai's voice blasted out of nowhere, stirring up a fluttery feeling in Summer's heart.

She crossed her fingers and held her hand out in front of her. "We *have* this," she whispered. "It's our destiny."

Tiernan and Alice crossed their fingers, too, holding them out so that all three of their hands touched.

"I know what *your* destiny is." Tiernan shot Summer a knowing look. "Travis Wyland."

"Maybe," Summer said with a smile. The truth was, she kind of had a feeling about that, too.

Laura G. and Kai were still talking, their inane DJ blather echoing through the wings, but Summer couldn't focus on their words.

"Okay, follow me." The microphone guy swept in out of nowhere. He put his hand on Summer's shoulder and gave her a forceful little shove. Behind his back, Tiernan leveled him with a death stare.

Then, just like that, she was back onstage with Alice and Tiernan, without even quite knowing how. Geoff, the clarinet guy, stood next to them.

"And, heeeeerre they aaaarre." Kai's voice blared full of phony enthusiasm. The audience burst into applause on cue. She heard someone scream "Pea Pod Experience!"

Summer felt woozy, as if her body were made of rubber— a combination of nervousness, lack of sleep, and the 250- milligram jolt of caffeine she'd had backstage.

"Okay, so let's get down to business," Kai said. "After careful review of the judges' notes—"

"That would be *our* notes, Kai," Laura pointed out.

"*The judges*—Laura G. and myself—have come to our deci- sion." Kai paused. "You ready to hear it, Houston?"

The audience's howl sent a rush of blood to Summer's head. With front row tickets, she'd finally be able to see Travis up close—to see what he looked like for real, as a human being, not the man-god she'd built him up to be in her mind. She could almost feel herself there, the stage lights spilling onto them as she screamed the lyrics to every song with Alice and Tiernan by her side.

"The winner is . . ." Kai made a drumroll noise with his lips. "Geoff Newman!"

The audience exploded, but Summer's body fell so still, she wondered if she might have stopped breathing. She forced her- self to look at Alice and Tiernan, then immediately regretted it. All she wanted to do was to get off this stage, to run back to the Pea Pod, and cry. Couldn't these people give them a little privacy?

"Congratulations, Geoff!" Laura G. approached him. They shook hands. "But before I hand over your ticket, I want to tell our audience about the conversation you and I had backstage."

Great. While they were backstage having a heart-to-heart, Geoff had been schmoozing the judges. *Talk about unfair.* Summer gave Alice and Tiernan a not-so-subtle look of disbelief. Alice's expression was blank, like a coma victim. Tiernan's face was twisted into a scowl.

"Anyway," Laura continued. "It would appear as if Geoff's playing a solo number both on and offstage."

"Tooting his own horn, so to speak," Kai added. The sound effects guy played a clip of a woman moaning in ecstasy. The audience groaned.

"Ignore him, Geoff," Laura scolded.

"Technically, the clarinet's a wind instrument," Geoff said, deadpan.

"Any-hoo," Laura went on. "As everyone here knows, we have *four* tickets to give away to the very special one-night-only Level3 show tonight, and Geoff only needs *one*, so, I did the math . . ."

"Uh-oh, there's math involved." Kai made a snoring sound.

All at once, Summer's breath came rushing back to her.

"Pea Pod Experience . . . turns out this might just be your lucky day after all. . . . You're going to Level3 tonight!"

The next thing Summer knew, her arms were entangled with Alice's and Tiernan's, the three of them hopping around the stage in a shrieking, crying clump, like a three-headed Miss America.

"Congratulations," said a voice from outside their circle of chaos. Geoff the clarinetist eyed them warily.

"You too," Summer called to Geoff, pulling herself free of the celebration. Alice and Tiernan collected themselves and added their compliments.

"So, I hope you don't mind me tagging along for the limo ride," he said apologetically. He didn't seem embarrassed by going to the concert alone, just concerned with cramping their style.

The idea came to Summer all at once. But when she opened her mouth to run it by Alice and Tiernan, she could see they'd had the same thought. Of course, this sent them all into violent hysterics. Geoff looked even more awkward than before.

"If y-you'd rather I do something else," he stammered, "I can—"

Summer kindly cut him off. "The limo's all yours, Geoff," she said, smiling. "My friends and I already have a ride."

"ROLLER COASTER"

ON THE UP SIDE,
I'M UNDER
CONTROL.

THE FAMILIAR THRILL
OF KNOWING
WHAT COMES NEXT.

THOUGH IT OFFERS NO SURPRISES,
THE ANXIETY, IT RISES,
THE HIGHER UP WE GO,
TILL THERE'S NOWHERE LEFT TO GO

AND I JUST FALL,
I FALL, I FALL,
OH, OH
I JUST
FALL.

—*from Level3's self-titled first CD*

Chapter Twenty-Three

IF ALICE DIDN'T KNOW BETTER, SHE WOULD HAVE SWORN THE PEA Pod sailed out of Houston on a cloud. For the past two hours, the mood in the van had been giddy delirium, interrupted only by their own spontaneous screams. In the middle of a sentence, one of them would see a sign for Austin and remember where they were going, how they had won.

"You guys, we're making great time." Summer fiddled with Coach Quigley. "It's only another hour till Austin."

Tiernan leaned her head halfway out the window, even though she was driving. *"'Don't tell me I'm gonna be late,'"* she sang into the wind. *"'Your p-p-parade will just have to wait!'"* A guy in a pickup blasted his horn as they whizzed past.

Driving into Houston, the flatness of the landscape had looked boring to Alice. Now the big Texas sky seemed wide open, full of possibility. She leaned down and rooted around for the Scotch tape in her craft box. Their map deserved a place on the wall, a permanent Pea Pod decoration. As she affixed her tape donuts to the back, she reread Tiernan's note. It was her third time reading it, but it still brought tears to her eyes.

"Tiernan, this letter is brilliant," Alice said. "It's so convincing."

"Whatever." Tiernan kept her eyes on the road. "I think it had more to do with that dog taking a whiz on Kai's leg."

"No way," Summer said. "It was all you, T-Bird."

Tiernan shook her head. "It was all of us."

Alice stuck the map in its designated spot, admiring her own handiwork on the collage for their final destination. Austin was the most straightforward of all the collages on the map—a photo of the band performing live, with cutouts of the three girls (age twelve) pressed up against the stage. Hours from now they'd be living this picture.

Looking at their smiling middle-school faces, Alice felt a pang of sadness for all the years of friendship they'd missed out on between then and now. There was so much catching up to do, so many blanks to be filled in. But for once she wasn't in a hurry. They had the rest of their lives to catch up. They had five hours to get to a show that was only an hour away.

Tiernan pulled off the exit. "Sustenance," she said, before Alice had the chance to ask.

It wasn't until she walked into the Mexican joint and inhaled the sweet corn smell of homemade tortilla chips that Alice realized how ravenous she was.

"You have the tickets, right?" she asked, sitting down next to Tiernan.

"OMFG! Stop asking me that!" It was a kindhearted tirade. Tiernan shot Summer an exaggerated eye roll. Summer smiled back at her. Another one of their familiar dances.

"What? Do you want to see them?" Tiernan challenged her.

"No!" Summer and Alice both shouted. But it was too late, Tiernan had already pulled down her scoop-necked shirt, revealing the little white envelope tucked inside of her little black bra.

"I'll come back," the waiter said, tossing their basket of chips so fast, half of them scattered across the wooden table. He was a dark-haired boy, their age, with braces and a Spanish accent.

Before he was two steps away they burst into laughter. The tiny bowl of salsa lay capsized in the sea of chips, and Alice picked it up and placed it on the table.

She could live forever right here in this moment, laughing with Tiernan and Summer, double-dipping their corn chips. It was allowed.

Suddenly she was overcome with a longing to talk to MJ. She'd missed her during the trip, but never so much as right now. She wanted to share the good news about winning the tickets, to tell MJ how much she loved her. And after she was done talking to MJ, she wanted to call her parents, too. She wanted to share this feeling with everything and everyone— the bird sitting on that tree branch outside the window, the old man in the cowboy hat drinking alone at the bar. Heck, she'd probably even learn to love UVM once she gave it a chance.

She pulled her phone from her bag. Better just to text MJ, since it was likely to be two a.m. in China, tomorrow or yesterday—she was too tired to remember which. But when

Reunited

she opened her phone, she saw that there was a text message waiting for her.

She didn't realize she'd gasped until she noticed Tiernan and Summer staring.

"Quentin sent me another text," she said, flinging the phone onto the table, like there was a chance it might detonate at any second.

"And you're not going to open it?" Tiernan looked dubious.

"I can't," Alice moaned. "One of you has to do it."

Summer pulled the phone toward her, sighing. "I may as well, seeing as how I *am* the resident expert on heartbreak around here."

It took Summer so long to read the message, Alice halfwondered if Quentin had forwarded her a copy of *War and Peace*.

"You're gonna want to read this," Summer finally pronounced.

Alice reached for the phone, her whole body turning to mush.

```
A, sorry bout that last message. Cell
phone confiscated. Tried to sneak it
then mom came back. ;) Meant to say
I can't stop thinking about you. I
can't. Don't try to make me. Q
```

I can't stop thinking about you. I can't. Alice read those words again and again as her whole body screamed with happiness. And to think she'd spent the last two days torturing herself, thinking she was the only one who'd felt that way, instead of believing what she'd known all along, instead of just trusting her heart.

"Oh, come on," Tiernan whined. "Hand it over already."

The waiter came back and took their order without making eye contact. Alice's excitement over Quentin had stolen her appetite, but as a gesture of apology to the waiter, she ordered the daily special.

"So, what are you gonna do?" Tiernan asked.

"Tell him we'll stop by on the way back," Summer said, with authority.

"But not at his house," Tiernan added. "You'll need a rendezvous point. Like a motel."

"No. No motels. Too sleazy," Summer said. "Someplace public, yet romantic. Like a park by a river."

"I don't remember seeing any rivers around there," Tiernan said.

"You guys, I'm sure Quentin and I will figure something out."

"Yeah, right." Summer sighed.

"Alice," Tiernan said with a smirk. "Even the president has cabinet members."

"So, if I'm the president, what does that make you guys? Undersecretaries of Love?"

Tiernan wrinkled her nose. "I prefer Chief Booty Call Strategists."

By the time their food arrived and Alice saw the slices of avocado stacked like a little green staircase, her hunger found her again. They had a long slow lunch, giggling over Quentin, speculating about which song Level3 would open with tonight. Tiernan had her money on "Unadulterated," their first big hit. Summer was sure it would be "Natural Causes." But Alice had a feeling it would be "Parade." Not that she needed more proof that the universe was back in flow.

An hour later they checked into a cheap motel on the outskirts of Austin. The room was small and worn, and no matter how much they cranked the AC, the temperature remained a steamy eighty-two degrees. Alice tried to fight off her post-lunch lethargy, but between her lack of sleep last night and the letdown from this morning's adrenaline rush, she was crashing hard.

She sprawled out on the bed next to Tiernan (already deep in a *Jersey Shore* coma) while Summer headed for the shower. Normally Alice would be too wired to kick back and relax before a big show, but she had to give herself a break sometime, didn't she? Plus, it was only 4:14. The concert didn't start until 7:00. And after thousands of miles and one disaster after another, things were finally going right for once.

But, just to be on the safe side, Alice hauled herself out of bed and lay out her outfit for the concert on the armchair in the corner—her favorite floral tank top, brand-new skinny jeans, and the gold dangling earrings she'd worn that night with Quentin. Then she set the alarm clock for 5:30 as a final precaution. On the slight possibility she actually *did* manage to drift off, that would still give them plenty of time to get ready. According to Coach Quigley, the Frank Erwin Center was less than five miles away from their hotel. But they were way too close to seeing Level3 to take any chances.

Alice woke up to the sound of Cartman screaming. It took her a full five seconds to realize that the noise was coming from the TV, where *South Park* was on, and not the alarm clock radio she was hitting repeatedly.

Then her eyes focused on the time. *8:05? No, it wasn't possible.* Alice lifted the clock to her face and pressed the alarm button. It didn't make sense. The alarm was still set to 5:30 p.m., just as she'd left it, a little red dot glowing next to the words "Alarm On."

That's when she saw the tiny white letters below it—p.m. Strangely, there was no red dot glowing next to them.

It hit her all at once—the alarm hadn't gone off because some jerk had set the clock to a.m. when it should have been p.m. A flutter of panic flew through Alice's chest as the clock blinked to 8:06 in her hand. She threw it down, leaped out of bed, and ran for the window, tearing open the curtains to reveal a sky washed in orange and pink. Sunset. At least it wasn't *actually* morning. Which meant they still had a shred of hope.

"Get up!" Alice shouted, but Summer was already sitting, her hair damp and curly from falling asleep with it still wet. She stared at the clock distrustfully, like she was about to hit it.

"What the hell?"

Tiernan pulled her pillow over her face and groaned, but Summer yanked it off of her.

"Dude!" Tiernan whined, opening just one eye. "There's a gentler way to—" But as soon as she saw the sunset through the window her mouth instantly shut and the other eye popped open.

"We need to move," Alice said with forced calm. "*Now.*"

They flung on their clothes in a haphazard manner. There were no touch-ups of makeup, no tiny rhinestone barrettes, no shimmering lotions applied to bare arms.

"Do you have the—?"

"Got 'em." Tiernan thumped her chest and they were out the door.

"In eight hundred yards, turn left," Coach Quigley commanded. *Damn his computer voice for being so tranquil.* The speed limit was thirty-five. Alice drove fifty.

"Maybe there's an opening act," Summer offered quietly from the back.

"It's not on the tickets," Alice said, hitting the gas so hard that the engine whinnied.

"Stop sign!" Tiernan shouted, and Alice jammed on the brakes.

"Let's just get there alive," Summer said coolly.

Let's just get there, Alice thought. To miss the show after everything they'd been through . . .

"Up ahead, bear right," Coach Quigley barked.

It was 8:15 p.m. The stadium was three miles away.

"I don't know." Tiernan sounded skeptical. "This doesn't seem like the right way, Alice."

"How do *you* know?" she snapped.

"I'm just saying, that road looks sketchy, doesn't it?"

But Alice followed Coach Quigley's directive and turned onto it anyway. The road led them through a brand-new industrial park—low concrete buildings on either side, dirt lawns sprayed green with grass seed.

"Alice, *slow down*," Summer said, this time more forcefully.

They'd reached the dead end of a cul-de-sac—where more identical buildings were in the process of being constructed.

"In six hundred yards, turn left," Coach Quigley said.

"There is no left!" Alice shouted back.

"I think this road's too new to be in his system. He didn't know." Summer defended Coach Quigley like he was a real person, with actual feelings.

"Turn around when possible." Coach Quigley answered back.

"Bite me!" Tiernan yelled, poking at his buttons. "Okay, he's going to find an alternate route."

Alice took a deep breath and held it. Her yoga teacher told her to use the image of her lungs filling slowly, like a balloon.

But when 8:17 gave way to 8:18, Alice's balloon nearly popped. *Why hadn't she double-checked the stupid alarm clock? Why had she let herself eat that huge greasy lunch? Why had she let herself get comfortable?* Constant vigilance—that was the difference between success and failure, the difference between the Ivy League and UVM.

"Up ahead, turn left." Alice turned around and followed Coach Quigley's new instructions, even though she didn't trust him anymore.

"Grab the map," she directed Tiernan. "We need backup."

"Our map?" Tiernan asked.

"No, *the* map. The original map. *My* map."

Tiernan dug through the box that had started off as a snack bin and somewhere along the road had turned into a junk drawer, full of hair scrunchies, flattened Kashi granola bars and trashy celebrity magazines with the covers ripped off. She pulled out the map and handed it to Summer.

"This map isn't detailed enough," Summer said. "We just have to trust Coach Quigley. We have no other choice."

By 8:26, they crossed onto the University of Texas campus, where the stadium was located.

"Look! Concert parking!" Tiernan gestured toward a yellow sign with an arrow pointing left.

Alice followed it, but when she pulled up to the parking garage another sign read LOT FULL.

Tiernan called out to the man in the little white booth at

the entrance. "Excuse me, sir! Is there another place to park around here?"

The man looked up slowly, like he needed the time to process her words. "Keep going straight," he said in a thick, indeterminate accent.

The second garage was three blocks away, and the only spaces left were all the way up on the fifth floor.

Alice ripped the keys from the ignition and jumped out of the van as though she were fleeing a burning building, racing across the polished concrete floor of the garage, the hollow *thwack-thawck-thawck* of her flip-flops echoing off the walls. Of course, these weren't the shoes she'd *planned* on wearing.

Together, they flew down five flights of stairs and burst through the garage's green metal door, breathless.

"Which way to Frank Erwin Center?" Tiernan yelled to a boy skateboarding down the sidewalk.

He pointed. "End of the street, take a right, and it's about a half mile up."

They ran off without even thanking him, charging down the smooth, empty sidewalks of the summertime college campus. The sun had dipped below the horizon, leaving only a watermelon slice of sky.

By 8:38, they could see the Erwin Center in the distance—round, bare concrete, illuminated by a halo of sun-yellow lights. They flocked to it like moths, slowing down only when their feet touched its perimeter. The place looked empty except for a homeless man muttering to himself and a couple of college kids loitering outside smoking cigarettes. Alice strained to hear to the music inside, but the only noise that came back was the thrum of the highway.

She was only fifty feet away from the glass doors when they opened with a sharp squeak and a boy and girl emerged, holding hands, the faint sound of applause and screaming in the background. The couple walked off as the doors *shush*ed closed behind them and the night grew silent again.

Alice walked closer, Summer and Tiernan at her side, the Erwin Center looming before them like an undiscovered planet. They were almost at the doors when they swung open a second time. A group of boys exited, all in jeans and stiff new Level3 T-shirts; behind them, an older couple, then a dozen or so college kids.

Summer slowed to a stop. "I think ... maybe ..." She let her voice trial off.

But Alice kept on marching. She wasn't about to stop just because some people were leaving early to avoid traffic. They could probably still make the encore. Springsteen's encores were sometimes longer than his shows.

Alice lifted her hand to reach for the door handle when the mass exodus began in full—increasing in force and noise by the second, like a human avalanche. Since there was nowhere to go, Alice just stood there, letting the mob surge past, all gleeful chatter and careless elbows. By the time she remembered to look for Summer and Tiernan, she couldn't find them any-where. Not that she was ready to face them yet.

Instead, Alice just stayed put, getting jostled by the crowd as they passed, as if it would take all fifteen thousand concert goers shaking her by the shoulders to finally get her to accept the truth.

"HOME"
KNOCK ON MY DOOR,
I'LL ANSWER.
RING MY BELL
AT TWO A.M.

AND IF I'M NOT AT HOME,
YOU CAN USE MY SECRET KEY,
'CAUSE IT'S STILL HIDDEN IN THE PLACE
WHERE IT USED TO BE.

—*from Level3's third CD,* Natural Causes

Chapter Twenty-Four

TIERNAN STOOD ON A CONCRETE BENCH ON HER TIPTOES, BUT even with the extra height, she still couldn't spot Alice in the crowd.

"Shoot. I think I lost her again."

Summer climbed up next to Tiernan, taking her shift at Alice patrol. "Don't worry." Summer sighed. "She's still just standing there."

"What the hell?" Tiernan asked, to no one in particular.

They'd been waiting for Alice for the last ten minutes, while all around them, happy, satisfied fans were practically rubbing it in their faces.

"I think we should just go over there and get her," Tiernan said.

"No." Summer's voice was firm. "Give her some time, and she'll calm down eventually. Just let her ease into it."

Tiernan rolled her eyes. Summer had *her* way of dealing with Alice's meltdowns. Tiernan had her own methods. "Screw that," Tiernan said. "It's time to bust a move."

She headed off into the crowd, elbowing her way through the throngs of people until she was close enough to grab Alice's hand. "Come on," she said, pulling Alice in the direction of the exiting mob. "Party's over. Time to go."

"No." Alice shrugged her off. "I'm not going back to that nasty motel room. I'm just not."

Suddenly Summer was behind them.

"It's okay, Alice," Summer cooed, squeezing past Tiernan. "Let's just get out of here and we can find someplace else to go." She wrapped an arm around Alice's shoulder, but Alice shook it off.

"I think I just need to be alone for a while, okay?" Alice said; then she stamped off into the flow of people.

Tiernan turned to Summer and shrugged. "I guess you called that one right."

Shockingly, Summer didn't rub it in. "She has my cell number. She'll call when she's ready."

By the time Tiernan and Summer had found their way out of the fray, Alice was at the end of the block. Even for a shorty like Tiernan, she'd been easy to pinpoint—the only person angrily storming her way through a sidewalk full of amblers.

"I think we better follow her," Summer said. "She's in a pretty delicate state."

And what about me? Tiernan wanted to ask. They'd *all* missed the concert. "Aren't *you* bummed about missing the show?" Tiernan couldn't help herself.

"Of course I am," Summer snapped. "But you know how Alice gets."

Tiernan felt a wave of anger surge through her chest, but she wasn't sure why. What did *she* care if Summer was looking out for Alice? It wasn't as if Tiernan wanted to abandon the poor girl. What exactly was it about Summer's thoughtfulness that Tiernan found so annoying?

Unless . . . A thought flashed through Tiernan's mind, making her stop in her tracks. What if that thing she was feeling wasn't annoyance at all? What if, after all this time, she was actually still jealous?

"What are you doing?" Summer turned around, ten paces ahead of her. "We're gonna lose her."

Tiernan started walking again, picking up speed until she caught up to Summer. Things felt different now that it was just the two of them, without Alice around to act as their buffer. Or maybe it was the lurking feeling that Tiernan needed to finish what she'd started on the stage back in Houston, only she didn't know how.

"I know you probably think that I'm babying Alice," Summer said, turning to face her. "And maybe I am. But you know what a perfectionist she is. You know how hard she can be on herself when things don't go her way."

Tiernan nodded.

"It's just . . ." Summer searched for the words. "You and I can deal with things in a way Alice can't."

Yeah." Tiernan laughed. "Probably because we're more used to disappointment."

"For your information, I'm pretty pissed off about missing the show," Summer declared.

"Well, so am I," Tiernan said. "I'm *super*pissed."

"I was on the verge of tears before," Summer said. "Seriously."

"I feel like screaming at the top of my lungs," said Tiernan. "Like randomly kicking people."

Summer sidestepped away from her, pretending to be afraid.

Tiernan went on, "I feel like biting a chunk out of my own arm."

"Ew." Summer groaned. "That's just disturbing."

Up ahead, Alice turned left into the heart of the college campus. Tiernan and Summer followed her, like the world's most conspicuous pair of spies.

"I hate it when Alice gets upset," Tiernan said. "It wigs me out."

"That's so weird," Summer said. "I was just thinking the exact same thing."

They walked in silence for a while.

"You know what I think?" Summer asked. "I think if you look back to freshman year when things went south between us, it was all about Alice being unhappy. You and I, we always had our little squabbles. But I never fought with Alice. Did you?"

Tiernan shook her head. "Never."

"And I was never jealous of Alice, either. Even though I

wished I could be more like her. You know what I mean?"

"Totally," Tiernan agreed. Even on the rare occasion that Alice freaked out (like tonight, or at that loathsome freshman dance) her intention was never to be hurtful or cruel, just to vent her feelings so that she could say her piece and move on. Unlike Tiernan, Alice wasn't afraid to let her emotions spill out freely. She wasn't afraid to speak the truth, even if it meant laying herself totally bare. Just the thought of being so vulnerable gave Tiernan goose bumps.

Summer continued. "You know what surprised me most about what you said, back in Houston?"

That I'm a liar? That I was the one who sabotaged our entire friendship? All the muscles in Tiernan's body seemed to cramp at once, but somehow she managed to both speak and keep walking. "What?"

"What shocked me most was that you, of all people, were actually jealous. I guess I always just assumed you never really cared about anything. You know, 'cause you act all 'whatever' all the time."

Tiernan smiled. "Ah, yes, my Whatever-ness. I own the trademark on that."

Summer laughed. "You know what the sad thing is?"

Tiernan shook her head. Up the block, Alice hung a left.

"I was always jealous of Alice and *you*."

"Yeah, right." Tiernan snorted. Was Summer just trying to make her feel better?

"No, really," Summer went on. "I always felt like you and Alice were closer friends than me and her or me and you."

"That's ridiculous," Tiernan scoffed. "In my mind it was the other way around."

"But Alice was always in the middle, wasn't she?"

Tiernan smiled. "The glue in our collage, so to speak."

"Hey, look!" Summer pointed up the street. "I think the glue's finally slowing down."

Tiernan watched Alice plod across the street to the garage where they'd stashed the Pea Pod. Her talk with Summer had left her feeling good, considering their circumstances. Suddenly a new fear hit her.

"You don't think she'd take off on us, do you?"

Summer turned to face her, wide-eyed, then they both broke into a run.

In the parking garage, they dodged their way through the line of cars jammed up by the exit and barreled up four flights of stairs. When they finally reached the top floor, Tiernan was relieved to see the Pea Pod right where they'd left it, with Alice sitting in the driver's seat.

They approached the van cautiously, as if Alice were a fly they were trying to trap inside a cup. Tiernan was almost at the driver's side window when she heard a noise that made her stop. Slowly she turned to Summer while the sound repeated itself—*Ch-ch-ch, shoop*—the halfhearted wheeze of an engine that won't start.

For a few seconds Tiernan and Summer just stood there, listening to Alice turn the key in the ignition again and again, until finally all the life had been drained from the battery and the engine only made a pitiful clicking noise.

"I think she left the headlights on," Summer whispered to Tiernan.

"Probably," Tiernan whispered back. "But you might not wanna bring it up."

Just then, Alice flung herself from the Pea Pod, her cell phone flying out of her back pocket and clattering across the concrete. "I give up!" She screamed at the rows of parked cars, or possibly the universe. Alice was in such a state, Tiernan wasn't even sure she'd seen them standing there.

"Hey," Tiernan said softly. "We can call Triple A if you want." She picked up Alice's cell phone and held it out, like she was offering a steak to a rabid dog.

But Alice just stormed off across the garage.

Tiernan shot Summer a look that said, *Your turn*, and the two of them took off after Alice.

"Listen, Alice," Summer began when they were in speaking range. "This isn't your fault. *All* of us fell asleep."

Alice stopped, turning to face them. "It just sucks, okay? This totally sucks! This whole trip has been nothing but a complete disaster from day one."

Tiernan wanted to argue with her, but what could she really say to that? *Getting the van stuck in the mud and ripping kudzu off a shed and having her mom crash their trip and Alice getting her purse stolen and missing the concert they all came to see was totally awesome! Woo hoo!*

"So what?" Summer sighed. "So things haven't exactly gone our way. It still doesn't mean you should blame yourself. It's not anyone's fault things ended up like this. It's like that John Lennon quote, 'Life's what happens while you're making other plans.'"

Alice narrowed her eyes at Summer as though she'd just spoken a foreign language. "What did you just say?"

Summer repeated herself. "I said, 'Life's what happens while you're making other—'" But she was cut off by Alice's howls of laughter.

Summer looked at Tiernan. Tiernan looked at the phone, still in her hand. Screw Triple A—she was calling the nuthouse.

"I'm sorry," Alice said, trying to suppress her giggles. "But I really hate that stupid quote." She wiped the tears from her eyes. "I guess I was just trying so hard to make things perfect, you know? Like if we had an amazing time, it just might fix things between us."

A small smile emerged from deep within Tiernan's layers of "whatevers." She'd spent so much energy convincing herself that the only reason she came on this trip was to run away from being grounded. But what if she was never really running away at all? What if, this whole time, without realizing it, Tiernan was actually running *to* something?

"I thought this whole trip was *beshert*," Alice continued. "The three of us being together again, seeing Level3 play. There were so many signs . . ." She let the rest of her sentence fade away.

"Maybe it is *beshert*," Tiernan began. "Maybe *this* is just what's meant to be."

She stared at Alice and Summer, their faces lit up by the fluorescent green light of the garage. It gave her that same woozy feeling she'd felt onstage back in Houston.

"Maybe Level3 was just an excuse," Tiernan continued. "But we just didn't know it."

Summer raised an eyebrow at her. "I think we all had plenty of excuses."

Tiernan laughed. "Yeah, so what else is new?"

Alice's phone rang in Tiernan's hand, startling her. The Level3 ringtone had seemed like a great idea when Alice had downloaded it over lunch. Now it made them all wince.

Tiernan looked at the caller ID and handed the phone to Alice. "Here you go. It's your parents."

Alice shook her head. "I don't want to talk to them right now."

Tiernan glanced at the ringing phone. Now that she was on a roll, she might as well apologize to the Millers, too.

"Then I will," Tiernan said, answering the call before Alice could stop her.

"Hey, it's Tiernan," she said, veering away from Alice and

Summer to give herself some privacy. "I just wanted to say sorry about the whole thing with my mom, and for putting you guys in the middle of it—"

Of course, she wasn't even halfway through her apology when Bill Miller told her she'd been forgiven. Anyway, he didn't have time to for Tiernan's true confessions. Bill was calling with more important news.

"'I've got a golden ticket!'" Tiernan skipped toward Alice and Summer singing the song from the 1970s *Willy Wonka and the Chocolate Factory*, her hand curled tightly around Alice's phone.

"What's that supposed to mean?" Alice looked curious.

"I can't believe your dad's letting me do this." Tiernan beamed.

"Letting you do *what*?" Alice asked.

Tiernan whistled the familiar melody. *I've got a golden ticket.*

"Oh, for God's sake, could you stop torturing us already?" Summer sighed.

"Okay, I'll give you a hint." Tiernan flashed a mischievous smile. "What's another word for *beshert*?"

Alice rolled her eyes. "I don't know. Destiny?"

"Nope."

"Serendipity?" Summer offered.

Tiernan shook her head.

"How long do we have to do this?" Alice asked.

"Keep going." Tiernan was enjoying this torture a little too much.

"Fate," Summer said. "Karma!"

"No and no."

"There aren't any more synonyms," Summer complained.

"There's at least one," Tiernan said, doing her best to sound coy.

She could see it hit Alice then, could tell that she knew but was afraid to say it. Alice swallowed hard, waiting for a heavy truck to rumble past. "Is it . . . *Providence*?"

"It is!" Tiernan chirped.

"As in Rhode Island?" Alice was still tentative. "The city where Brown University is?"

Tiernan smiled wide. "Your parents just got the letter!"

"IN OUR HANDS"

YOU SAID THE STARS
WERE IN OUR FAVOR
THE NIGHT THAT I MET YOU
UNDER THE STARS.
BUT THE VERY NEXT DAY,
MY FORTUNE COOKIE WAS EMPTY.

OH, HOW WE LAUGHED,
BUT YOU STILL WOULDN'T TRADE ME
MY FUTURE OF NOTHINGNESS FOR YOURS,
NO MATTER HOW HARD I BEGGED,
EVEN WHEN I TRIED TO STEAL IT FROM YOUR HANDS.

—from Level3's second CD, Rough & Tumble

Chapter Twenty-Five

FOR THE SECOND TIME THAT DAY, ALICE SHRIEKED WITH JOY. Summer and Tiernan joined her, the three of them holding hands and jumping up and down and screaming just like they'd done a few hours earlier when they'd won the tickets.

"They had some long apology about sending your acceptance letter to the wrong address, twice," Tiernan explained when they'd stopped squealing. "I told your dad I'd let him fill you in on the details."

Alice's head was spinning. She couldn't wipe the smile off her face if she tried. Everything was working out like she'd wanted. Well, *almost* everything.

"Let's go celebrate," Summer said. "Let's go into the city. See what Austin's like."

Summer was right. They could deal with the Pea Pod later. Right now, Alice had too much happy energy to waste it waiting around for Triple A. And there was no way she was going to spend another minute in that awful motel room.

"Let's do it!" Alice said, leading the way out of the garage and back onto the college campus.

"You know, Providence is only about an hour from Boston," Tiernan said. "You can come up and stay with me at Emerson for the weekend if you want."

"Or with me," Summer chimed in.

She'd been a student at Brown for a whopping thirty seconds and already she was spending her weekends away. Alice wasn't entirely sure whether Summer and Tiernan would ever really visit her, or if it was just the heat of the moment talking, but at least she wasn't afraid to admit that she *wanted* it to be true.

Maybe her friendship with Tiernan and Summer was like waiting to hear from Brown. She'd ended up getting what she'd hoped for, just when she'd finally let it go.

"Seriously, though." Tiernan was still making plans. "You can take the train from South Station to Providence for, like, only ten bucks."

"But what about the Pea Pod?" Summer asked.

"Oh, I think we've spent enough time in the Pea Pod," Alice said.

"Alice!" Summer and Tiernan each gasped in mock horror.

"What? You know it smells like butt in there."

Then the three of them dissolved into laughter as they stumbled along the clean, wide sidewalks of the UT Austin campus. Even if her friendship with Tiernan and Summer didn't last beyond this trip, it still felt good to be sharing this moment with them. And how could she plan for the future now? In two more months, they'd be off at their own college campuses, each of them starting a new chapter in their lives.

Alice slipped her arm through Summer's. "Travis doesn't know what he's missing."

"Damn straight," Summer said with a laugh.

"Seriously." Tiernan linked herself onto Alice's free arm. "If he'd seen you shaking your *thang* in the front row, you actually might have had a shot."

Summer smiled. "You know, you guys, it's nice to have other people who actually believe in my fantasy world."

"Hey, that's what friends are for, right?" Tiernan asked.

The word made Alice's eyes well up. *Friends.*

"Speaking of fantasy worlds," Tiernan began. "I want to hear about your dream date with Travis again. I always liked that one the best. And you always told it so well; you made it sound like a novel or something."

Summer gave them a sly smile. "Sorry, girls. That dream date's no longer available. I changed it."

Alice gasped. "You did not."

Summed nodded. "Earlier tonight. In the motel room. Before I fell asleep."

"Soooo?" Tiernan teased. "Is it rated NC-17 or something?"

"You wish," Summer said. "But, no, it's just Travis and me, riding his motorcycle through the desert."

"The *desert*?" Alice asked.

Summer shrugged. "I've never been there before. Anyway,

he's riding really fast, and I'm holding on tight. And he's taking me someplace that's a surprise. Someplace he's not telling me till we get there."

"Like one of those spas where you can take a mud bath?"

"I don't know," Summer said. "That's when I fell asleep."

Alice laughed. "Okay, T, your turn. What are you and Luke up to these days?"

Tiernan smirked. "Three words: Japanese sex hotel."

"Classy," Summer said. "Very classy. Okay, Alice, you're up."

Alice didn't want to be a buzzkill, but at the moment she couldn't even *consider* fantasizing about someone other than Quentin.

"Hate to disappoint you ladies, but my daydreams only involve my *real* boyfriend," Alice teased. "Now that I might actually have one."

"Wait a minute." Tiernan stopped abruptly, pulling them all to a complete standstill since their arms were still linked. "Where *are* we?"

Alice had been so lost in the moment, she'd assumed the grass they were walking on was a park. But now that she looked, she realized it was the on-ramp to the highway.

A car flew past blaring its horn.

"Turn around when possible," Summer said in her best Coach Quigley voice, which, of course, sent all three of them into convulsive laughter, until they were doubled over on the strip of grass by the breakdown lane.

320   HILARY WEISMAN GRAHAM

Alice was just catching her breath when she noticed a van pull up beside them, its hazard lights blinking as it came to a stop.

"You guys . . ." Alice sat up to get a better look. The van was the Pea Pod's double, only canary yellow. Just like the vintage VW Level3 used to tour in when they were first starting out, back when Ryan's mom had to chauffeur them around to gigs because they weren't old enough to drive. *But it couldn't be . . .*

Just then the back door slid open, revealing Luke Dixon, the drummer for Level3, crouched in the back.

"You girls are aware that you're hanging out on an on-ramp, right?" Luke asked.

Alice stared at him, like a mute girl with a brain injury. There was Luke Frigging Dixon, two feet away from her. And—*holy crap!*—there was Travis glaring at them skeptically from the passenger's side window. Alice leaned forward to steal a glimpse of Ryan behind the wheel, but all she could see was the back of his head. One look at that soft, brown wavy hair was all it took to make the thought *Quentin who?* flash through her mind.

"Our c-car broke down," Tiernan stammered when nobody else spoke, her voice an octave higher than usual.

"Is it an invisible car?" Luke asked, looking around.

"No," Alice managed to utter. "It's actually exactly like this one. Except mine's green."

"The Pea Pod," Summer added. "We left it back in the garage by the show."

Luke shot Ryan a glance. "Well, we can give you a lift into town if you want."

"Sorry." Somehow Summer had managed to not only sound coherent, but also to stand. "But we have a strict policy about not accepting rides from strangers."

It took Alice a good five seconds to realize it was joke. But as soon as she did, she burst into hysterics again, with Summer and Tiernan joining in right along with her.

Level3 just stared at them, the looks of bewilderment on their faces quickly changing into genuine concern at the sight of three giggling lunatics flailing around next to the highway on-ramp. But before they could ask another question, the girls were already making their way over to the van. Luke eyed them all warily, as if he was considering withdrawing his offer. So Alice quickened her pace and scrambled inside before he could change his mind.

Being a twin to the Pea Pod, the van felt as familiar as home.

"You really have a green 1976 VW bus called the Pea Pod?" Luke asked.

Tiernan leveled him with a look. "You think we'd make something like that up?"

"Hard to say," Luke answered, looking entirely unconvinced.

"Well, this here is the Banana Boat," Travis said, patting the dashboard.

"We know." Alice smiled shyly.

Introductions were awkward. Alice had to bite her lip not

to say "duh" each time the boys told them their names.

"So, were you guys at the show?" Ryan asked.

By the time their third laughing fit subsided, Travis had turned around in his seat to glare at them.

"Just how baked are you?" he asked accusingly.

"Not at all." Summer sniffled. "I swear. We're completely normal."

"Yeah, right," Luke scoffed. Ryan and Travis exchanged looks.

"So, how'd it go?" Tiernan asked. "The show, I mean."

"Actually . . ." Luke ran his hand through his hair. "It was pretty damn sweet, if I do say so myself."

Alice smiled. She was happy they'd had a good show, even though she hadn't been there to see it.

"So, where do you want us to take you?" Ryan asked.

"Right here's pretty good," Alice said, startled by her honesty. This time all six of them shared a laugh. While Summer wasn't looking, Alice caught Travis stealing a glance.

"Ryan's having some people over," Travis said. "At his mom's place. Just a few of our old friends from Austin. It's pretty lowkey."

"We're kicking it old school," Luke added. "Hence, the van."

"Anyway, you're welcome to come along if you want."

If Alice didn't know better, she would have sworn her heart stopped beating for a solid ten seconds. She looked searchingly at Summer and Tiernan, both of whom seemed to be doing a very convincing job of appearing casual while their heads popped off.

Summer nodded. "Sure, I guess we could stop by."

Oh, thank God for Summer.

"Can you girls keep a secret?" Travis asked.

"Travis." Ryan said his name like it was a reprimand.

"Come on, dude, relax." Ryan and Travis exchanged a look. "We just officially decided we're going back in the studio this fall," Travis continued, and smiled. "And next summer, we're thinking of going out on tour."

"You mean you're getting back together?" Alice asked breathlessly.

"Yeah, something like that," Travis said. "We'll see how it goes." His tone seemed awfully casual, but Alice could see in his eyes how excited he was. Summer and Tiernan were absolutely glowing. If Level3 was getting back together, that meant they'd have other chances to see them play.

Ryan stayed focused on the road. "Things got pretty rough, post breakup." His voice sounded hesitant, like he was afraid of sharing too much. "But it seems like it's worth it to get back on that horse and give it another shot."

"Same thing, only different," Luke said.

Alice smiled. "Well, here's to second chances," she said, raising an invisible champagne flute in a toast.

"To second chances!" Summer and Tiernan repeated in unison, clinking their imaginary glasses with hers.

Not even the best of their childhood Level3 fantasies had ever been as good as this. Then again, reality (in spite of all its imperfections) was always better than any daydream.

Alice didn't want to get her hopes up about the rest of the night. And yet, how could she possibly keep her expectations in check when she was heading off into the night with her three favorite rock stars and her two oldest friends?

Alice took a deep breath, making a mental list of all the things that could potentially go wrong. Ryan's party could be awful. The guys could turn out to be jerks once she got to know them. Or Level3 could think *they* were the jerks. Or maybe the night would be totally amazing, but the girls would have to live the rest of lives knowing that their very best moment had already passed them by. Which, of course, would inevitably bum them out, causing things to fall apart between them all over again, and Alice's friendship with Summer and Tiernan wouldn't last past the drive back to Walford.

Alice exhaled.

No, there was no need to make plans right now or to worry about what might come next. Not when the bright lights of Austin glittered with possibility. Not even with the knowledge that this perfect moment would someday come to an end. The night was still young. And to Alice, it felt like the beginning.